P9-DMP-784

FROZEN REIGN

FROZEN REIGN

KATHRYN PURDIE

KATHERINE TEGEN BOOKS
An Imprint of HarperCollins Publishers

Katherine Tegen Books is an imprint of HarperCollins Publishers.

Frozen Reign
Copyright © 2018 by Kathryn Purdie
All rights reserved. Printed in the United States of America. No part of this book
may be used or reproduced in any manner whatsoever without written permission
except in the case of brief quotations embodied in critical articles and reviews. For
information address HarperCollins Children's Books, a division of HarperCollins
Publishers, 195 Broadway, New York, NY 10007.
www.epicreads.com

Library of Congress Control Number: 2018941661
ISBN 978-0-06-241242-3

Typography by Carla Weise
18 19 20 21 22   PC/LSCH   10 9 8 7 6 5 4 3 2 1
❖
First Edition

 FOR MY BROTHER MATTHEW,
keeper of my left kidney. Without you,
I never would have written this trilogy.

FROZEN REIGN

 CHAPTER ONE

DYING SUNLIGHT GUIDED MY STEPS FROM THE CONVENT porch to the locked gate. I breathed in deeply, trying to trap the scent of forest pine in my nostrils. The stench of sickness hung about me as I passed the hospital tent.

The soldiers' coughs rang dimly on the evening air. Though I gradually outdistanced the sound, I couldn't shake the vivid image of blood on their handkerchiefs and pillow slips. I'd scrubbed them with lye soap until my fingertips peeled, but some stains wouldn't fade.

An outbreak of consumption shouldn't strike at the cusp of autumn. Rampant illness was a marker of winter. "A bad omen," a superstitious soldier had whispered to another across his cot. "We're going to lose both wars."

A basket of rye bread, hard cheese, and apples bumped against my hip as I quickened my steps. Over the last four months, our rations from Torchev had increased to feed the regiment Anton left to protect us here. The extra food hadn't gone unnoticed by the peasants from Ormina, however. They often congregated at the convent gate to beg. I gave them what I could each day, hoping to prevent another full-scale mob from forming. Sestra Mirna, Nadia, and I couldn't defend ourselves with only a few soldiers well enough to aid us.

I pressed forward. My heart pounded as I scanned the road beyond the gate. On days the courier came, this was the time he rode in. I was foolish to hope for letters. The ones that arrived were always for our regiment's lieutenant or Sestra Mirna. Never me.

I reached into the pocket of my blue dress and felt the tattered flaps of the small, waxed envelopes inside. They once contained seeds, one for roses, one for lilacs, and one for violets. I'd found them at different times among our ration supply. The only messages I'd received from Anton over the past four months had been slipped inside. They were brief notes, not addressed to me or signed by him—nothing to give away the secret guarded by those left behind at the convent: I was alive. In fact, every note, written in Anton's bold and long-sweeping hand, was the same: *For the Auraseers.*

Flower seeds were a romantic gesture, I'd told myself, a sign Anton still loved me after all my betrayals. But nine long weeks had passed since any seeds had made their way into our shipments. Their absence made my doubts creep in. Auraseers, the notes had said, not Auraseer. Not even a simple S to hint at

Sonya. Perhaps I was wrong, and it wasn't Anton's handwriting, after all.

Maybe he'd never forgive me.

The convent door shut behind me. I glanced back. "Do you still keep those little envelopes in your pocket?" Nadia smirked, throwing a shawl around her shoulders. Her burn scars shimmered in the last rays of sunlight and trailed down half her face and neck, along with her swirling tattoos.

I withdrew my hand from my pocket. "I don't know what you're talking about."

"Really, Sonya?" Nadia took her time catching up to me. Sestra Mirna had insisted we walk together to the gate. Safety in numbers. "I don't need any special power to interpret your love-lorn expressions. You wear your emotions like you're at the front of a garish parade. How do you think I fooled you for so long?"

"I don't know." I tossed my dark blond braid behind my shoulder. "You'll have to teach me the fine art of deception so I can think like a proper liar." While we'd journeyed together over the summer, Nadia had pretended to have Auraseer abilities. The truth was she'd lost them during the trauma of the convent fire. A fire I had caused.

She swept nearer, her jade eyes leveling on me. "I can think of worse sins than lying."

I knew full well she was baiting me. She laid these traps like clockwork, but I only saw them as opportunities to strike back. The two of us were like flint and steel, sparking whenever we came together. "Oh, yes? What?"

"Betrayal." A strand of Nadia's shoulder-length raven hair caught in the corner of her mouth, at the edge of her condescending smile. "Something we have in common. And *you* set the example, so you should stop acting so superior."

"Betrayal?" I scoffed, though my gut needled. It was true I'd betrayed Anton. I'd overpowered his will and sided with Valko in a desperate attempt to halt the Shenglin invasion, but I'd been shot, proving my loyalty to the fledgling democracy. Was that enough to pay for my mistakes and earn back Anton's love? "I was trying to save Riaznin. You were only grappling to become sovereign Auraseer."

"At least I've never burned a convent to ashes."

"That was an accident."

"Everything is with you, isn't it? Even slitting my mother's throat."

I flinched, recoiling from the slap of her words. Our brief conversations always ended at this breaking point—Nadia's mother, Terezia Dyomin. The countess had been a supporter of Valko's. When she'd threatened me, our argument escalated until my emotions bled into her and she killed herself. Not my intention, but my fault all the same. "That's not how it happened," I answered quietly, all the bite in my voice gone.

Nadia's eyes glistened with a sheen of tears. She glanced away, setting her jaw with a little lift of her chin. "You know, I think you can handle a few peasants on your own today." She spun back toward the convent. "It isn't as if anything interesting happens around here, anyway."

I sighed, letting her leave. Sestra Mirna didn't need to know I went this once to the gate alone.

I walked the remaining thirty yards to where the gate stood near the edge of the forest. No one was here. Not even a single soldier stood guard. Even before many fell ill, they had been slacking off. Ormina was on the west coast of Riaznin, farther from the Shenglin invasion and the growing discord of the civil war. Perhaps our regiment thought we were safe here, despite the two wars. I could never feel safe. Not with Valko alive.

My stomach reflexively tightened where he'd shot me during the convent battle. The wound had healed, but I'd never forget the pain.

The wind keened through the branches, a wolf howled in the distance, the forest buried the last rays of sunlight deep within its clutches, and a rustle drew my gaze. A small noise. I expected to find a jackrabbit or a fox. Instead, a hooded figure stepped out from the shadows of the tree line, fifty yards away. A woman. The hem of her skirt caught the brambles, and she paused to tear it free. Then with a glance behind her, she advanced closer, taking care with her footing so she didn't make another sound.

I adjusted the basket of food on my arm. She must be ravenous to take such pains to go unnoticed, though no other peasants were anywhere to be seen. Clearly she didn't want to share.

"Open the gate," she said when she was fifteen feet away.

She spoke quietly, just loud enough for me to hear. Her words lilted with a light accent.

"I can't," I replied. I'd welcomed a starving madman inside the convent last winter, and the tragedy that followed had taught me to temper my compassion with prudence. "But please take this." The basket wouldn't fit between the bars of the gate, so I stooped to pass each piece of food through to the other side.

The woman crept nearer, but didn't crouch to receive my gift. Her autumn-brown eyes were large as they focused upon me. "Sovereign Auraseer?" she asked.

My heart stopped. None of the peasants knew who I was—who I'd *been*. If Feliks or Valko found out I was here . . . if they knew I was alive . . . I swallowed hard. Feliks and Anton used to be revolutionary allies, but once the democracy had been established, the two men had vastly different ideas of how it should operate. Feliks had taken control of the Duma ruling council and tried to blackmail me into using my power to prevent further uprisings. I'd ultimately refused. I'd also committed enough crimes to merit my own death sentence. Still, Valko was the greater threat. For all he knew, he'd already succeeded in killing me. He wouldn't hesitate to do so again.

"Who are you?" I stood, retreating a step. I could see her face now in the twilight. She appeared to be a little older than my age of eighteen, and her haunted, deep-set eyes and fair complexion were vaguely familiar.

Her mouth twitched into a frown just as she was on the

verge of smiling. She tilted her head, perplexed. *"Où est ton aura?"*

The nape of my neck prickled when she said *aura*. I had the unsettling sense she knew even more about me than I wished.

A dull sound rose above our voices. The shuffle of a tired horse. My gaze snapped to the road, anticipation zinging through my palms.

The girl gasped. The whites of her eyes rimmed her irises. *"Laisse-moi entrer!"* She grabbed the gate bars and shook them.

I didn't understand. "It's only the courier." I pointed in the distance, watching for the rider to clear the bend. But before he could, another person emerged from the forest, following the girl's path. The shadowy contours of his body loomed large and intimidating.

The girl reached through and seized my arm. *"Aidez-moi!"* Her fingers felt ice cold, though the evening was warm. *"S'il te plaît*, Sovereign Auraseer!"

Esten. She was speaking Esten. I recognized the nasally tone of her vowels and rolling *R*s.

Her hood fell back, revealing her auburn hair. Its distinct shade, along with her nationality, finally jogged my memory. She was the Auraseer that the Esten emissary, Floquart de Bonpré, had claimed ownership of, the unfortunate girl he'd abused. I'd met her in the palace during the ball on Morva's Eve. Somehow she'd escaped him.

I pulled the gate key from around my neck and ran to the

lock. The girl raced beside me on the other side. Who was pursuing her? I couldn't imagine a high-ranking nobleman like Floquart prowling about this forest for a girl. I stole a glance down the road, my doubts now heavy about the rider. Was he really the courier? His horse had turned the bend, but the rider wasn't near enough to identify.

I turned the key in the lock. The shackle popped. I loosened the chains wrapped around the gate bars. The girl assisted me, hands fumbling.

"*Arrêtez!*" The man from the forest shouted. He was less than a dozen yards away. His hair hung in greasy blond locks. His matted beard didn't grow along a scar cleaving his chin.

The girl whimpered, tugging on the chains. "Do not stop!" she rasped. "He will not kill me. He wants me alive."

My stomach gave a sickening drop. Suddenly I understood. "Bounty hunter?"

"*Oui.*"

Fear and revulsion flooded my bloodstream. I'd had my own dealings with bounty hunters. Every encounter was as brutal and horrifying as the last. They were known to be merciless. Taking someone alive might just as well have meant taking them broken.

The bounty hunter sized me up with a quick, sweeping glance. I wasn't fierce-looking like Nadia, and I didn't have the build of a fighter. Unintimidated, he grinned.

"Help!" I cried at the top of my lungs, because what more

could I do? I had no weapon, and he was bound to have several. "Help!" I shouted again, rattling the gate to pry it open from the chains. I'd failed this same Esten Auraseer before. I wouldn't do it again. After Floquart had called off the hopeful alliance between Estengarde and Riaznin, he and his entourage left the palace in haste. I'd missed my chance to free the girl he'd treated like a slave.

Hooves pounded down the road as the horse and rider broke into a gallop. "Sonya? Is that you?" My frenzied mind couldn't place the man's voice. He couldn't be the courier, who didn't know my name. "What's happening?" he asked, unable to see the bounty hunter with the forest blocking his view.

The Esten Auraseer squeezed one shoulder through the gap of the gate.

A horrible clang sounded.

She jumped back as a dagger bounced off the bars and thudded to the ground. The sharp blade had been a breath away from striking her—from striking me.

Panic lit my veins. "Kill him!" I shouted to the rider.

"Kill who?"

"Just—kill—him!"

The rider must have advanced far enough to spy the bounty hunter, for his horse whinnied, hooves skidding as it came to a stop. "You, there! What are you doing? Lower your weapon. Let's—let's talk this through, all right?"

Talk? I peered around the wedged girl to see who thought

talking would help our situation.

Once I saw his elongated features, my mouth went slack. *Tosya.*

Tosya, my oldest friend. Tosya the *pacifist*. I hadn't seen him since the night of the convent battle. He'd left with Anton, fast on Valko's trail. I made a quick study of his lanky frame. I doubted he even had a whittling knife on him. He couldn't save us. And I couldn't protect him.

"Tosya, he's a bounty hunter!"

Tosya froze in his saddle. He had suffered an arrow to the leg the last time he'd met a bounty hunter. "I have money," he said frantically, bargaining with what this man must have valued most.

The Esten man broke into a deep chuckle, surveying Tosya's patched clothing. Poets weren't paid by the revolutionary governments they inspired. *"Tu es un pauvre imbécile."*

Tosya swallowed and turned beseeching eyes on me. *Why aren't you doing something about him?* the sharp look he gave me said. I didn't have time to explain. The bounty hunter advanced toward the girl. She cried out as she desperately fought to push through the iron bars.

Shouts and coughing radiated behind me. Soldiers. At least two of them. I prayed their muskets were loaded and they wouldn't collapse before they reached us.

The Esten Auraseer fully squeezed through the gate.

Rage lined every edge of the bounty hunter's face. He barked a string of Esten words. The girl flinched, quaking beside me. With one hand, the bounty hunter cocked his arm back to fling his knife. With the other, he beckoned her forward.

"She belongs to Feya now," I yelled at him, stalling for time. "She has sanctuary at this convent." I wasn't sure if he cared about the holy grounds of the Riaznian-worshipped goddess of Auraseers, or if he even understood a word I was saying.

Thirty yards behind me, the soldiers sprinted nearer. The bounty hunter was quickly losing his opportunity to seize the girl. He could throw his dagger, but unless his aim was perfect, his blade would ricochet against the bars again.

Running out of strategies, he turned on Tosya and raised his knife.

I sucked in a sharp breath. "No!"

The bounty hunter's jaw went hard and inflexible. Again, he motioned for the Esten Auraseer, but his eyes were trained on me. He wanted *me* to give her up in exchange for Tosya's life.

I gripped the girl's arm, my instinct to protect her wavering. I scarcely knew her, but Tosya was like a brother to me.

She met my gaze, eyes wide. I didn't try to hide my guilt. She couldn't know what I was thinking.

She most certainly couldn't know what I was feeling.

I didn't soften my grip, but I couldn't make myself drag her forward. I wouldn't give the bounty hunter anyone, especially an Auraseer.

A crack of gunfire shuddered the air. One of the soldiers

had fired. The lead ball managed to clear the gate, but it missed its target. Still, the bounty hunter hastened back and sheathed his knife.

"*Voyante misérable!*" he shouted at the girl. "*Nous n'avons pas finis.*"

He whistled with two fingers, a horse call. A few seconds later, his stallion galloped out of the forest. The bounty hunter deftly mounted him, then raced away into the cover of trees.

My tension released like the cork off a bottle of wine. The Esten girl burst into sobs of relief. I cast away the last of the gate's chains. Tosya rode onto the grounds. He leapt off his horse just in time to catch me in his arms. I squeezed his torso with all my strength, my body shaking, my head pressed tightly against his chest.

He gave a jittery laugh and patted me on the back. "Never a dull moment at the convent, is there?" he said, a total contradiction of Nadia's earlier claim.

As if the thought of Nadia called her forward, I heard her cry, "Tosya!"

She raced across the convent grounds to meet us, quickly assessing the guards locking the gate and the quivering girl in our midst. She panted to catch her breath, her gaze anchoring back on Tosya. "Are you all right?"

His jaw muscle flexed, and he gave a stiff nod. Tosya and Nadia had developed feelings for each other over the summer while the three of us journeyed together. But if he still held any sentiment for her, he didn't show it. He'd saved her life during the battle at the convent, but that was before he learned she'd betrayed me to Valko. Directing his attention to me, Tosya asked, "Would you care to introduce me to your friend?" He regained enough composure to offer a kind smile to the Esten Auraseer.

"Of course." I turned and found her staring at Nadia as if she'd seen a ghost. "I'm sorry," I said, tucking a loose strand of hair back into my braid. "I don't know your name." I'd never learned it during her fleeting time at the palace.

She forced her hunched shoulders back, but her posture remained stooped. "Genevie."

"Genevie, these are my friends, Tosya and Nadia." *Friend* was a generous word for Nadia.

Genevie fidgeted and gave them a small nod of greeting.

Nadia didn't seem to notice her unease. Instead, she bit the corner of her lip and took a step toward Tosya. "Let me help you stable your horse."

He flinched away and grabbed his stallion's bridle. "I've got it. See you in a little while, Sonya. Nice to meet you, Genevie."

Nadia's crestfallen face almost made me pity her. I touched Genevie's arm. "Come on. Let's get you inside."

We ambled back to the convent, walking in silence. Nadia eventually fell into step behind us. I couldn't think of anything to say. Genevie unnerved me too much. She kept staring at me, then back at Nadia, her brow twisted in confusion. My cheeks burned hot. I knew what she felt when she gazed into my hazel eyes. Nothingness. A pitch-dark void.

She wrapped her arms tightly across her stomach. "What has happened to both of you?" she finally asked. "Your auras . . . *elles ont disparu.* They are gone."

I shut my eyes. Stopped short. Her words shouldn't have hurt so much. She only spoke the truth. But it was the first time since I'd lost my ability that I'd been in the presence of anyone who could actually sense aura.

It made me feel dead inside.

I spun around to Nadia. "Sestra Mirna needs my help in the hospital tent," I blurted. "Could you help Genevie get settled?"

Before she could answer, I rushed away.

CHAPTER TWO

"HOLD HIM STILL, SONYA!"

"I'm trying!" I pinned one of the soldier's flailing arms beneath my knee on his cot. Sestra Mirna held his other arm while I braced his head as he convulsed. Sitting on his legs to quell his kicking, the sestra brought a cup of warm water seeped with garlic, salt, and cloves to his mouth. It tasted terrible. I knew, not because I sensed the bitterness on the tongues of the other sick men, but because I'd sampled it for myself in the convent kitchen. At least in that small way I understood some of what they were suffering. I felt nothing from their auras. Or anyone else's. I hadn't since Valko had shot me.

I pried the soldier's jaw open. Sestra Mirna tipped in the drink. He coughed and gagged, but we didn't relent. The herb water dribbled down his chin. He hadn't swallowed anything.

"Pinch his nose and hold his mouth shut," the sestra commanded.

I turned exasperated eyes on her. How many hands did she think I had? Nevertheless, I managed to stretch my fingers to clasp the bulb of the soldier's nose while wrapping my other hand beneath his jaw and across his wet lips. His convulsing worsened. My muscles cramped as I struggled to restrain him.

He was so dehydrated that his body had fallen into a severe state of shock and confusion. He mumbled of giant spiders crawling on the canvas walls of the hospital tent and called Sestra Mirna and me demons with red eyes and clawed hands.

"Swallow!" Sestra Mirna shouted, her wrinkles cutting deeper into harsh lines. The soldier's gaunt face flushed a muted red, all the color his deathly pallor could muster. Unable to breathe, he finally gulped down the drink.

"One more sip," I said, leaning to his ear and speaking quiet and low. "You need every last drop."

He gagged down the rest. A few moments later, the last of his seizing stopped.

I fell back on my knees and inhaled a shaky breath. Around us, the coherent soldiers among the sick helplessly watched their comrade. Eleven men were in here. They stared with wide and feeble eyes. Perhaps they felt grief for their comrade or shock at his seizure or fear that death might also be coming for them. Whatever their emotions, I could only guess. Had I felt them, I would have been able to help each of them better. Know what they needed. Bridge a connection to their auras and give them hope. I would be able to do *something*—something more than feel utterly useless and incapable.

I swallowed a sting of threatening tears. *My power will return. It has to.*

That was my mantra. I'd physically recovered from the trauma of being shot, so it could only be a matter of time before my gift for sensing aura would recover, too.

"Let's get him a new blanket," Sestra Mirna said, her voice rattling on a thin breath. She seemed to have aged another year in the last hour. Exhaustion was taking its toll on all of us.

I took another moment to compose myself, then stood and pulled off the sheet draped over the soldier. Blood spotted the cloth from his coughing. I threw it in the basket with the dirty linens, and Sestra Mirna helped me spread another blanket over him. When we finished, she smoothed a lock of gray hair off her brow. "You should leave now. You've been in here all last night and most of today."

"As have you. I'll rest after you do."

She shook her head. "The soldiers are stable for the time being. I'll lie down on a spare cot. Go wash up and put something in your belly. Make sure Nadia hasn't scared off the new girl while you're at it."

I shifted on my feet. While I wanted to see Tosya, I wasn't anxious to face Genevie again. Or to feel even more hollow inside. "Are you sure?"

She nodded, rubbing the base of her throat with one hand and making a shooing motion with the other.

She must be thirsty. I poured a cup of water and handed it to her. "What are we going to do about the bounty hunter?"

"I'll speak to the lieutenant." The sestra took a sip and glanced across the tent to the middle-aged man with a salt-and-pepper mustache. He lay fitfully sleeping. When he'd taken ill, the soldiers who were well—only eight men—had slacked off even more. Although Anton had left over fifty soldiers to guard the convent, Feliks, who had become the major general of Free Riaznin since the onset of the civil war, ordered thirty back to Torchev two months ago. "We'll make sure guards stand watch at the gate at all times and keep a patrol around the grounds. The bounty hunter should stay away, but if he doesn't, Genevie will be able to warn us."

How I wished I could have, too. I had no ability to protect anyone here.

I walked to a basin of fresh water and scrubbed my hands with tallow soap. Its mutton fat lathered without any burning from the slaughtered sheep's lingering aura. My hands felt numb without that sting of death.

A cot creaked as Sestra Mirna sat down. A hanging lantern shone over her. Even under its warmth, her skin looked pale. I couldn't tell whether from weariness or concern. I hoped she'd rest like she said she would. "Did the courier ever come by?" she asked. "We should have received another letter by now. How long has it been since—?"

"Nineteen days." A tremor ran through the length of my fingers.

After a spell of hesitation, Sestra Mirna said, "Sonya?"

"Yes?" I noted the protective way she folded her arms across her waist. Even though the courier never brought letters from Anton, she knew I clung to my foolish hope. It was just as futile as our attempts to locate Dasha. Who knew where Valko had taken his little sister and what things he was manipulating her to do with her power?

"Be careful with your heart, child." Sestra Mirna's eyes tightened gently, the way they did when her scolding softened to an affectionate reprimanding. It was a look she'd often given to Dasha and Kira, back when the little girls lived here and were safe. "This civil war could last for years. Driving out the Shenglin could take longer. Anton is governor of the largest city in Riaznin. Don't expect what he can't give."

CHAPTER THREE

THE MOON CAST THE CONVENT'S WHITEWASHED WALLS IN wolf gray. I quickened my steps away from the hospital tent, glancing over my shoulder at every small noise. The bounty hunter could be near, and I'd have no warning. I reached the door, wiped my shoes on a bristled mat, and hurried inside.

Nadia's and Genevie's voices wafted down the stone corridors, along with the clang of pots and clink of dishes. They must be preparing a late dinner in the kitchen. I moved in that direction when a shadow stirred on my left. I startled, instinctively feeling out for an aura, only to be met by my frustrating inability.

My eyes adjusted to the dim light of one candle and focused on a pair of long legs in patched-up trousers near the bottom of the narrow staircase. "Tosya?" I came nearer, touching the banister.

He sat on the lower steps, his sleeves rolled up, his elbows on his knees as he picked dirt from his fingernails. "Oh, hello," he said. The wood beneath him creaked as he looked up at me.

"What are you doing over there?"

"Just waiting for my best friend." He winked, though his smile was delayed.

"Anton is your best friend."

"That's debatable. He's not as pretty."

I couldn't laugh, not with the thought of Anton pinching my breath. I sat down beside Tosya. "Have you seen him?" I asked, twisting my fingers in my lap.

"We parted ways a few weeks ago so I could join the Romska Greater Council." The nomadic tribes convened annually, and this year's meeting place was near Ormina. "Motshan sent me with herbs to help you treat the consumption."

"He knew we had an outbreak?"

"He keeps a closer eye on you than you think."

Warmth flooded my limbs at the thought of the Romska chief and my distant blood tie to the tribes. "I didn't know Motshan kept *any* kind of watch on me," I confessed. The idea of nomads lurking about the woods wasn't bothersome—being remembered felt nice—I was only disappointed I hadn't sensed their presence myself. "What did the elders decide during the Council?" I asked. "Will they allow a tribesman to represent them on the Duma?"

Tosya preened, straightening his vest. "You're looking at

the first Romska governor."

"They elected you?" My mouth stretched into a wide smile. "Tosya, that's wonderful!"

"It's not official yet. Anton still needs to gain the approval of the Duma."

"I'm sure he will." Anton had been pressing the issue with the other governors on the ruling council of Riaznin since last spring. "So is Anton in Torchev?"

"Last I heard, yes."

My stomach fluttered. "He . . . didn't give you a letter for me, did he?"

"You know he can't write you any letters." Tosya bumped my knee with his.

"I know." My shoulders wilted.

"Letters can be intercepted, and if the emperor found out you were alive—"

"*Former* emperor," I corrected. I'd never call Valko my sovereign again. The brief thought of him surfaced the dregs of his aura, though they were only memory. His hatred, sorrow, obsession, and fear—echoes of what I'd felt in the moment he'd shot me—still rattled inside the drum of my chest. I hated to think of Dasha with Valko now, exposed to his poisonous emotions.

"Doesn't feel so former anymore," Tosya muttered.

At his resentful tone, my insides folded. I never felt this distraught around my oldest friend. Tosya was my escape from the harshness of the world. He made me smile and relax and forget my worries. But I could no longer feel his easing energy, and, for the first time, that made Tosya seem like a stranger. "I miss your aura," I murmured, my throat aching, my words more for myself than for him. I didn't realize my slip until he drew back to study my eyes. Could he see how empty I was inside?

"What do you mean?" he asked, the long planes of his face stretching as he lifted his brows.

I shook my head and stood to leave, but he caught my hand. Reluctantly, I turned to him, but I couldn't make myself admit to my lost gift.

"She's like me now," Nadia interjected. We spun around to find her a few feet away, at the entrance of the corridor leading to the kitchen. She lifted her chin.

Shame burned my cheeks and stung my eyes. *Accept your fate*, Nadia had told me just yesterday. *You're broken, just like you broke me.*

"You've lost your power?" Tosya asked, breathless. I fidgeted under the pressure of his unblinking gaze, desperate to escape the weight of what I couldn't feel from him, whether it was overwhelming pity or staggering repulsion.

I couldn't answer. I felt like a moth caught in a jar under Tosya's scrutiny, his emotions out of reach on the other side of the glass.

"Is dinner ready?" I asked Nadia abruptly. When she nodded, I managed a smile that opposed Tosya's downturned mouth. "Wonderful. Shall we?"

"But—? Are you—?" He made vague gestures at me. "Will you be—?"

"All right?" I supplied. "Of course. My gift will return soon enough."

"Yes, just like mine has." Nadia snapped her fingers. "Poof! So simple." Tosya narrowed his eyes at her, and her smirk fell.

"I'll wait for you in the kitchen, Sonya," he said, brushing past Nadia as he advanced down the corridor.

She lowered her head and rubbed a stain on her apron. "He hasn't forgiven me," she said once he was out of earshot. "He's been hiding in this foyer for over an hour, no doubt waiting for you. Genevie sensed him enter."

Without knowing if Nadia was hurt or jealous or confused, I was at a loss for how to comfort her, or even if I would have done so despite the constant barbs between us. "Apologies go a long way," I said, walking past her. "Maybe you could start by telling him you're sorry."

"You should teach me how," she murmured. I paused to look at her face, dim in the corridor. Her expression was unreadable. "You've had to beg forgiveness for so many things."

Her voice came quietly, only cutting with a dull knife rather than her usual sharp steel. I couldn't tell whether she was mocking me or sincerely pleading for my help, so I walked on.

In the kitchen, I found Tosya sitting at the table. He awkwardly sipped at his soup while Genevie stood in the farthest corner, wiping already clean bowls with a dish towel.

I crossed the kitchen, and she shrank back, pressing herself against the slab. When I halted, she released a shaky exhale. "*Pardonne-moi*," she said. "I cannot feel your aura—yours or the other girl's. I am still taken by surprise."

"That's all right." I offered a smile, trying not to feel like the aberration I was, and started stacking the bowls she'd pretended to dry. "Have you eaten yet?"

She reached for a tumbler of water with trembling hands. "I am only thirsty."

It took me a moment to understand why. "You sense the sick soldiers?" When she nodded, jealousy scalded the lining of my stomach. Ridiculous, but I couldn't rationalize it away. I would have taken upon myself the infirmities of those scores of men just to feel any aura again.

"They need so much water." Genevie rubbed her throat. "Nothing satiates them."

"I know." *But not like she does.* "They'll be sick for weeks. You should eat. All I found in your knapsack was a few berries."

She nodded, but her gaze drifted to Tosya.

"He won't do you any harm. We grew up together. I trust him with my life."

Genevie swallowed and slowly unhitched herself from the wooden slab where she'd been working. We ladled soup from the pot hanging over the hearth, and then sat at the table across from Tosya. He passed Genevie the black bread with a nonchalant smile and minimal eye contact, which seemed just the right balance between kindness and disinterest. Her shoulders relaxed. I gave Tosya's foot a little nudge of thanks, and the side of his mouth lifted.

As I took my first taste of soup, I didn't cringe from the ham hock flavoring the broth. The auras from slaughtered animals no longer plagued me. Still, my throat constricted, and I offered a silent prayer to Morva, acknowledging the beast's death. "How did you escape Floquart de Bonpré?" I asked Genevie, searching for something to talk about.

She blanched and gave a small laugh. "How did *you* escape Emperor Valko?" she countered.

Fair enough. If I was going to bring up her past abuser in our first real conversation together, she had every right to bring up mine. "I convinced him to relinquish his throne and left Torchev before he declared it was his again."

Tosya snorted, choking on his drink. "It wasn't that simple, but I do like your version, Sonya."

Genevie glanced between us, and though we didn't elaborate, she must have sensed the marrow of my history with Valko. She couldn't feel my shame for briefly being infatuated with the emperor before he turned vicious, my hatred because he'd killed my friend Pia and later shot me, my regret for never defeating him—at least not in any sustainable way—and my infuriation because, without my power, I couldn't. But Tosya knew me and my story well; his emotions would at least echo a dim recollection of what I'd endured.

Genevie swallowed a small bite of bread. "I was never bound to Floquart with chains," she explained, finally answering my question. "But he owned me, according to Esten law. He had bought me when I was fifteen. He made me feel worse than his property. I felt . . . *épouvantable*." Her eyes roamed the kitchen as she searched for a word we'd understand. "Tarnished. Worthless. I never dared to leave him, not until after we visited the palace in Torchev. On the night of the ball, I felt your pain, Sonya, when the emperor hurt you. It was so like my own each time Floquart . . ."

Her lips quivered. She mashed them together and picked at the end of her fraying sleeve. Even without sensing her aura, I understood a small part of what she'd suffered. Still, I'd only been Valko's servant for four months, not four *years*, if I'd guessed Genevie's age correctly.

"I finally gained the courage to run away," she continued. "I planned my escape for months after I returned to Estengarde. Until the bounty hunter found me, I believed I was free."

"We'll do everything we can to keep you safe here," I promised, though my stomach twisted at the thought of the bounty hunter looming in the woods. Floquart must have offered him a generous reward if he had tracked Genevie across the border. I doubted he would give up his quest so easily.

The room grew quiet, save for the popping embers in the fireplace. Nadia entered the kitchen and dished herself a bowl of soup, her gaze deftly assessing our somber expressions. She was quicker at picking up emotional cues than I was; she'd dealt with the loss of her abilities longer.

She sat beside Tosya, giving him a berth of two feet on their bench seat. He shifted another inch away. Face composed, masking any hurt she may have been feeling, she asked Genevie, "Have you told them of the Auraseers in Alaise?" Alaise was on the other side of the Bayac Mountains, the capital city of Estengarde, where the king lived.

I turned curious eyes on Genevie. "What about them?" My knowledge of Esten Auraseers was limited, but I did know they held no respect among their countrymen. Some were sold as slaves, like Genevie, and others were cast out of society to scrape a living for themselves, unable to marry or receive wages by any legal means. Many ended up living on the streets as prostitutes. Under the empire, Riaznian Auraseers had been given no liberties to speak of, either, but at least we'd been fed, sheltered, and tutored in the convent.

Genevie sat up taller. Some of the fragility she'd shown seemed to break away, hinting at the strength of a coal-pressed diamond beneath. "I am not the only person who will need sanctuary in this convent."

"Some Auraseers are banding together to escape their masters," Nadia added. "Genevie didn't act alone."

"Four others escaped with me. Two of them should arrive any day. When Floquart's bounty hunter caught our trail in the mountains, I snuck away in the night and raced ahead to keep my friends out of danger."

"What about the other two Auraseers?" I asked.

Genevie's lips paled. "Sandrine and Zophie never made it out of Alaise. They were caught and arrested. I fear they have been executed by now."

"I hope you and the others didn't travel all this way to suffer a similar fate," Tosya said in his frank but gentle way. "Riaznin is at war; the convent may not be a safe place for much longer."

Genevie's brows twitched when he addressed her, but then she exhaled and composed herself. "If Shengli overtakes Riaznin, your Auraseers will be protected. The Shenglin revere the gifted. And if your democracy falls in the civil war, Auraseers will be trained once again to become guardians to the emperor. *Que será, será.* No matter what fate befalls your nation or whatever war you may lose, my friends are safer here than in Estengarde."

"The convent doors are open to any Auraseers." I touched her arm. "Your friends may take their chances for refuge here. I'm sure Sestra Mirna will welcome them." To the sestra, *all* Auraseers were born blessed by the goddess Feya, to whom this convent was dedicated.

Genevie's gaze dropped to her spoon. She stirred her soup in a slow circle. Was she feeling shy or nervous? "I didn't expect to find you here, Sovereign Auraseer." Her autumn-brown eyes warmed as she looked up at me. "We have stories of Auraseers like you in Estengarde—*les grandes voyantes*, we call them— but until I met you, I thought they were myth."

The nape of my neck prickled. How could she know about the power I once possessed to alter other people's emotions? It was a carefully guarded secret, known to only a few, so I wouldn't be exploited for my abilities.

When I said nothing, only stared at her with parted lips, she explained, "On the night of the ball, I felt more than your pain when the emperor hurt you. I felt you change inside and grow stronger. I felt you change *him*—his aura—so he stopped hurting you. Later, I learned how Emperor Valko gave up his throne to offer freedom to his people. That went against all his attributes. So I believed—I hoped—you played a role in overthrowing him." Her mouth curved a little, the first time I'd seen her smile. It transformed her countenance and brought life to her eyes. "You inspired me. You have inspired so many Auraseers in Alaise."

Tosya grinned and jostled my leg under the table, but I felt numb, even to my own emotions. "You told them about me?" I asked Genevie. Already two Auraseers had been executed, likely because of my so-called inspiration.

"You have helped us see we deserve better," she replied. "We will not find freedom in Estengarde, but we can escape and wish for it here. *Nous essayons.*" She shrugged. "At least that is what several of us are trying to do."

I held my breath. "How many Auraseers are you talking about?"

Her eyes drifted over the table as she mentally calculated. "Close to twelve. But maybe they will encourage more. Your story is powerful."

"But *I'm* not." My heart thudded painfully in my chest, my numbness shattering. "Not anymore." Genevie knew what I was now. She felt it, the void in me, the wall I couldn't break down around myself. Auraseers in Estengarde were endangering themselves because a *grande voyante*—I—gave them hope. I felt responsible to protect them, just like I was desperate to protect Dasha from Valko, and Kira from the dangers in Torchev. But how could I?

"Nadia says you were shot and almost killed." Genevie bit her lip, rubbing the splintering stem of her wood spoon. "*Tu pourrais toujours guérir.* Maybe . . . you will heal."

Her voice was gentle, but it struck with the force of gunpowder. For months, no one but myself had expressed any faith that I would recover. Now, hearing someone else say the words, I realized how false and empty they were, how unalterably wounded I was. I stood, feeling a sudden urge to escape her expectant gaze. "Would you please excuse me? I promised Tosya I would take him on a walk to see the convent grounds." I'd done no such thing, but I didn't want to be alone with my thoughts. Tosya was safe company.

He blinked, his spoon frozen on its journey to his mouth. "In the dark?" Clearly, he hadn't forgotten the bounty hunter.

"The moon is bright, and the guards are out. Sestra Mirna has seen to that. Shall we?"

"Um . . . all right."

❧❧❧

Tosya strolled beside me, his hands in his pockets. His toes kicked the occasional pebble as I guided him along the path encircling the convent. The moon was almost full and gave us the light I'd promised. My guard eased up regarding the bounty hunter. I felt safe in the company of Tosya, pacifist or not. Besides, two soldiers were in sight, walking the grounds on patrol.

A racking cough came from the hospital tent, but from where we stood, the dreary smell of antiseptics didn't reach us. I breathed in the earthen, decaying fragrance of the forest in its first turn of autumn.

"All this is new," I said, pointing to the rebuilt east wing of the convent. "A bell tower used to be up there. The girls said it was haunted because Auraseers had been hung from its rafters. That was before Sestra Mirna's time, back when Auraseers were punished by death when they refused to serve the Ozerov emperors." I tilted my head up and gazed longingly. "But I loved the bell tower."

"You were always one to be drawn to scenes of morbid tragedy."

I gave Tosya a one-handed shove, and he chuckled. "Yuliya and I would sneak up there," I said, "and no one would bother us. We could see all the way to the Ilvinov Ocean. It reminded me of that story from your book of folktales."

"The Golden Fish?"

"No, *The Sea King and Vasilisa the Wise.*"

Tosya peered up at the spot where the bell tower used to be, and then burst into laughter.

"What's so funny?" I grinned, even though I didn't know what had set him off.

"Of course you would like that story—Vasilisa kills the sea king and rescues the prince. It was self-prophecy, you reading that."

"I hope not." I wrapped my arms around myself. "That

version left out the part where the sea king resurrects himself, Vasilisa loses her magic, and the prince is left to fight his demons without her help."

"A rather depressing twist."

"Believe me, I know."

We shuffled along the path. The air grew cooler, and the wistful song of a nightingale rose on the breeze. "So it's really gone, then, your power?" Tosya asked. "You feel absolutely nothing? Not a spark of my winning charm or intolerable vanity dancing through your veins?"

"Not even your irritating intelligence."

Tosya smiled, then rubbed the back of his neck. "You know, Genevie is right—your story is inspiring. It doesn't matter that your power is gone. What you did for the revolution while you had power was enough. It's giving these Esten Auraseers hope. It could give *many* people hope."

I contemplated him. I'd once wished to be recognized for the role I played in Valko's abdication. I'd wanted to be seen as someone important like Anton, a prince turned governor, or Tosya, the poet who penned the poem that sparked the revolution. Now all I wanted was to be useful, no matter who knew. "I don't want to give people hope if I can't do anything more to help them."

"Do you really miss your abilities? You never wanted to be an Auraseer, much less one who could feel the dead and overpower another person's emotions."

"That was like wishing I didn't exist."

"Well, what if I could never write a poem again?"

"Then you'd know how I feel."

"And I would still be Tosya. Or is that all I am to you, a poet?"

I folded my arms, resistant to what he was driving at. I would never be satisfied with myself this way. A person couldn't be made whole from broken, missing pieces. "What I miss most is simply feeling what others around me feel. I'm blind without that." I could do without the stronger gift I once had, although it was what I needed most to save Dasha. "If I could at least sense aura, then I could feel danger coming. I could protect the convent, maybe even track Valko." Whether I'd wanted to or not, I'd always felt his aura stronger than any others, a beacon of darkness.

Tosya laid a hand on my shoulder. "You are more than an Auraseer, Sonya."

"What if I don't want to be?" My voice carried on a frail thread of air, thin as spider silk. "How can I help anyone now?"

"Do you think the Esten Auraseers will care if you've lost your abilities? What they want is a new start, a life of their own choosing. You can help them find it here. That can be *your* new start, as well."

I cast my gaze at the convent. I had no intention to remain here forever. After these wars ended, I still hoped for a life with Anton in Torchev.

If the wars *ever* ended. If Anton still loved me.

"Of course I'll help them. But if you start calling me Sestra Sonya, I might slug you."

Tosya chuckled and draped a lanky arm around me. "I wouldn't dream of it, Sestra Sonya."

CHAPTER FOUR

"Do you ever regret your vows to Feya?" I asked Sestra Mirna the next day as we slowly climbed the staircase in the west wing. Nadia had taken over for her in the hospital tent, and I'd insisted on walking her to her bedchamber to make sure she finally lay down to rest. She probably hadn't slept last night, like she said she would. She still looked bone-weary and pale.

She came to a sudden stop halfway up the steep flight, her back hunched as she gripped the railing and coughed, panting for breath.

"Are you all right?" I reached out to support her. She was getting too old for all these stairs. I needed to talk to Nadia about moving her into one of the vacant rooms on the ground floor.

The wrinkles between her brows cut into two deep slashes as she turned her head to me. Was she hurting, as well as struggling to breathe? "That is not something an Auraseer should *ever* ask a sestra," she said, disregarding my last question.

Oh. She was angry.

"I'm sorry." Heat prickled to my cheeks. "I didn't mean to offend you." I was still learning all the etiquette of the convent. I hadn't lived here most of my life, like Nadia. "I only wondered why you chose to dedicate your life to serving Auraseers. I should have phrased it that way."

Sestra Mirna released a rattling sigh, and her forehead smoothed to its usual canvas of careworn lines. She returned her gaze to the rest of the daunting flight ahead of us and started climbing again, one painstaking step at a time. "I suppose when life closes enough doors on you, your feet take you to where one last door remains open. You either walk inside or walk an endless path of misery."

I frowned. That sounded like a harsh ultimatum. "Those are the only two choices?"

"For me they were."

I looked askance at her and studied the map of wrinkles on her face, wondering what hard experiences in her life had wrought each crease and furrow. Had they been anything like mine? "How will I know, then?"

"Know what?"

"When I've come to my last open door?" My voice betrayed a tremble of desperation.

Three stairs from the landing, Sestra Mirna paused again,

this time to look at me. Her weary eyes warmed, and for a moment, I pictured her younger and vibrant and beautiful. "You will know, Sonya. Trust me. Crossing that threshold will take every last measure of your courage and fierce desire to fight." She reached up and took my face in one of her firm and weathered hands. "So stay courageous, my child. Stay strong."

It seemed like she was asking me to promise her something, and the look in her fervent gaze made that request feel urgent, though I couldn't say why. So I drew up taller and answered, "I will." She patted my cheek and climbed onward.

Her words stayed with me long after I'd helped her to her room and baked bread in the kitchen and boiled more herb water for the soldiers. They stayed with me while I went to check on Genevie in the upstairs study hall.

The pleats of her simple green dress swayed as she paced near the window, where she kept watch for her two Auraseer friends to arrive. This room offered the clearest vantage of the front grounds and the road beyond.

As I walked to her, I paused at the two desks my best friend, Yuliya, and I had often sat at. They still remained side by side. In the hidden recess beneath my old inkwell, I'd scratched my name. On her desk, in the same spot, Yuliya had etched a primrose bouquet. A lump formed in my throat. I promised myself I'd lay more flowers on Yuliya's grave.

"Would you like something to eat?" I asked Genevie, pushing away from the desks and wiping my hands on my apron.

"No, *merci.*" She leaned on the window ledge as she gazed

outside. Her auburn hair gleamed red in the sunlight. Another reminder of Yuliya, whose hair had been ginger.

"Can you sense anything yet?"

Genevie shook her head.

"How far *can* you sense?" When I'd had my power, my range of awareness was long—I could have felt aura from here to the first few trees in the forest—but no other Auraseer I knew of besides Dasha had abilities that strong.

She pursed her lips. "To the end of a large room, like the palace ballroom in Torchev, if I concentrate."

That wouldn't help us much if the bounty hunter was prowling nearby. "Maybe you can learn to cast your awareness wider. I could teach you."

"*J'en doute.* I trained under Madame Perle, the personal Auraseer to the king. My abilities are as refined as they will ever be." She smiled gently—whether to humor me or put me in my place, I didn't know. "Not all of us are special like you."

I laughed. The sound rang so falsely in my ears. "I'm not special. Not anymore."

She turned to study me. In her eyes, I saw Yuliya's gentility and Pia's brightness. Genevie couldn't replace them—I wouldn't want her to—but maybe I had room in my heart for one more friend. "*Où est-ce?*" she said, her brow wrinkling. "It has to be there. You could not be alive without aura." She came over and squeezed my hand with a light but steady pressure. "Do not worry, Sonya. We will find a way to help your aura breathe."

"How?" I asked, both skeptical and curious. I'd tried just

about everything. Nadia and I even brewed a strong batch of relaxing herbs several weeks ago, hoping they would reconnect us to our deepest senses, but they only made us sick.

"I don't know." She tilted her head and sighed. "If only you could meet Madame Perle. She has a rare talent."

"Rare?" I frowned at her. "How rare? Like mine and Dasha's?" The thought of someone else with our abilities sent my heart pounding—not out of kinship, but fear.

"Madame Perle has a different power. She can feel so deeply into another person's aura that she falls into a trance, a state of meditation that allows her to sense the emotions of memories that person may have forgotten."

I cocked an eyebrow, openly staring at Genevie. I'd never heard of such a gift in an Auraseer.

"Perhaps you are . . . *refouler*"—she tried to think of the right word—"suppressing some deep emotions, and that is why your aura is hiding. Maybe they are attached to your buried memories." She crossed her arms. "What is the earliest thing you remember as a child?"

"The flagstones in my parents' garden."

"How old were you?"

I shrugged. "Five or six."

"That is late for a first memory. What about your parents? What memories do you have of them?"

"None, but that's because they sent me to live with the Romska for my safety."

"At what age?"

"Seven."

"Your memories become vivid after that?"

I slid my hands behind my back. "Is that really so unusual?"

She nodded, her brows raised. "Did you know a child's . . ." She cast about for the right word. "*Personnalité?*"

"Personality?"

"Yes." She grinned, amused at how the two words were almost identical. "A child's personality is established by age six. Think of all you have forgotten before then that made you *you.*"

I considered her. Maybe she was onto something. Being separated from my parents at such a young age must have been traumatic. Had I blocked my childhood memories to protect my heart? What if I'd also unwittingly blocked my aura in order to protect myself? The two incidents might be connected. "You really believe this Madame Perle can help me? Wouldn't I have to emit my aura in order for her to sense it?"

"You *do* have aura." Genevie clasped my hand. "It is only sleeping. If anyone can awaken it, it is Madame Perle. She can help you reconnect with yourself through your deep memories." Genevie's autumn-brown eyes and closed-lipped smile reflected the confidence underlying her quiet voice. It dissipated the tension I'd held in my muscles for so long.

For the first time in four months, I felt rational, sustainable hope that I could be made whole again.

Just as I started to ask more about Madame Perle, Genevie's

fingers stiffened in my grasp. Her shoulders hitched, like an agitated cat with its hair on end. "Something is different," she said.

It took me a moment to realize what she meant: she *felt* something different. I broke into a wide grin. "Have your friends arrived?" I moved to look out the window, but Genevie wouldn't let go of my hand.

"No, it isn't them." She bowed her head in concentration. "There are many. One aura radiates strongest. It surges with a tremendous sense of pride and satisfaction . . . but it feels wrong somehow. *Ça me rend malade.* It is making my stomach turn."

With a shaky breath, I pulled away and squinted through the window. Past the leaded panes, a regiment of at least sixty soldiers were coming through the gate. Our guards had let them in. Of course they had. These men wore the same red-and-gold uniform of Riaznin, along with a blue sash, denoting their affiliation with the new democracy.

For one brief moment, I ignored Genevie's warning and hope flared in my heart. Was Anton with them?

His face flashed to the forefront of my mind. I pictured the straight slope of his aristocratic Ozerov nose. His kind and fathomless brown eyes. His marble-cut cheekbones and the thin sculpt of his upper lip. I felt his warm hands on my waist. The remembrance of his strong and luminous aura.

I scanned the men, searching for his dark hair, broad shoulders, and regal posture, but I found him nowhere.

A movement below me caught my eye, close to the convent

porch. One of the soldiers had ridden ahead of the others. He wore a plumed general's hat. I couldn't see his face, not until he glanced up.

I gasped and jumped back from the window. All the muscles in my body stiffened, and my blood ran colder than the governor's icy blue eyes.

Feliks.

I whirled around to Genevie. "We have to wake up Sestra Mirna!" I whisper-shouted, though Feliks couldn't have heard me. "He can't know I'm alive!"

"Who?" Genevie peered out the window for herself.

"General Kaverin." I tightened my fists. "I don't have time to explain, but if he knows I've survived and am powerless, he'll never let me live."

"Why do you think he has come here?" Genevie asked.

I shook my head, rushing for the door. "The convent is an outpost for the army. Maybe enemy forces are nearby. Feliks could have brought his regiment here to prepare for battle."

As I reached for the handle, the door flew open. Tosya stood there, panting on the threshold. His olive skin had paled to a sickly green. "Feliks is asking for you, Sonya."

My heartbeat skidded to a stop, then broke into galloping race. "Tell him I'm dead!"

"Too late. One of the convent soldiers slipped up and said you were here."

I stumbled back a step, clenching my hands in my hair. "What do I do?"

He reached out with his long arm and grabbed mine. "Run! I'll help you escape."

He yanked me into the upstairs corridor, and we fled toward the back stairs. Soldiers emerged on the landing. We turned and rushed the other way, but at the opposite end of the corridor, more soldiers stormed up the main staircase.

We backed up slowly. Panic constricted my chest. Each breath came harder than the last.

The plume of Feliks's general's hat rose above his soldiers' as he came forward. The men stepped aside, letting him pass. Once he laid eyes on me, his mouth hitched in a half grin. The disturbing sense of satisfaction Genevie had felt within him showed plainly across his smug expression.

"Auraseer Petrova," he said, his cunning gaze raking over me. "What magic you possess. It appears even the former emperor cannot kill you."

CHAPTER FIVE

"WHO TOLD YOU I WAS—?"

"Alive?" Feliks motioned for one of his soldiers to draw up an armchair in front of the fireplace. They had moved me to the convent library, where a fire was already crackling in the hearth, and dragged along Tosya and Genevie, no doubt to threaten them if I became difficult. Feliks still believed I had my power to alter emotions, otherwise he wouldn't have traveled three days from the capital during wartime to retrieve me. "Some of the soldiers who used to be stationed here confided the truth when they returned to the city."

My fingers curled in the folds of my skirt. "They promised to keep that a secret."

"*Whom* did they promise? Anton?" Feliks sat down and leveled his gaze on me, seated across from him on a worn couch between my friends. "Not everyone treats the governor of Torchev like a prince anymore. There are other Duma councilors they must answer to—above all, their general." He leaned back and crossed one leg over the other. He reminded me so much of Valko then, an arrogant ruler on his throne.

"Does Anton know you've come here?" I asked, fighting to steady my erratic heartbeat. The Anton I knew—the Anton who loved me—would have protected me at all costs.

"No, I'm afraid he doesn't. The Duma saw fit to send Governor Ozerov on a lengthy mission just before I left, so the timing worked out rather well."

I glanced at Tosya to see if he knew what Feliks was talking about, but he shook his head, his eyes mirroring my worry. "What mission?" I asked. "If you've endangered Anton in any way to make me—"

"It's a *diplomatic* mission, so you have nothing to fear. Anton is far too valuable an asset for me to compromise. His ties to Estengarde—"

"You sent him to *Estengarde*?" My voice pitched high. Alaise, the capital city, was a two-week journey to the west, sometimes more, depending on road conditions in the Bayac Mountains pass. "Why would you send him so far when the wars are here?" Feliks had to have a justifiable reason besides getting Anton out of the way. He was a practical man, if nothing else. Then it struck me: "You want him to forge an alliance." The alliance Valko had failed to achieve last spring.

Anton had a time-tested relationship with King Léopold, who had protected him when he was a child living in hiding near the border of Estengarde. It was all a part of Anton's father,

Emperor Izia's, plan to one day foster an alliance between nations. At least that's what Valko suspected, for he had spent his childhood on the opposite side of Riaznin, living near Shengli, where Izia had made a similar arrangement with our eastern neighbors.

Feliks's hands spread wide. "Free Riaznin is strong, but the former emperor has now amassed support from one-third of our nation. We cannot hope to conquer his armies *and* the invading Shenglin without more help. One war is taxing enough. We need the Esten alliance . . . and we need you."

Tosya stiffened beside me. Genevie stared intently at Feliks, surely scouring his aura, though I doubted he held any secret sentiments. Feliks's motives had always been transparent. He was a man driven by a vain sense of righteousness that allowed him to rationalize the most extreme measures he took to uphold justice.

He pulled his sleeve cuffs taut. "I see no need to mince words, Sonya. I'm willing to forgive your numerous trespasses—above all, treason—for your cooperation."

"You want me to be your weapon in both wars," I concluded with a grim nod. While Feliks knew I couldn't bend the emotions of a large group of people, I'd shown I *could* influence individuals in high positions. At least I once could, but that power was long gone.

"To have a fair fight, we need a powerful Auraseer, like the one Valko has."

"Dasha." My stomach tightened. I pictured the little girl,

her delicate features, large gray eyes, and dark, waving hair. Valko was surely fashioning her into the weapon he'd once dreamed I could be. "What has she done?"

"What *hasn't* she done?" Feliks replied. The tassels of his epaulettes danced as he gave a humorless laugh. "No one but another Auraseer can say for certain, but Valko is rumored to bring her everywhere. She is seen before and after battles. Dasha rides with him while he parades through towns, recruiting his army. People fear her. Some have seen her use her power. Dasha has become a symbol of Valko's reclaimed reign."

I swallowed hard, feeling more helpless than ever. Feliks believed I could outmatch a seven-year-old girl, but I couldn't, not even to save her. "You're a fool to think you can control me. I could compel you and your regiment to leave here and ride as far as Abdara if I had the mind to."

"Could you, now?" Feliks smirked and leaned forward. "I imagine that would require an extraordinary level of exertion. What would it take, I wonder, to sustain it?"

I'd gone too far with my bluff, but it didn't matter. "You don't have any real leverage, and you know it. This discussion is pointless." At the very least, Feliks had to believe threatening my friends at the convent wouldn't get him anywhere. As far as he knew, I had the power to persuade him to back down. I'd done so before.

"You're forgetting who *isn't* here," Feliks said, one step ahead of me. "A little someone I found living in appalling conditions in Torchev."

I wasn't following.

"Have you forgotten young Kira so easily?"

My ribs contracted like prison bars across my lungs. I inwardly cursed Feliks with every foul name I could think of. "What have you done with her?" He knew I loved Kira like a sister, just as I loved Dasha. I should have predicted this was the card he would play.

His grin broadened, his manner as cool and indifferent as his glacier-blue eyes. "I have her detained somewhere; that is all you need to know. She is safe for now."

Genevie turned her mouth to my ear. "He is lying," she whispered.

My heart gave a hard pound of alarm. I turned to her. "How?"

"Take the other Auraseer out of here," Feliks barked at his soldiers.

"Wait!" I clutched Genevie's arm, but two men dragged her out of the library. Feliks couldn't have heard what she'd said to me, but he was suspicious all the same. Clearly, he didn't want more than one Auraseer in here, reading the intentions behind his words. If only I could. He'd lied about Kira, but which part? Was he holding her hostage or not? Was she truly safe?

"Do I have your attention now?" Feliks asked me. "I'm not asking for your help, Sonya; I'm requiring it. Free Riaznin needs you. Not only as a weapon, but to be our *symbol*, just as Dasha is Valko's."

"A symbol?" Dizziness flashed through my head. I couldn't think clearly. Not with Kira in possible danger. "How?"

"That part is simple. Just ask your friend here, the 'Voice of the Revolution.'"

I blinked, frowning at Tosya. The "Voice of the Revolution" was a title the people had given him because he'd penned the poem that sparked the revolution. But what did that have to do with me? "What is Feliks talking about?"

Tosya turned his hands up. "I have no idea." Still, a slight tremor ran across his forehead. Was he afraid, or was he hiding something? No, he was my best friend.

Feliks motioned to a soldier, who brought forth a traveling bag. Feliks unbuckled it and withdrew a slim, forest-green book. He held it up for us to see. My breath caught. Embossed on the cover was the title *Sovereign Auraseer*.

Tosya jumped to his feet, crossed to Feliks in three strides, and snatched the book away.

A few soldiers stepped forward, but Feliks held up a hand to stall them. "Go on," he urged Tosya. "Read it for yourself. Another excellent poem."

Tosya fumbled through the pages, and his shoulders fell. He dragged a hand over his face.

"I don't understand," I said, a terrible foreboding wrenching deep in my belly. "Did you write that, Tosya?"

Our eyes met, and his dark brows rose helplessly. "I write a lot of things, Sonya. I told you, you had an inspiring story," he said, shame creeping into his voice. "But I swear to you, I never published this. I would never endanger you like that." He whirled on Feliks. "Where did you get this?"

"From *you*, naturally." Feliks folded his hands in his lap. "You're a terribly unguarded person, if you must know the truth. Your belongings were easy to confiscate. After I learned Sonya was alive, I had you tracked, seeing as you two are close friends. I never imagined the gem you would give me." His fingers fanned out, pointing at the book. "You see, above all, the people in Riaznin need hope. In their terror of being conquered by the Shenglin, they're turning to the old ways—to Valko. They see his regime as the strongest, the most capable of driving out the Shenglin. We need to show them that the democracy is stronger."

Dread trickled into the pit of my stomach. I rose on shaky feet. "Tosya," I said, my pulse thundering in my ears, "what did you write in that book?"

He exhaled, briefly squeezing his eyes shut. "Everything."

"Everything?" I repeated, my tone severe.

"Everything you did for the revolution," he clarified, lowering his gaze as he passed me the book.

My hands trembled as I flipped through it. I fought to breathe. It revealed all that I feared. My power to manipulate emotions. My role in persuading Valko to abdicate. How I'd felt a legion of auras during the One Day War—all the emotions of the peasants storming the palace—and forced Valko to feel them. On the last page of the book was a drawing: Valko cowering on the ground while I held his crown aloft in the air.

My legs threatened to give way. I stumbled backward to sit on the couch before my knees buckled. This couldn't be happening. Feliks had threatened to exploit my power in the past, but never publicly. "This isn't the only copy, is it?"

Feliks grinned, seeing I was catching on. "Before I left, I saw that the poem was distributed throughout Torchev. Soon it will spread to farther reaches of Riaznin. Even now, people are reading about the sovereign Auraseer who once saved them and will save them again. And those who can't read . . . well, that picture there should suffice."

"But"—Tosya kneaded his brow—"the people don't know Sonya is alive, right?" I didn't need to be an Auraseer to see the dying hope on his face. He must have known Feliks was too clever to miss a detail like that. The general wouldn't have gone to the trouble of publishing and distributing this poem if people thought I was dead.

"Did you miss the last line of the book?" Feliks gave him a secretive grin. "I hope you don't mind, Tosya. I took the liberty of writing that small part myself."

Fully baited, I turned to that page. Tosya leaned over me to read it too.

Now she rests at the convent of Auraseers,
waiting for the day her people need her once more.

I closed the book. Hunched over. Buried my head in my hands. "You don't know what you've done," I said to Feliks.

Word would spread. Valko would find out I was alive. He'd have me hunted and killed. I wouldn't be able to defend myself. Or save Dasha. Or anyone.

The door to the library flung open. Sestra Mirna stood there in her nightgown and an untied robe, her body tense. Even her toes clenched white on the floorboards. "What are you doing here, General Kaverin?" Her tone sounded fierce, though it rang weakly. She looked younger, more vulnerable without her gray hair tied back into a kerchief. It hung in wiry waves past her shoulders. "You leave Sonya alone. She has sanctuary in this convent."

"Yes, if she chooses it," Feliks replied matter-of-factly. The embers in the fireplace sparked behind him. "But after everything she and I have discussed, I believe she will see reason and come with me. Sonya is needed in Torchev."

"She will do no such thing. She's needed *here*. You can't—"

My hands dug in my scalp. "I have no power anymore!"

"Sonya!" Sestra Mirna gasped and started coughing. She brought her handkerchief to her mouth as her eyes rounded on me. I'd just revealed the secret we'd worked so hard to protect.

Feliks's studied me carefully. "Lying won't help anyone, Auraseer Petrova, most certainly not your young friend, Kira."

"I *am* thinking of Kira," I snapped. The sestra's eyes widened another fraction at our talk of the little girl. She tried to speak, but she couldn't stop hacking. "You'll let her go if you know the truth. When Valko shot me, I nearly died. And when I woke up, my abilities were gone. *All* of them. I can't even *sense* aura anymore, let alone overpower people. Why do you think I've remained hidden here?"

I met Tosya's fearful gaze. He knew what I'd just done by confessing. My life was now forfeit. Feliks would see me hanged for treason. But I had to accept my fate. Better to die this way, before any harm could come to those I loved. "You've made a terrible mistake by publishing that poem," I told Feliks. "I'm not that person anymore."

He was quiet for several moments, then he stood from his armchair and straightened his sleeves. "Does she speak truthfully?" he asked Sestra Mirna.

Her eyes rimmed with tears—whether from coughing or in fear for my life, I couldn't tell. The sestra had grown to care for me these past months, but I'd never known if that care extended to love, not when I couldn't feel it.

How desperately I wanted to feel it now.

At length, she shut her weary eyes and nodded.

Feliks's mouth flattened into a vicious line. His painstaking plan had come to nothing. He walked back and forth in front of the fireplace, scratching his jaw, his gaze fast on me. At length, he inhaled a determined breath and planted his feet. "You'll still be our sovereign Auraseer."

"What? No, I—"

"The people don't need to know that you're powerless."

"How can I keep a secret like that?" I asked, exasperated. "They'll find me out, and I won't be able to help anyone. Valko will come for me. He'll kill me, and your fabricated symbol will be destroyed, along with the people's hope."

"We will protect you from Valko."

"How?" I threw up my hands. "He has Dasha."

That silenced him.

The poor sestra was still coughing with great agitation. I rushed over and brought her forward to sit on the vacant armchair. While she held her handkerchief at her mouth, her other hand squeezed mine in a bone-crushing grip. We both knew I'd spoken the truth to Feliks—he had no use for me. Now I was only a liability. He would execute me like the ruthless leader I knew he was.

I wanted to say something comforting to Sestra Mirna. *If Feya has appointed my death, we must accept it.* But my mouth ran dry. My heart squeezed in a vise of fear. Had I really survived Valko's attempt to kill me just to die at the hands of another tyrant?

"Someone in Estengarde can restore Sonya's power," Genevie said from behind me.

I spun around to find her standing in the doorway. One of the soldiers flanking her saluted Feliks. "Please excuse the intrusion, General. She promised you'd want to hear her."

Feliks's cunning eyes hooded. "*Who* can restore Sonya's power? How is that possible?"

She took a tremulous step forward and balled her shaking hands. "The king's prized Auraseer has a special talent," she said, and quickly explained what she'd earlier told me: Madame Perle could sense beyond the block in my aura and find a way to release it. The claim was far-fetched—there was no real proof Madame Perle could cure me, but Genevie was trying to spare my life. If Feliks thought I had any hope to recover, he might allow me the chance.

I regarded him, wondering what the slight curl of his mouth meant. Did he find Genevie ridiculous, or was he seriously considering her? Perhaps he needed a more reliable plan. "I can also strengthen Anton's delegation," I blurted.

"Oh, yes?" Feliks cocked his head. "How so?"

"I'll travel to Estengarde and help him gain the alliance. Genevie says I'm respected there." Feliks didn't need to know that only the Auraseers in Alaise held me in esteem.

He scoffed. "No Auraseers are respected in Estengarde."

"Just as none were respected in Riaznin—not until me." How arrogant I sounded, but Feliks knew it was the truth. He'd published Tosya's poem to make sure of it.

Sestra Mirna's grip softened in my hand. Her coughing had quieted some, but her shoulders continued to rack. Hopefully any concerns she had over me were easing. Feliks would let me live. Genevie gave me a small nod to confirm his shifting emotions.

"Very well, then. You may go to Estengarde," Feliks said. "I'll spread word to our people that their sovereign Auraseer is guaranteeing a strong alliance."

"Guaranteeing?"

Feliks ambled over to me. "I'm giving you this one chance, Sonya. Regain your power and become the person I've promised to Riaznin. Prove yourself by securing this alliance. If you fail, I'll have no choice but to sentence you for your crimes." He leaned close to my ear. "And if saving your own life doesn't persuade you, just remember Kira and everyone else in our nation. You've gone to great lengths to aid them before. Surely you'll do your best not to let them down now."

The sestra went rigid and made a horrible wheezing sound. Confused, I dropped to my knees beside her. She squirmed, fighting to breathe. Alarmed, I pounded on her back.

Her handkerchief fell away from her mouth.

It was covered in blood.

My heart shot up my throat. How long had she been ill? Why hadn't she told me?

"You have six weeks to travel to Estengarde and return to Torchev," Feliks said, showing no concern for Sestra Mirna. "Those are my terms."

Tosya grabbed a flask off one of the soldiers and rushed over to the sestra's other side. He tried to make her drink, but she only choked on the water.

I clutched her arm. Squeezed her hand. I didn't know what to do. She needed a physician. But *she* was the convent's physician. Our nurse. Our everything.

"Six weeks does not allow for slower travel through the mountains if the snow comes early," Genevie said, wringing her hands by the doorway, unsure how to help.

"These wars won't wait any longer," Feliks replied. "We need Sonya back before the Shenglin conquer any more cities and Valko gains more supporters. Six weeks, Sovereign Auras-eer," he told me, "or I'll send an army to track you."

I opened my mouth to tell him what I thought of him—how could he be so insensitive while Sestra Mirna suffered?—but I never uttered a word. The sestra went quiet. Her head dropped forward. Her eyes closed. Her body slumped in the chair.

My stomach went rock hard, then I started to shake.

Please, Feya, tell me she's only fainted.

I leaned over her. Tears slipped down the bridge of my nose. I needed to feel her aura now more than ever. Why couldn't the goddess grant me that? "Genevie?" My voice cracked as I turned to her in pleading. She could feel what I couldn't.

She stood with her hand clamped over her mouth. Her eyes were red with emotion.

What emotion?

She finally pulled her fingers away. "Oh, Sonya," she said, gasping with a little sob.

My chest burned with a crushing exhale. Why was Genevie crying when she couldn't feel my heart breaking?

"I am so sorry," she whispered. "Your sestra is gone."

I shook my head twice, refusing to believe her. My vision blurred with building tears. Sestra Mirna wasn't dead. She was a survivor. She'd outlasted the ague last winter, as well as the convent fire and Valko's attack. Consumption couldn't take her. She was too strong. She was the one holding us together here.

Tosya's arms came around me. A ragged cry tore from my lungs. His sympathy cemented the agonizing truth.

Sestra Mirna—the protectress of so many, the long devotee of the convent, the woman who ruled her own domain with relentless strictness and surprising flickers of deep affection—was truly gone.

CHAPTER SIX

I TOUCHED TWO FINGERS TO MY FOREHEAD THEN MY HEART, making the sign of Feya. The sun drooped low, gilding the convent grounds with copper light. I sat kneeling in the graveyard beside a mound of freshly overturned earth. Feliks and his soldiers had departed right after he'd given me my ultimatum of six weeks, but I'd put off traveling to Estengarde to wait the customary three days to bury Sestra Mirna. She deserved her full burial rites.

Scanning the crowded graveyard, I wrapped my arms around my waist. So many people had died here. Auraseers from the convent fire, as well as those who had passed away from last winter's ague. Other Auraseers I'd never known from long ago, moss and lichen growing over their stone markers. Yuliya—the yellow flowers I'd planted for her peeked up at her carved name. Loyalist and revolutionary soldiers from the convent battle. And now those who'd died from the consumption. I wondered how full other graveyards in Riaznin were growing. How many more people would lose their lives while my power remained stagnant?

Hot tears rolled down my cheeks. If I'd had my abilities, I could have sensed Sestra Mirna was ill. I would have tended to her. Insisted she rest more often. Refused to let her nurse the soldiers. She'd caught her death while giving Nadia and me other chores, ensuring we weren't in the hospital tent too long. Was I so blind without my power that I couldn't realize what she'd been doing?

I cupped a handful of dirt over her grave and closed my fingers tightly over it. "I promise to do what you'd do in my place. I'll bring Dasha and Kira back here safely."

I wandered back to the convent and passed the wash line, where my laundered clothes hung to dry. All my preparations for Estengarde were in order, though I still felt so unready to leave. Sestra Mirna's presence still dwelled within these whitewashed walls, just out of my palpable reach. I climbed the stairs in the west wing. Close to the infirmary, in a section of the house that had survived the fire, I found the sestra's bedchamber.

Her smell of calendula and beetroot wafted over me, making the space feel even more alive with her. I could almost feel her hand on my cheek, her voice whispering that I would be well again. She'd tended to me night and day while I recovered from the gunshot wound. She'd held me when I'd cried, fearing

Anton would never come back.

I wished I had expressed to her how much she'd meant to me while she was alive.

I found a brush on top of her mirrorless dresser and, setting down my candle, ran my fingers over a few trapped strands of her gray hair. All I felt was its wiry texture past the stiff bristles. No lingering aura. Heartsore, I withdrew my hand and turned away.

The room looked painfully bare for someone who had lived here over half of a century. The only shelf held a prayer book and a small idol of the goddess Feya, even simpler than my old wooden one. No pictures hung on the stone walls. No mementos rested on her bedside table. A simple carved chest sat at the foot of her bed. It reminded me of the one in the library where the sestra had stored the Auraseers' birth certificates and correspondence with the empire.

Kneeling with my candle, I lifted the chest lid and found a stack of wool blankets. I removed them, one by one, searching for a deeper imprint of Sestra Mirna's time in this world. At the bottom of the chest rested a ribbon-tied bundle of letters, as well as a journal. Opening the cover, I found inside a genealogy of the convent's Auraseers. On the last written page, my name, along with my dead parents and brother, was scrawled, along with our shared birthplace of Bovallen. Why had she kept such detailed records of all of us? Some Auraseers had more than three generations back listed in this journal.

I traced my mother's name, *Alena*, trying to remember

anything more from my childhood. My family's faces. Our home. Even something else from our garden besides flagstones. But, as always, I came up blank.

I set down the journal and looked at the bundle of letters. Would it be disrespectful to open them? I debated for a minute, then decided that learning more of Sestra Mirna's history would help me honor her.

My half-burned candle melted to a nub by the time I'd finished reading. I couldn't stop, not even to stuff the letters back inside their envelopes. Onionskin paper littered the floorboards. I sat with my knees tucked to my chest, and my head leaned back against the bed's mattress. My mind spun, vividly awake, though the hour was late. The sestra's life fascinated me.

"What is that you're reading?"

I jumped to see Nadia in the doorway. Unlike me, still in my dress from the day, she was wearing her nightgown. The candle in her hand underlit her face, catching on the uneven, ropy texture of her burn scars.

Once my heart started beating again, I processed the tone of her voice. Not scornful, not accusatory, just curious. She hadn't spoken to me since the sestra had passed away. Maybe she felt as guilty as I did for not knowing the sestra was sick.

"Love letters," I replied.

Her jade eyes lowered to the maelstrom of paper on the floor. "Truly?"

I held out a page. "Did you know Sestra Mirna once planned to marry a farm boy named Feodor?"

Nadia came over and sat beside me, skimming the paper for herself. "What happened to him?"

I released a pensive sigh, as weighty as the story I'd just gleaned through all my reading. "Feodor's mother was an Auraseer. She and his father kept that a secret from the empire and instructed Feodor to do the same. But they were found out, the entire family was executed, and Mirna Sorokina became Sestra Mirna of the convent of Auraseers."

I studied Feodor's name in Sestra Mirna's beautiful handwriting, feeling a new kinship with her. My parents had also been executed, like the sestra's lover and his parents, for the same reason—hiding an Auraseer from the empire. It was a tribute to her love for Feodor that Sestra Mirna dedicated her life to protecting Auraseers.

Nadia picked up another page and shook her head in wonder. "I never heard her speak of any of that, not even to the other sestras, and, believe me, I eavesdropped plenty."

"I never imagined such tragedy had brought Sestra Mirna to live her life here."

"Tragedy brings us *all* here, Sonya," Nadia replied with no malice, only the bare truth. "This convent was built to hold the broken."

I tugged my knees tighter to my chest. "That farm boy's mother was so much older than I was when the authorities found her." As far as I knew, I was the only girl in all of Riaznin's history to be brought to the convent at the late age of seventeen. Bounty hunters collected most Auraseers many years younger.

"Do you think it's possible many of us go undiscovered?"

"I don't know . . . I hope so. At least that would mean some Auraseers lived freely."

"But they wouldn't have any training," I said. Nadia didn't understand, like I did, how difficult life could be when you had no rein over your abilities, how other people's auras could drive you to the brink of insanity. She hadn't writhed every time a woman bore a child or shrieked when a boy killed a rabbit for supper. The sestras had taught her, from a young age, to govern her emotions and separate herself from other auras.

"So it's better to be owned for the sake of an education?" Nadia asked, a sliver of her abrasiveness returning.

"Of course not." I rested my chin on my knees. "But what if you could choose both—have liberty *and* learning?"

The scarred side of Nadia's mouth creased as she pursed her lips. "You think anyone would *choose* to live at this convent? You hated living here as much as I did."

I shrugged. "We were miserable because we had no freedom, not because of these walls."

Nadia scoffed, taking up her candle as she pushed to her feet. "These letters have filled your head with roses, Sonya. Beware the thorns. There is nothing in this place for anyone who hasn't lost everything."

⁂

I couldn't sleep in the hour or two remaining before the daybreak, so I packed away Sestra Mirna's treasures and paced the floor. I needed to be thinking of Estengarde—I would leave tomorrow with a few soldiers who were well enough to accompany me—but my sleep-addled mind overflowed with images of a thriving convent, its rooms filled with smiling Auraseers who studied together and walked the halls in accord.

When my candle burned out, I stooped to light a fire in Sestra Mirna's fireplace, only to find it coated with a thick layer of ash. I couldn't leave it be—the sestra deserved better—so I spread out a linen sheet before the hearth and swept the ashes onto it, then I polished the black off the hearthstone. Arms sullied to the elbows and nose itching and smudged, I folded up the sheet like a knapsack and carried it outside.

The morning sun greeted me past milky dawn clouds. In the middle of the convent's front courtyard, I shook out the ashes. As the linen sheet came billowing down, I spied a horse and rider advancing to the convent. I couldn't make out the man's face from the quarter mile away, but his horse was snow white. One of the three troika horses.

Anton.

My grip went slack. The sheet rippled to the ground. My heart pummeled a hailstorm of percussive beats against my rib cage. I raced three steps toward him, then halted, sidestepping, backtracking, fairly spinning in circles.

He can't . . . I can't . . . I can't let him see me like this.

I whirled toward the convent, then skidded to a stop as Tosya and Genevie stepped outside. One look at Genevie's all-seeing gaze sent me running for a tall maple bordering the outer walls of the grounds. Yuliya and I had sometimes hidden in its branches to skip our classes. Hitching up my skirt, I climbed halfway up, then remembered Genevie couldn't even sense my aura to know what had come over me.

"Sonya!" I glanced down to find Tosya staring up at me like I'd gone mad. "What in the names of all the gods you worship are you doing?"

I clung to the tree's trunk, my feet planted on a shaky branch. "I'm so dirty, Tosya," I whimpered lamely.

"And you thought you'd bathe with *sap*?"

My knees knocked together. My head prickled with light-headedness. "Tell him I went to the village, all right?"

"Tell who?"

"Anton!" I whisper-shouted.

Tosya didn't move for a moment, then he abruptly strode away, likely to view the road for himself. When he returned, his footsteps came slower and a boyish smirk crossed his face. "Am I to understand that you're hiding in a tree from the boy you love—the boy you haven't seen in *four months*—because you're dirty?"

"He's supposed to be in Estengarde." I climbed up another branch and straddled it, wiping my black hands on my skirt to no avail. "I thought . . . I thought I'd have more time."

Tosya shook his head at me. "Yes, imagine all the baths you could have had."

I moaned and rested my forehead against the tree trunk.

"Or is this about your power?" He crossed his arms.

The bark dug deeper into my skin. "He doesn't know it's

gone, Tosya." I sounded like a child. I felt like one.

He gave a long, belabored exhale. "Sonya . . ."

"You don't understand. I won't know what he's feeling." Anton had been hard enough to read, even when I'd had my abilities. Now it would be nearly impossible. I wouldn't know if he'd forgiven me. Or if he still loved me.

Anton's horse, Oriel, galloped in past the convent's gate. I cursed and scrambled higher up the maple. "Don't tell him where I am!"

Tosya mumbled something incomprehensible. I only made out the word *ridiculous* before he left me again.

Past the spindly branches at the crown of the tree, I watched as Anton swept onto the convent grounds like a princely dragon slayer straight from Riaznian myth.

His waving, dark hair had grown two inches longer since I'd last seen him; the front locks hung near to his chin when they used to fall across his eye. He'd grown a short beard, making him look at least five years older than his youthful age of nineteen. All his traveling had wrought him leaner and more muscular. His cheekbones protruded with sharper relief against his chiseled face, and his rolled-back sleeves revealed sinewy, tanned arms.

While I didn't want him to see me yet, I yearned for the stalwart strains of his aura, the patient notes that hummed along my nerves and soothed my troubled heart. My chest ached that I was unable to draw him into me and hold his energy there, where it belonged.

He leapt down from his horse and gave a quick embrace to Tosya, as well as a nod of greeting to Genevie. I couldn't be sure from up here, but his expression seemed pensive. He exchanged a few words with Tosya, glanced around the grounds, pointed down the road to a small company of men who had traveled with him, then looked up at the convent. He scrubbed a hand over his face and walked inside.

Genevie whispered something to Tosya, looking at the tree I was nestled in, and struck a path for the hospital tent.

Tosya scratched the nape of his neck, feigning casualness as he meandered back to the maple I was hiding in like an ash-drenched squirrel. "A ruble for your thoughts?" He poked his head under a low-lying branch.

"Ten for your aura," I countered. "Or Anton's. Or anyone's."

He spread his empty hands wide. "I'm afraid you don't have that kind of money, dear Sonya."

Resigned, I climbed down the branches. Tosya looked hopeful for a moment, but then I hopped down and ran for a small orchard in the back of the convent.

"Where are you going?" he demanded, tired of my games.

"Thank you for covering for me!"

"You can't hide forever," he called in a singsong voice. "Ten years with the Romska should have taught you that."

CHAPTER SEVEN

I WASHED MY HAIR IN A LITTLE DITCH THAT RAN THROUGH THE orchard and did my best to scrub my body, hoping my ash-coated blue sarafan wouldn't make me filthy again. I told myself I wasn't wasting time. I'd have to bathe before my journey tomorrow, anyway, and I was already packed with my food provisions wrapped. As my hair dried, flowing loose in dark-blond waves to the lower ridge of my spine, I dipped my toes in the water and gazed at my rippling reflection. The day passed this way: me staring at hazel eyes and wondering where all my courage had gone. I had stood up to tyrants, silenced courtrooms, and wrestled violent auras inside me. Why couldn't I face the boy I loved?

Why had Anton stopped here, anyway? Ormina was three days out of the way from Torchev to the mountain pass.

Was he still going to Estengarde? I hoped so and feared so.

I wanted to be with him, but didn't. Not if everything was lost between us.

Through the tree canopy above, golden flecks of sunlight turned to shimmering silver moonlight. Still, I didn't move from the orchard. The glow of a lantern approached, bouncing leafy shadows about its circumference. I stiffened until I heard Genevie's voice calling, "Sonya?"

I slowly stood and turned around. Genevie wasn't alone. Nadia was with her, two lines creased between her brows. No doubt she was annoyed she had to come out here at nighttime to find me.

Genevie smiled and tilted her head. "Your hair is pretty like that."

"Doesn't it look ravishing with my dress?" I twisted back and forth at the waist, displaying the sooty fabric.

"Your prince will like it."

"Shh." Nadia nudged her.

I frowned, studying the sly glimmer in Genevie's eyes, all the more pronounced by the lantern's flame. "What's going on?"

"It was meant to be a surprise," Nadia said.

"What was?" My stomach knotted with misgiving.

"*Tu verras.*" Genevie pulled a large handkerchief from her pocket. "Come and find out."

When I made a small moan of resistance, Nadia rolled her eyes and grabbed my arm.

71

I tugged at the blindfold over my eyes. "Is this really necessary?"

"No," Nadia replied. "We just like confusing you."

I pressed my lips together against a terse remark. "Are we almost there yet?"

"Yes."

The coolness of the convent's stone walls surrounded me, but I couldn't place our destination within. "Is this surprise your idea or Anton's?" I asked, the toe of my shoe catching on the corner of a rug.

"Anton's," Genevie said. I could hear the smile in her voice.

"Hmm." I imagined what he'd reveal once the game was up. Maybe a map of Riaznin flagged with provinces, cities, and villages that had managed to defend themselves against the Shenglin invasion and not declare allegiance to Valko in the process. But that might only be three or four pitiful flags. Nothing to celebrate.

Genevie spun me in three circles, then pulled me a new direction. After fifteen more steps, she did it again, continuing to guide me deeper inside. Soon I was completely disoriented.

We turned a corner and entered a new space. I sensed the vastness of the room by the far-reaching echoes of our footsteps.

"*Arrête.*" Genevie touched my arm. "We are here."

She removed my blindfold and let go of my hand. My gaze settled on the brightest spot before me, a large panel of windows, its curtains drawn open. The moonlight spilled inside and illuminated the well-ordered rows of oak tables and sur-rounding river-rock walls.

I was in the dining hall, the most magnificent room in the convent, simple as it was.

The door clicked shut behind me. Genevie and Nadia had disappeared.

"Sonya," Anton said.

I shivered with a sudden rush of warmth. I hadn't heard his voice this close to me in what felt like ages. It rumbled softly in its deep and resonant octave. Glancing to my left, I saw him in a dim recess of the room.

He walked nearer, hands behind his back, and my heart raced, sending a flush of fire to my cheeks. He'd shaved his beard, combed back his hair, and brushed the dust from his homespun green kaftan, the inconspicuous clothing he'd jour-neyed in.

My throat ran dry, caught up as I was in drinking in the sight of him. I'd imagined this moment for months, me running into his arms as he whirled me around, both of us weeping with happiness. But now I couldn't move. My joy felt buried beneath my pulsing anxiety.

Anton withdrew his hands from behind his back and offered me a bouquet of delicate-blue aster and a shy smile.

I reached for the flowers, then resisted, pressing my hand to my stomach. "Anton, I . . . I need to tell you something."

"I know you lost your abilities." His voice was steady, gliding on waveless water. "Tosya told me."

My mouth unhinged. A terrible concoction of humiliation and fury brewed in my gut. "Oh, yes? Well, then I'll kill him."

"You might regret that."

"Doubtful."

"You were on the verge of telling me yourself just now."

"Which was *my* right, not his."

"I agree, though you should know I tortured him for the information."

I snorted and crossed my arms. "How, by threatening to steal his quill? He probably caved immediately."

Anton's grin spread to his eyes. "You're even more beautiful than I remembered."

I froze, searching his face, aching to sense what I couldn't feel inside him. "How can I be," I whispered, unable to support my breath, "when I feel so empty?"

"Sonya . . ." Was it pain or regret that laced the edge of his voice? Did sympathy or fatigue weave through his gilded brown irises? "Please," he said, "take my hand."

After a beat of hesitation, I offered him my half-curled fist. He threaded our fingers together. Our physical connection released a slow exhale from inside me. I'd forgotten how perfectly I fit against him, the heel of my hand in the cup of his palm.

He led me across the room to the open floor before the windows. I found myself staring at the leaded panes of glass. They were new. I'd broken the old ones when I'd fallen outside in the snow, moments before the convent fire raged out of control. "Will you pretend something for me?" Anton asked.

"What?"

"See those three candles?" I followed his gaze to a branching candlestick on a nearby table. "Imagine scores more around us, washing everything in golden light. The breeze against the windows is violin strings." He pulled me nearer and tipped his head. "If you listen closer, you'll hear the flute and oboe in the orchestra. They're playing a Riaznian waltz. I'm wearing a fine kaftan"—he broadened his shoulders—"and you're in an elegant silk dress. These wildflowers are roses from the garden beside the palace orchard. And this stone floor is smooth and shining marble. It makes you feel like you're walking on glass."

"Sounds very imperial," I said, though I clung to the beautiful spell of his words.

Anton broke into a warm chuckle. "I suppose it does." He set down the aster bouquet on a table and reached beside it to pick up another arrangement of flowers that were woven into a delicate crown. They reminded me of the hawthorn blossoms I'd worn at Kivratide, back when I'd had such naive hope for peace after Valko abdicated. Anton had later given me another crown, red with poppies, once I was stable after being shot. I'd found them when I regained consciousness. I'd feared they meant he was saying good-bye forever. "Do you know what I've been thinking about all these months?"

I contemplated him, genuinely curious. "Perhaps you wish you and I could return to the way things were before . . ." *Before we rushed into this revolution.* "Is that what all this is about?"

He shook his head, eyes lowered as he idly touched one of the flower petals. "I wish I'd danced with you at the Morva's Eve ball."

I swallowed, suddenly timid and warm and far too wobbly on my feet. "Oh."

He met my eyes again. Something about his gaze sent heat through my body. It cascaded from the tips of my shoulders down the lengths of my arms to the very ends of my fingertips.

He approached me. Past the leaded glass, the moonlight traveled over him, painting rippling shadows across his body. "I admired your courage in asking me to dance that night, despite the shock of the court ladies. You were so beautiful. I didn't dare hold your gaze for fear I would reveal my aura and what I truly felt about you. That was the first night you hinted at any affection for me, but I didn't trust it. I was afraid."

"I scared you?"

Anton placed the flower crown on my head, his fingers trailing down to the sensitive spot behind my ear. "Very much. You still do."

His scent of musk and pine brought me back to our journey in the troika from Ormina to Torchev, back in our first days together, when I was learning to trust him. "Even powerless?"

"Sonya . . ." His thumb brushed my cheekbone. "Do you think I love you because you're an Auraseer?"

I shrugged, glancing down at the ashy folds of my dress. I supposed I didn't think that, not when I forced myself to be rational. But Anton had endured so much by leading a revolution and dealing with the never-ending fallout. If I were still gifted, I could be helping him. "I wanted to be more for you."

The warm press of his lips lighted against my brow. He tenderly lifted my chin, and the tears trapped in my lashes fell. "And I wanted to give you a peaceful life in Riaznin," he said, his own eyes shining, "but I wouldn't trade that for this life with you, just as you are."

Months of pent-up tension released from the tight space between my shoulder blades.

I drew a deep and sustaining breath. *Just as you are* echoed in my mind.

His hand slid to cradle my cheek. "Let me give you what I can . . . my heart and this quiet moment that no one can steal from us, not even Feliks." When my posture sagged, he nodded. "Tosya told me everything." A shadow of rage crossed Anton's face, but he swallowed, striving to compose himself. "When the Romska warned me Feliks was coming here, I rode back to make sure you were safe."

My stomach twisted, thinking of the ultimatum the general had given me. "I don't know how I'm going to—"

"I promise we'll find a solution together."

"Did Tosya also tell you about Sestra Mirna?" I bit the inside of my cheek against the sting of threatening tears.

"Yes." Anton leaned his forehead against mine. "I'm so sorry." His hand cupped the back of my head, and he ran his fingers through my hair. "You've endured so much. But for now, please, let me give you respite."

The comfort he offered felt tangible enough to fold myself in. All our troubles would exist in the morning, but for an hour or two, we could allow this world to narrow to us, a boy and a girl in a moonlit room.

Stepping back, Anton swept into a graceful bow. "May I have this dance, Sonya Petrova?"

I sniffed and cracked a smile. "If you don't mind getting covered in soot, I would be honored, Anton Ozerov."

He drew me close to him, one hand wrapping around my back, the other extending my arm. The silent orchestra started playing a new waltz, and our feet swept into its one-two-three rhythm. "Do you know what else I wish?" he asked.

"Careful, you might end up with more regrets than I do."

"I wish I'd kissed you in the troika."

My smile tempered and heart fluttered. "Truly? You didn't seem very keen on me back then."

"I was good at deceiving you. I remember so vividly when you were nodding off to sleep. Snowflakes kept melting on your lips. I'd guarded myself against you, but in that moment, my feelings got the better of me. I'm surprised my aura didn't wake you."

I tilted my head as we revolved. The moonlight and the candles swirled behind us. "Tell me what you felt. I miss knowing."

He looked away to the window, then back at me, boyish

and shy, maybe even a little embarrassed. "Mostly afraid," he confessed.

My brows lifted. "More fear? I have a gift for bringing that out in you, don't I?"

"I'm not finished," he said. The warm print of his hand seeped through the back of my dress as he drew me nearer. "I was afraid at the level of admiration I already felt for a girl I'd just met—a girl I thought I could never have." He stopped dancing, and my dress swished about my ankles. "Sonya, a moment ago, you said you wanted to be more for me. But that girl you were, unaware of any revolution, sleeping with my mother's blanket wrapped around her, the snow glistening in her hair . . . she has always been enough."

My skin warmed, bathed in a glow that radiated from deep within me. I loved him. I adored him. Stronger than ever before. I searched for the right words to express how much, but all I managed to say was, "Are you going to kiss me now? Because I'd really like for you to kiss me now."

He grinned, giving the slightest pout. "I was rather hoping you would kiss *me* now, what with that romantic story I just told."

A bubble of laughter tickled up my throat, but I didn't release it. I was too enraptured by the candlelight and how it caught on the divot above Anton's upper lip. My voice went a little hoarse when I replied, "Perhaps we can compromise."

We drifted nearer in sweet slowness and sealed off the

small gap between us. His hands wound through my unbound hair. Mine found purchase on the hardness of his chest. Our noses softly bumped, then our lips.

We got to know each other again, taking our time, remembering the gentle push and pull of our rhythm, the way he tipped his head whenever he drew breath, and how he let me guide his mouth for my consent to draw the kiss deeper.

At length, he tucked my head against the curve of his neck, and I wrapped my arms around his torso. "Somehow we're going to be fine, you and me . . . this nation. I won't let us lose what we've fought so hard to attain."

I let his words sink into me as we held each other, clinging on to that hope, the breeze singing against the windowpanes like the high, faint strains of a violin.

 CHAPTER EIGHT

NADIA JOSTLED ME AWAKE THE NEXT MORNING, SO EARLY only a hazy promise of sunlight caught in the weave of my bedroom curtains. It was the day our party was going to set off to Estengarde. "I've decided to stay," she announced.

I could scarcely see her face in the dimness. I didn't trust I'd heard her correctly. "What?" My voice was still thick with sleep. Nadia and I had been arguing over whether she should remain here ever since Feliks left. She wished to meet Madame Perle, too, but we didn't want to leave Genevie—someone unfamiliar with the convent—alone to wait for the other Esten Auraseers, especially with all the sick soldiers and the possibility that the bounty hunter was still lurking nearby.

"I have something to show you." Nadia lit the candle on my bedside table. The rest of my grogginess vanished upon seeing Sestra Mirna's journal in her hands. I propped myself up on my elbows as Nadia knelt next to the bed and laid the book on the edge of my mattress. She opened it to a ribbon-marked page where Sestra Mirna had written *Yuliya Aliyeva* in her bold and deliberate handwriting. "Look at this genealogy." Nadia tucked her raven hair behind her ears and pointed to the names that branched upward from Yuliya—her parents, grandparents, great-grandparents, and some distant aunts and uncles. Other spots were left blank where Sestra Mirna must not have yet deduced who belonged there. "You see this great-aunt here, *Verusha Kovrova*, and the marking beneath her name?"

I rubbed my eyes and focused on the underscoring line. All the names on the page had one, except this woman's line was embellished with two angled points on the right end, like an arrow with two arrowheads. "The same marking is also below Yuliya's name," I said.

"Yes. Two angles nested side by side. It's an ancient symbol for Feya."

My spine tingled. "You think Yuliya's great-aunt was an Auraseer?" Feya wasn't the supreme god in Riaznin's pantheon, even if we treated her as such in the convent. She was the goddess of prophecy and Auraseers.

"I know she was. The name, Verusha, sounded familiar. I searched and found it on one of the older gravestones here at the convent."

Curious, I sat up and pulled the journal in my lap, flipping through the pages for more symbols of Feya. Every so often I found more than one in a family. "Dasha and I both descend from the Romska," I said. "Motshan told me that's why our power is—*was*—similar. It looks like Sestra Mirna proved that other Auraseers are also connected through their ancestry." Chewing my lower lip, I added, "Do you think the empire asked Sestra Mirna to keep this record so the bounty hunters could find us more easily?"

"Yes, she did whatever possible to help them capture us."

I stared at Nadia in dismay until her sardonic tone finally registered.

She rolled her eyes. "Wake up, Sonya. Do you really think Sestra Mirna would have done anything to endanger us?" She climbed up beside me and brought the candle with her. "Look, the page for Dasha names Katerina Ozerova as her mother. Sestra Mirna made a vow to the dowager empress to keep that knowledge a secret. She wouldn't write it in a public record."

I leaned back. "Then the sestra kept this journal for her own purposes."

"So *she* might one day find new Auraseers," Nadia added, showing me places where the genealogies branched downward to girls and women who were alive today, among them first and second cousins of Auraseers who had recently lived in the convent. "Sestra Mirna dedicated her life to Feya, not to the empire or even Riaznin. She wanted this convent to be a sanctuary for all Auraseers."

"It *should* be a place of refuge—especially with our nation at war—but only for those who *choose* to come here."

"Yes." Nadia's jade eyes were fire bright, reflecting the candle and what seemed to be a new conviction inside her. "So that's why I'm going to stay. I figure I have one of two choices: tag along with you and feel even more unimportant and useless, or do something meaningful here." She thumbed the deckled edges of the pages. "This book lists the birthplaces of possible Auraseers. I'll write to them. If they want to be trained and given protection, I'll offer it."

"What if your letters get into the wrong hands?" If Valko won the civil war, he'd seek to own all Auraseers again.

"Tosya has asked some of his Romska friends to help deliver them." When Nadia said Tosya's name, she slightly averted her gaze. The two of them were barely on speaking terms, but his offer of assistance was a good sign that he might forgive her one day. "No one should suspect any tribespeople of being couriers. The nomads are known to keep to themselves."

I studied Nadia, the most ambitious girl I'd ever known. "Will all of this make you happy? Running a convent isn't what you imagined for your life."

"Who else is going to do it—you?"

I lowered my gaze.

She fell quiet for a moment, idly chasing her finger through the candle's flame. "I always thought becoming sovereign Auraseer was the most girls like us could hope for. Now I see how narrow-minded that was. If I'd have gotten what I wished for, I would have still felt owned and boxed in. I deserve more. All of us do. We should have the chance to live up to what we're really capable of. That's what I want to be a part of now—providing a safe place and an education for Auraseers, so we can become what the empire tried to deny us."

I reached out and clasped her hand. She stiffened under the affectionate gesture—we'd never had an easy relationship, never shared the kind of embraces Pia and I had exchanged so freely—but Nadia's fingers gradually relaxed under mine. "I should be here helping you," I said. "The convent is almost empty of Auraseers because of me."

"But you need to go to Estengarde."

I gave a small nod. "I *promise* to teach you what I learn from Madame Perle."

She grinned sadly. "My scars run too deep for healing, I think." My eyes fell to the ropy striations along her skin, though I knew she was speaking of her emotional trauma. "Your duty to Auraseers is larger than this convent. The fire here was horrific, but perhaps Feya's hand was in it. You became sovereign Auraseer instead of me, and because of that the emperor abdicated the throne." Nadia drew a long breath and turned her hand over so it cupped mine. "Riaznin needs *you*, Sonya." She squeezed my fingers. "I don't begrudge you that anymore."

Two hours later, I stood outside the convent, fussing with my mare's bridle one last time. Finally satisfied, I brought down Raina's head and leaned my own against the auburn star on her brow. Beneath her sunny smell of hay, there was wintry peppermint, honeyed dust, and sweet grass. Despite all my anxieties about this trip, a thrill of excitement ran up my spine. I itched for adventure after all my months at the convent. "I'm glad you'll be with me, girl." I rubbed Raina's long white neck.

A warm hand touched the small of my back. "Ready?" Anton asked.

I startled, not knowing he was so close. In the past, I would have sensed him coming by his aura. I eased my guard and leaned into him. "Yes."

His regiment of eleven soldiers was already on horseback and awaiting his lead. Tosya was with them. He planned to find the Esten Romska, who lived in the Bayacs, to see if they'd be willing to welcome the Riaznian tribes across the border in case our nation became too dangerous for the nomads during wartime.

I pulled up into Raina's saddle, and Anton mounted Oriel. Nadia stood on the convent porch, her arms wrapped around her waist. My chest constricted when I didn't see Genevie. I wished I could have told her good-bye.

As our party headed for the open convent gate, I heard the sound of another horse trotting behind the others. I turned to find Genevie riding out from the convent stables.

"She's coming with us?" Tosya asked.

My brow wrinkled. "Not that I know of."

Genevie's cheeks were flushed when she caught up to us. She ducked her head, passing through the soldiers, until she reached me. "I cannot let you go alone," she said.

"I'm not alone." I looked at the men around me.

"You have no Auraseer, no one to sense danger coming."

I swallowed, stung by the reminder that I had no ability to do the same.

"Valko might come after you when he finds out you're alive," she added.

"And if *you* come with us, you might set that bounty hunter on our trail."

She cast a worried gaze at the forest, but then tightened her hands on her reins. "I can warn you about him, too. I know the mountain roads better than any of you Riaznians. And in Alaise, if the king refuses to let you meet Madame Perle, I know a secret way into her chambers. I promise to be valuable to you." Her eyes were large, her brows peaked, I didn't know whether in anticipation, pleading, or fear.

"Why are you so eager to return to the place you ran from? If Floquart finds you—"

"I'll disguise myself." Genevie reached across our horses and took my hand. "*S'il te plaît*, Sonya. This is important to me. Esten Auraseers are still trying to escape. I want to help them, just like you are trying to help your people."

I snuck a glance at Anton. From where he sat on his horse, a few yards ahead of us, he couldn't hear our hushed voices. He wouldn't like the idea of someone joining our party to do something illegal. It would hurt our chances at achieving an alliance.

"You have inspired me," Genevie continued, taking a deep breath and holding it. "I want to be brave like you."

Another weight of pressure dropped on my shoulders. This

was partly why I was so resistant to be a symbol of hope to people. It only encouraged them to do foolhardy things. If Genevie was arrested in Estengarde, I'd feel responsible. But how could I deny her her desire to help her people when that's what I was setting out to do, as well? "What about the Esten Auraseers on the way to the convent?"

"I've talked to Nadia. She'll take care of them. I have to think about the others in Alaise."

I deliberated, flexing my boots in Raina's stirrups. "Very well." Who was I to tell Genevie she couldn't join us? "Just let me be the one to tell Anton about your plan to help more Auraseers escape, all right?"

She nodded, breaking into a radiant smile. "Thank you, Sonya."

I tamped down the flare of misgiving in my belly. "You're welcome."

I knew full well I was leading my new friend into danger.

I only hoped I could help her escape it.

CHAPTER NINE

I URGED RAINA FORWARD AS SOON AS THE PATH WIDENED SO I could ride beside Genevie again. She would be the first to sense an ambush. She'd be the *only* one to. All kinds of threats could be out here: enemy soldiers, the bounty hunter, Valko, or even Shenglin spies. I especially worried for Anton. He may not have been the major general of Riaznin's armies, like Feliks, but he was still an important member of the Duma and the driving force behind the revolution. As such, and with only a small company of soldiers to protect him, this journey needed to be as inconspicuous as possible. We crossed main thoroughfares only when necessary, which meant the narrow trails often forced us to ride single file.

Our company made a quick stop at midday when the horses needed water. Anton and Genevie ducked beneath a shady tree to study a map. I followed, anxious to be useful, though I had no knowledge of the roads.

Drawing near, I caught the last fragments of what Genevie was saying, something about a quicker route to the western pass through the Bayac Mountains.

"I agree traveling through forestland gives us a straighter course," Anton replied. "And, yes, the trees would grant more cover, but they'll also slow us down. We'd have to pick our way through thickets and unknown terrain. No villages are nearby, so there may not even be hunting paths in those woods." He pointed to a miniature cluster of sketched trees.

I leaned forward to have a closer look, when someone burst out from behind a tall shrub.

I shrieked like a child, then saw it was only Tosya. I smacked him in the arm. "Don't startle me like that."

"I found blackberries!" he said, opening his hands to show me.

"Shh, the whole forest will know we're here."

He rolled his eyes. "Relax, Sonya. Genevie will tell us if anyone is nearby."

She glanced up with a modest smile. "We are alone for now, so Tosya is free to shout about his berries."

"You see?" He jostled my shoulder.

I shrugged away. "Genevie can't sense as far as your voice can carry. Take a care to not get us all killed, will you?"

He jutted out his lower lip in a mock pout. "If I'm going to die, I'll do so with my belly full of this glorious fruit." He popped a blackberry in his mouth and sauntered back the way he came.

"I still think we should follow the coastline until we reach the western foot of the Bayacs," Anton continued, unconcerned with the nuisance that was Tosya. "The Shenglin aren't likely to go to the very edge of our empire, not while they still have other strongholds to conquer en route here."

"What about your brother and sister?" Genevie braced a hand on her hip, though somehow the gesture didn't look argumentative. She had a gentle way of asserting herself. "Can Dasha track your aura? Sonya said her ability is strong."

"Dasha doesn't know Anton well enough to single out his aura like that," I cut in.

Anton's jaw muscle ticked and a look of hurt crossed his face. I immediately regretted my words.

"But Dasha would be able to feel *all* your auras if she got close enough," I said, unable to shut my mouth. "Valko will inevitably find out we're going to Estengarde—Feliks is spreading the word—so Dasha could try to track us, regardless."

"Then it doesn't matter which route we choose." Anton rubbed the bridge of his nose. "We can't base our decision on avoiding them. We'll continue down the coastline." Folding the map, he strode away and called for his soldiers to saddle up again.

That night, after we'd traveled till sundown, we pitched our camp between the cover of two tall boulders on the shore. The ocean waves lapped at the sand, and a few soldiers chattered around the crackle of a dying campfire. Others rustled in nearby tents as they prepared for bed. I left the tent I was sharing with Genevie, crept over to Anton's tent, and peeked inside. He had already removed his boots and was sitting in the cramped quarters while unbuttoning his kaftan. The hot glow of the lantern limned his chest muscles with golden light.

I knelt outside the entrance and held the tent flap back. "I'm sorry about Valko and Dasha . . . her especially. I'm here if you ever need to talk. I just wanted you to know that."

Anton shifted nearer and caught the ends of the soft cords dangling from the neckline of my nightgown. He pulled me close until our lips touched, a moth-wing flutter of a kiss. "I know. I'm not trying to hold my feelings back from you; I just don't like to confront them, I guess."

"It's all right to be angry," I said, coming inside as he made room for me. "Anyone in your place would be at the betrayal of a brother."

"I'm not just angry with Valko. I'm angry with my father for driving this wedge between our family in the first place. If Valko and I had been raised together, everything might be different." Anton sat down on his bedroll and scrubbed his hand over his face. "I'm angry with my mother for living a double life and never telling me I had a sister. I'm even angry with Dasha, though that makes me feel more wretched than anything. She's only a child. But still, she bears my mark." He rubbed the lynx-shaped birthmark on his forearm. Years ago, a Romska fortune-teller foretold that whoever shared the mark would be soul-fitted to him and bring him great joy. "I thought it meant Dasha and I would share a deep and wonderful connection," he said, "but she must hate me now—Valko would have taught her that. I know what will happen if they ever find me. Valko will try to kill me, and he'll use Dasha to help him do it." Anton's eyes were pools of amber as he met my gaze. "He'll do the same to you," he added, a slight quiver in his voice.

I scooted over beside him and interlaced our fingers. "I won't let that happen."

He turned his head toward me, the stubble on his jaw a tender scratch against my brow. "*We* won't let it happen," he murmured. "You can't carry the weight of all Riaznin on your shoulders."

"Then let me carry *you*," I said. Anton represented our dream of Riaznin to me. If he died, it would fail.

He smoothed a strand of hair off my face. "You already do, my love."

He leaned forward to kiss me, but just before his mouth met mine, the flap of the tent flew open. Genevie crouched outside, her skin chalk-white, her pupils large. "He is close," she rasped, barely able to speak.

"Valko?" My heartbeats fired in rapid percussion.

She shook her head, her hand at the base of her throat. "The bounty hunter. And he is not alone."

Anton and I scrambled to our feet. At the same time, a girl's ragged cry shuddered through the night.

Anton grabbed his musket from the corner of the tent. His fingers flew as he loaded it. "Stay here," he told me and Genevie and scrambled outside.

My muscles ached to run after him. He might get himself killed. "Who just screamed?" I asked Genevie. "One of your Auraseer friends?"

She shook her head, her body quaking. "I do not recognize her aura, but it resonates like an Auraseer. *Elle a peur*. She is terrified."

The girl shrieked again. She sounded younger this time, her voice higher-pitched. "Sonya!" she cried. "Help me!"

Adrenaline scorched my bloodstream. *Dasha?* Was Valko here, too?

A knife lay in the corner of Anton's tent, where his musket had been. Without second thought, I snatched it and raced out into the night.

CHAPTER TEN

THE ROCKS ON THE SHORE STABBED MY BARE FEET AS I WOVE through the tents. I scarcely felt the pain. Some of soldiers, half-dressed from sleeping, ran past me, muskets in hand. I followed them toward the screaming.

Past the two boulders we were camped between, moonlight poured onto a wide beach with glossy rocks. I sprinted after the soldiers, who had turned left toward a bend in the shoreline. A cluster of pines towered there.

One by one, they halted as they arrived at the trees. Some drew aim with their guns, but no one fired.

My lungs burned as I hurried to catch up with them. Once I was close enough, I saw what they did. Chin-length hair. Protruding ears. Doe eyes. I blinked to be sure she was the right little girl.

Not Dasha. *Kira.*

I stopped running, frozen like the others. Ten feet away,

the Esten bounty hunter held a gleaming dagger at the young Auraseer's throat.

Tears streaked Kira's cheeks. Her terrified gaze implored me. She must have thought I held power. She'd seen me use it to stop a street riot in Torchev. I tried to harness that ability now, but the black void inside me was as thick as ever. Despair flooded my limbs. What could I do to save her?

"Let her go!" I demanded. "She's only a child." Only ten years old. Why was Kira out here, so far from Torchev?

The scar on the bounty hunter's chin stretched as he sneered. "*Ce rat?*" He clutched a fistful of Kira's hair and pulled her head back. The edge of his blade pressed closer to her neck. Another rush of tears spilled from her eyes. "*Donnez-moi Genevie pour elle.*"

Genevie, he'd said. My toes clenched on the rocks. He must be asking us to give her to him. But how could we trade one innocent life for another?

The soldiers were looking at me. They couldn't decide what to do, either. They didn't know Kira, and they barely knew Genevie. But Kira had called *my* name.

"There must be some kind of compromise we can make, something else we can give you," I said, stalling, though I didn't know to what end. Tosya and I had tried to bargain with this man at the convent gate and failed.

"Release the little girl!" Genevie shouted. I turned to find her not far behind me. She walked closer, her eyes narrowed on the bounty hunter, though her shoulders shook. "*Prenez-moi.*"

She pointed to her chest. She was giving herself up.

"No!" I caught her arm.

"Let me go, Sonya," Genevie said calmly, belying the terror in her eyes. "You know I can't let him hurt someone else when he came for me."

She pulled out of my grasp, and I let her. *I let her.* I didn't know what else to do.

I watched helplessly as she walked forward, trying not to stumble on the uneven rocks. Her nightgown fluttered on the ocean breeze.

Five of the soldiers who'd brought muskets kept careful aim on the bounty hunter as Genevie neared him.

"*Baissez vos armes!*" The bounty hunter nodded his chin at our men.

"He wants you to lower your weapons," Genevie said.

No one budged. The bounty hunter tightened his grip on Kira's hair, and she whimpered.

"Do as he says," I told them, dropping my knife. It clattered on the rocks.

Reluctantly, the soldiers set their muskets on the ground.

Genevie took three steps closer to the bounty hunter until she was within his reach. He carefully let go of Kira's hair, but didn't remove his dagger from her throat. Instead, he grabbed Genevie's arm. Dragged her close. Then, in one swift motion, he swapped girls, releasing Kira and bringing Genevie to the edge of his blade.

Kira broke into sobs. She ran for me, and I caught her in my arms. Her fingers dug into my back as she wept. "It's all right," I said, smoothing her mussed hair. "You're safe now." I swallowed and looked up at Genevie. She wasn't.

My heart lurched as the bounty hunter dragged her backward into the darkness behind the trees. Her gaze grew hollow, lifeless, defeated. Not only was Genevie in the clutches of a merciless bounty hunter, but she was also going to become the slave of an abusive master once more.

I'm so sorry, I wanted to tell her. She'd helped me in what I'd thought was an impossible situation. She'd given Feliks reason to spare my life and had granted me a chance to regain my power in Estengarde. But here I was. Unable to help her in return.

The bounty hunter pulled her back another step, then froze. I didn't know why.

A low voice pierced the silence. "Let the girl go." *Anton.* My chest surged with hope.

He emerged from behind a nearby tree and pointed a musket at the bounty hunter's head.

The man hesitated. Anton walked forward and pressed the barrel of the gun against his temple.

The bounty hunter winced and lowered his dagger hand. Genevie immediately fled from him, back into the circle of our regiment.

In the brief moment as Anton watched her go, the bounty hunter ducked and spun, dodging the musket and swiping out his blade for Anton's legs.

"Anton!" I shouted.

He jumped back and kicked, knocking the dagger out of the bounty hunter's grip. Anton retrained his gun on him. "Move again and I'll be forced to shoot," he warned. "Soldiers, tie him up." One removed his belt and bound the man's hands behind his back. "You are under arrest," Anton declared.

The bounty hunter thrust out his chin. "I have my right to a bounty," he replied, surprising me by speaking in Riaznian.

"Not in this country," Anton snapped. "Aside from that, you threatened to kill a child."

The bounty hunter scoffed. "She's just an Auraseer."

Anton's hands fisted, and Kira buried her head against my stomach. The bounty hunter must have seen or heard her do something that gave away her ability.

"Gag him," Anton commanded his soldiers. As one stuffed a handkerchief in his mouth, Anton told another, "Run to camp and bring back a strong rope. I want this man tied to a tree and guarded at all times."

After the second soldier departed, Anton rubbed the back of his neck and glared at the bounty hunter, who managed an oily grin around his gag.

Anton sighed, meeting my worried gaze. What were we going to do, send the bounty hunter back to a Riaznian prison with some of our soldiers or drag him with us to Estengarde? Either option endangered our party.

I looked down at Kira, whose attention had drifted from the bounty hunter. She was watching Genevie and feeling what I couldn't: my friend's distress. I saw it for myself as Genevie sat hunched over on a large rock several feet away, turned from the bounty hunter and slightly rocking and mumbling. Moonlight glanced off her wet cheeks.

Suddenly her shoulders perked. Her head rose. She turned to meet Kira's empathetic gaze. As they stared at one another, I imagined their comfort and relief. Several days had passed since Genevie had been in the presence of another Auraseer—several months for Kira. I ached to be a part of their shared understanding, the peace it must have given them. How I wished I could have given them just as much.

Kira's doe eyes shifted from Genevie to me. The skin between her brows puckered in confusion. Maybe even fear. "Where are you, Sonya?" she asked. "Why are you hiding from me?"

❧⚬✦⚬❧

I sat with Kira at a campfire Tosya had built between the boulders. From here, we couldn't see the trees where the bounty hunter was bound. Genevie had returned to our tent, but Kira was too hungry to sleep. She'd already eaten two bowls of lentil soup, and now she nibbled on a piece of bread from my knapsack, her fingers trembling.

"Are you cold?" I asked, adjusting the blanket around her.

She shook her head, but her nose was still pink from her continuous crying. Silent tears kept falling from her eyes. "I didn't even feel his aura," she confessed, "not until it was too late. I was so excited to find your camp. I only felt the soldiers' auras." I nodded with understanding, knowing how blinded by sensation one could be when latched on to the wrong person's energy. "But I never found *your* aura. . . ." The crease in her lower lip smoothed as she pressed her mouth closed.

"It's all right." I squeezed Kira's hand. I'd already explained what had happened to me, why I felt dead to her when I was clearly alive. She couldn't stop staring at me. I tried not to feel self-conscious. I probably scared her more than the bounty hunter had. For Kira, there was no precedent for someone like me; she hadn't seen Nadia since before the convent fire. "How did you find us?" I asked, striving to act normal, to prove I was the same Sonya, with or without my aura.

Was I?

"Were you riding on horseback before the bounty hunter found you?" I pressed. That was the only way I could fathom how she'd traveled so far from Torchev.

She swallowed another bite of bread. Her chestnut hair, matted as it was, glowed golden in the firelight. "General Kaverin took me from my parents."

My mouth parted. Hatred burned in my stomach. "Feliks kidnapped you?"

"No. My parents, they—" Kira's voice broke, and she took a deep breath. "When the general came to ask for my help, they said he could have me for money." She swiped a hand under her eyes, then rubbed her palm on her tattered skirt. Her parents were poor peasants, but they could have at least patched her clothes. I wasn't surprised they'd sold her. They'd never loved, only feared, their Auraseer daughter. Ever since Sestra Mirna was forced to return Kira to her mother and father after the empire fell, the little girl had lived in neglect.

"But then you escaped from Feliks?" I asked.

She nodded. "When we got close to Ormina, I heard him talking about you. His aura scared me—I knew he was going to do something bad. So I found a sharp rock, and while his soldiers were sleeping, I cut the ropes they'd tied me up with."

As I listened to her, I finally understood why Genevie had sensed Feliks was lying. He'd said Kira was in his custody, but by the time he arrived at the convent, she'd already escaped. One stitch of my anxiety loosened. At least Feliks couldn't threaten her anymore. Still, there were people in Torchev and beyond that must have read Tosya's poem by now, people who were depending on the sovereign Auraseer for an Esten alliance necessary to defeat Valko. If I didn't prove myself, Feliks would have me killed.

"Why didn't you go to the convent?" I asked.

"I did, but the soldier at the gate said you'd already gone. He also said Sestra Mirna had . . ." Kira bowed her head, hiccupping with a sob.

I put my arm around her, aching to sense what she was feeling. I felt so alone in my grief, so inept to comfort her.

"I was afraid Feliks might come after me," Kira continued, "and I knew I'd only feel safe with you." Guilt seized me as I realized she'd endangered herself because she'd thought I had power. "So I followed your trail."

I couldn't believe she'd caught up to us on foot. I supposed we *had* traveled slowly, picking our way through narrow paths in the woods, but it was still a tremendous feat. "You're an incredibly brave girl, Kira."

She cracked a shy smile and shrugged. "I was mostly scared."

I rubbed her back and kissed the top of her head. "That makes you even braver."

⁂

"Can you spare any men to return Kira to the convent?" I asked Anton a little later that night. We stood with Tosya at the mouth of the two boulders. A few minutes ago, I'd taken Kira to the tent I shared with Genevie and left her in my friend's care.

"I hate to thin our regiment," Anton replied, his hair ruffling in the salty breeze. "We only have eleven soldiers. If we're attacked, we'll be lucky if we have enough men to defend us. For that same reason, Kira might be safer in our company than if she travels back with only one or two soldiers."

"You really think we should take her all the way to Alaise?" I asked. Estengarde was a dangerous place for Auraseers.

"How will you explain to the king why Kira is part of your delegation?" Tosya added before Anton could answer.

He gave a rough sigh. "I've no idea. For that matter, how will I explain that we've arrested an Esten bounty hunter for reasons the Estens don't understand?" Anton folded his arms. "I wish I could spare the men to take the bounty hunter back to the nearest prison in Riaznin. But that's in Isker, three days away. Too far."

"Maybe you need to judge and sentence the bounty hunter here," I suggested as delicately as possible. In other words, execute him. There were definitely grounds for that in Riaznin; he'd threatened to kill two girls. But when Anton and Tosya turned to me with eyes that said I'd suggested something of the highest injustice, I squirmed. "What? In times of war, surely that's considered lawful."

"I can't rationalize killing a man unless there is no other way," Anton replied. He turned the collar of his cape up against another chilly breeze and glanced over his shoulder toward the cluster of pines where the bounty hunter was being held captive. "I'll spare two men to take him back to Isker," he said at last, resigned but determined, "but not any others. Kira will travel with us. We can't lose two days taking her back to the convent."

I nodded, though I feared we were making a mistake by sparing the bounty hunter's life.

We packed up camp at daybreak. Anton tasked two men to escort the bounty hunter away. They tied him to his saddle and one of their horses to his. When they pulled the handkerchief out of his mouth to readjust the gag, his lip curled at Genevie. "*Saluez vos amis pour moi*," he told her. She flinched.

"What did he say?" I asked as the two soldiers rode away with him.

"Say hello to your friends for me," she replied.

I frowned. "What did he mean by that?"

"I do not know." Genevie rubbed her arms. "But when he said it, his aura stung me." Her eyes followed the departing party, and she shuddered. "We are not safe while he lives."

CHAPTER ELEVEN

The dry autumn air chapped my lips and sent our regiment detouring for fresh water far too often. The weather was unnaturally hot for the season, even when the ground began to incline, nearing the Bayac Mountains. I tried to relax. The bounty hunter was gone, and if Dasha and Valko were following us, surely they'd have caught up by now. While we labored to be covert, they could have ridden fast. Still, I couldn't dissuade the dread trailing me like a living thing, making my stomach lurch whenever something shifted in the landscape.

Our encounter with the bounty hunter had put us all on edge. Anton gave me his brass flintlock pistol to carry, while he took to wearing a musket across his back. One night in his tent, he taught me how to reload the pistol. "Now the musket," he said, sliding the gun over. "They're temperamental and like to misfire."

Settled behind me, he guided my fingers over the ramrod.

"Push the ball to the very end of the barrel as quickly as possible. The gun won't fire if the ball isn't in the correct spot. But you also don't want to smash the ball. Lead is soft, and if the ball's misshapen it won't hit your target." Together, we slid the ramrod down the barrel. Anton wiggled it. "There, do you feel that placement?"

"Yes."

"Feel for that placement every time, and listen carefully for your musket to fire. If guns are blasting all around you, you may miss the sound. If by chance your musket *does* misfire, don't reload it until you dislodge the first ball. Soldiers have been found dead with a dozen balls crammed inside their barrels."

I nodded, withdrawing the ramrod. "I'll master it," I said, unable to fight a twinge of resentment. I wouldn't need to learn how to handle a gun if I'd had my power to bend emotions. If I at least had my simpler ability to sense aura, I could feel out threats at greater distances than Genevie and help us in that way.

Anton's lips brushed my temple. "Of course you will. I just hate having to teach you all this. Feels like I'm training you both to kill."

"You are teaching us to protect ourselves," Genevie said, seated cross-legged in front of us. She'd been practicing with the pistol while I worked with the musket. "There is an important difference."

Anton and I quieted as we watched the progress she was making. Her hands flew fast, her jaw set in determination, as she loaded the flint, black powder, and ball, then primed the flash pan. The warmth was gone from her eyes, replaced by a cool gleam that made me shiver.

"*J'ai terminé.*" She held up the gun, awaiting Anton's approval.

He nodded slowly and reached out to lower the barrel, which was inadvertently pointed at us. "That was . . . impressive."

Color rose to Genevie's cheeks, and she looked herself again, though I couldn't tell if she was blushing with pride or embarrassment. She swallowed, nodding at the weapon in my hands. "May I try the musket?"

Two days later, we arrived at the great watchtowers on the western front of the Bayacs, the border of Estengarde. Here, Anton took no pains to be covert. Better for our presence to be heralded to the Esten king as soon as possible.

He presented his identification papers to the guards, and after a debate that lasted three hours, they finally granted us permission to complete the remaining journey to Alaise, the capital city, which would take eleven to twelve more days if the weather held.

When we passed the border, our regiment's corset-tight tension unraveled. At last, we were in Estengarde. In Riaznin, we'd had to be careful, not knowing if we'd encounter friends or foes. But here we were guests, protected from our own people. The relief emboldened me. As we made the steady climb up the foothills of the Bayacs, the great teeth of its rocky ridges towering in the distance, I nudged Raina and rode closer to Anton.

His grip on Oriel's reins let up, allowing pink to flush his knuckles as he waited for me and Kira to catch up. She had been sharing my saddle ever since her encounter with the bounty hunter. "We're already more than halfway there," Anton said to us. "The Bayacs will slow us down, but afterward, it's only a two-day ride to the capital."

As we pressed forward, he told me and Kira of the wonders of Estengarde, the two lover gods they worshipped, the snails they ate as delicacies, and the white powder they dusted through their hair. Kira giggled. "Are you lying about the snails?"

Anton grinned and spread his arms wide. "Search my aura for any deception. Snails really aren't that bad." He shrugged. "Cook them with enough butter and garlic, and they taste like mushrooms."

Kira pulled a face. "Mushrooms are disgusting."

Soon thunder rumbled and rain came. It wasn't a nuisance until midday. Until then, our regiment pushed through. Most found the moisture a refreshing change from the dry heat. One soldier couldn't help tipping back his head every minute or two, opening his mouth to drink. But an hour later, the clouds darkened and the water fell in angry sheets. Lightning struck a tree only thirty yards away, and Anton pulled us off the narrow road to shelter under a few trees. But the rain still flooded past the crisp autumn leaves. Beneath us, the ground swiftly turned to mud.

"I know a place nearby where we can go," Genevie said. She led us across the road, down a slippery gully, and around a rocky outcropping of the foothills. "This is where I last camped with Éliane and Marguerite." She pointed to the dense spruce forest ahead, and I remembered what she'd told me at the convent: she'd separated from her Auraseer friends to protect them when the bounty hunter had caught her trail.

The rainfall let up as we entered the thick forest. Our surroundings grew dim and quiet as the needle-laden branches closed over us. "There is a level area over here where we can pitch our tents." Genevie nodded to her left and turned her steed that way. Our horses trailed after her. "Here we are," she called back, skirting a wide trunk.

As I urged Raina forward, Genevie made a small cry and Kira went rigid in my lap. I jerked Raina to a stop and drew a shallow breath. What were they sensing that I couldn't? "Is everything all right?" I asked Genevie. I couldn't see her.

Kira gripped my arm with shaking fingers. "Something is very wrong, Sonya."

My pulse tripped. "Who's out there?" All my nerves stood on end.

"No one but Genevie."

I didn't understand. Cautiously, I nudged Raina until we finished rounding the tree. A few feet ahead, Genevie sat on her horse with her back to us. She held perfectly still, her head frozen as she gazed upward.

Kira saw them before I did. She released a shrill scream.

Two corpses dangled from a high branch, their faces gray and mottling. Women.

I couldn't breathe. My gut wrenched in horror.

Soldiers from our regiment galloped into view. Then Anton. When he saw the dead Auraseers, he pulled his reins so hard Oriel bucked.

Genevie's gaze didn't break. She clumsily slid off her mare and stumbled closer to the women. She reached up and touched one of their boots. A quiet sob racked her shoulders.

They must be Genevie's friends. The other Auraseers.

"Marguerite," she cried on a fragile gasp of air.

The rain pattered on the canopy. No one spoke. Kira wept softly, feeling Genevie's pain. It must have mingled with her own horror. One of the dead women hanging above stared down with milky-white eyes. I swallowed hard. "Look away, Kira," I whispered, turning her head to me.

Tosya drew up beside us. I hadn't noticed him ride in. He reached for Kira, and I passed her over to him with trembling arms. *Thank you*, I tried to say, but couldn't speak. He nodded with understanding and pulled her into his saddle. With a click of his tongue, he guided his horse away, riding deeper into the forest and removing Kira from the awful scene.

Genevie turned around, her face wet with tears. "*Aidez-moi*," she said, her voice hoarse. When no one responded, she clenched her hands and shouted, "Do not stand there. Help me! They need to come down. We have to get them down!"

Her hysteria snapped me into action. I jumped off Raina and rushed over to her. "Genevie." I tried to embrace her, but she twisted away.

"He did this!" She sobbed. "My friends didn't have a bounty on their heads. They were worth nothing to him!"

I held her back as the soldiers climbed the tree to cut the ropes.

"He could have let them go!" She sobbed and pushed against my grip on her. "Why didn't he let them go?" Her keening cries tore at my heart. "I'm sorry." She stared up at the two Auraseers. "I'm so sorry."

Tears welled in my eyes. Pain pierced me. I felt for Genevie deeply, even without sensing her aura. Her shock was my own.

❦

In our tent I sat beside Genevie as she lay on her side. I sang her Romska songs and smoothed back her auburn hair. Tosya had given Kira his tent to sleep in and staked it near the one he'd be sharing with Anton. Separating Kira from Genevie for the night would be a kindness, we agreed. Seeing two dead bodies had been traumatic enough without adding the burden of Genevie's grief.

Now Genevie stared at the wall of our tent, her gaze numb and disillusioned, or so I imagined from her vacant and withered expression. "It wasn't your fault." I squeezed her shoulder.

"I know." Her voice cut raggedly from hours spent crying.

"It is the bounty hunter's fault. It is Estengarde's fault."

I lowered my head and gently drew away my hand. It was my fault, too. I'd never asked for Genevie's friends to believe I was a *grande voyante*. Still, my example had encouraged them to run from their masters and meet their terrible fates.

Marguerite's dead and clouded eyes still stared down at me. Éliane's stretched and bruised neck shot bile up my throat. I swallowed and focused on the comforting sounds of the dwindling storm, the intermittent rainfall on the ceiling of our tent, the wending breeze across the rippling canvas.

"I lost my friend Pia in a similar way." My voice caught when I tried to say more. I drew in a shaky breath of surprise. How easily I was able to connect to Genevie, even without my awareness. "A bounty hunter brought her to Valko, although she was innocent, and the emperor executed her just to bait her lover." My eyes blurred, remembering Pia's beautiful radiance. She'd brought joy to my dark days as Valko's sovereign Auraseer. "I understand more than you may think."

Genevie blinked slowly, her only reaction to my words. "Do you think it is wrong to seek revenge?"

I contemplated her. "Maybe." Valko's smug grin and razor-sharp glare blazed to mind—the look he'd given me when he'd abducted Dasha. "But it isn't wrong to seek justice."

Her face held its stony expression, but a tear slid down her cheek and onto her nose. She didn't wipe it away.

I clasped her hand, holding it firmly, though her fingers fell slack. "You're not alone." I knew what I needed to do. It became as clear as a cloudless sky. And it shouldn't have taken the death of Genevie's friends for me to see it. I should have given her my commitment the first day we'd met. "I'm going to help you."

She turned her head to me. "Help me do what?"

"Free the rest of your friends."

CHAPTER TWELVE

OVER THE NEXT SEVERAL DAYS, TOSYA KEPT A KEEN WATCH for signs of the Esten mountain tribes—tokens tied to branches, subtle carvings on tree trunks, arranged patterns of stones off the sides of winding roads. That was also how the Riaznian Romska communicated with each other, so other caravans could track their whereabouts during their continuous travels. But Tosya found nothing, and his usually optimistic demeanor started failing. I could understand why. Motshan and the other Riaznian Romska chiefs were counting on him to find the mountain tribes' secret footholds in the Bayacs.

One day in the chilly peaks, our narrow road crossed the switchbacks of another path in the great mountain range. Tosya brought his horse, Hanzi, to a halt by a wild cypress and a stunted oak tree. "I should venture off alone, even without a sign," he told me.

"That's a terrible idea." I shivered against an icy wind, my cloak cocoon-wrapped around my shoulders. "You can't wander off directionless. In a year, you couldn't cover all the ground of the Bayacs. Besides, winter will soon be upon us. You'll catch your death all alone up here."

Tosya gave me a lopsided grin. "I'm a nomad. I'm built for hard travel."

I leveled my gaze at him. "You're a nomad spoiled by spending your winters in the southlands." Already, his teeth were chattering. "You wouldn't know what to do if a snowstorm hit you."

"Obviously build a snowman. I'm not dense."

I snorted and my chest warmed. Even Kira, riding with me, cracked a smile. She'd barely spoken since the day we'd stumbled upon the dead Auraseers. "I refuse to let you leave right now, Tosya." I raised my chin. "I'll drag you behind me with a lasso if I have to."

He chuckled. "No need to get violent." With a grumbling sigh, he cast his gaze over the switchbacks one last time. "Very well. I suppose if I can't find the mountain tribes on the way to Alaise, I can try again on our return journey."

But three days later, just off a forking path, he finally located a clear sign of the Esten Romska: a rope of painted beads strung around a tree branch, and two slashes carved on the trunk. It meant the tribe's camp was two days in that direction. Tosya prepared to leave at once.

As I handed him some of my rationed food, ensuring he had enough, he kept staring at me and nibbling at the corner of his mouth. Was he nervous to travel on his own? No, his mood seemed to involve more than mere worrying over himself. Misgiving knotted through my stomach.

He cleared his throat. "I should take Kira with me."

I dropped the salted venison I'd been wrapping in a handkerchief. "What? No."

"Think about it, Sonya." He knelt and picked up the meat. "Kira will be safer with the nomads than if she goes with you to Alaise."

"We won't tell the Estens she's an Auraseer."

"And how will Anton explain to the king why he's brought a child with his delegation?"

My mouth parted, then closed. I had no idea.

Horse hooves clopped behind me and picked their way up the rocky path. I glanced over my shoulder and startled to see Kira riding with Genevie. When had they paired up? Kira was supposed to be riding with Anton today—his idea so I could rest from riding so cramped in the saddle.

I scrutinized Genevie's relaxed demeanor and Kira's easy smile. The little girl looked up at me and waved. I exhaled slowly, relieved to find them doing so well together. I'd labored to keep them apart, trying to protect Kira from Genevie's grief. But I'd underestimated the sisterhood of Auraseers, the comfort of their shared and echoed ability.

Yearning throbbed in my chest. I glanced away and wrapped my arms around myself. "How can you guarantee the Esten tribes will welcome Kira this time?" I asked Tosya. "She doesn't have Romska blood." That was the reason Motshan hadn't admitted her into his Riaznian caravan last spring, even though I'd begged him to. I was worried about Feliks threatening her even then.

"That was different," Tosya replied. "Motshan didn't feel it was right to take Kira from her parents. I'm confident the Esten tribes will help me look after a stranded child. When you and Anton are finished in Alaise, you can come back here for us." He pointed down the forked path. "I'll make sure there are signs all the way to the encampment. We'll wait here to travel back to Riaznin with you."

I sighed, my nose stinging in the cold mountain air. I felt a personal responsibility to watch over Kira, but I knew in my gut Tosya was right; she would be safer with the Romska, at least until I'd regained my power. If that ever happened.

"Treat her like you would a sister," I said, surrendering to what was best for Kira. "Like you would treat me."

He smirked. "You mean tease her relentlessly and write a poem that exploits her abilities to all Riaznin?" When I didn't laugh, he scratched his head under his wool cap. "Too soon?"

"Much too soon."

He sobered and touched my arm. "You know I'm very sorry about that, right?"

"I know."

"But I wouldn't have written it if I didn't believe every word."

I lifted my eyes and held his gaze.

"The people need a symbol to rally around, and whether you like it or not, you're inspiring."

"Even without my power?"

He shrugged. "Still inspiring, still powerful." I scoffed and shook my head. "You're more empathetic than you think, Sonya"—Tosya jostled my shoulder—"or else you wouldn't be so gentle with Genevie or concerned about Kira. You're attentive when they grow quiet. You help them before they ask. You could help Riaznin, too, just the way you are."

He enveloped me in one of his brotherly hugs that made me feel like we were children again, like I was safe in his care, even if everything else in the world felt like it was falling apart. "May Feya watch over you until we meet again," he said, acknowledging the goddess I'd grown to believe in. "If she's real, she'll help you. You're Riaznin's best hope."

Kira jumped off Genevie's horse and ran to me. "Sonya, did you see that waterfall off the road?" Her cheeks flushed a cheerful pink. "Genevie says we'll see an even bigger one tomorrow!"

My chest ached, and I glanced at Tosya. He gave me a reassuring nod. I knelt before Kira and took both her hands in mine. "I'll be sure to tell you all about it when I see you again."

Her smile fell. I saw the moment she finally absorbed Tosya's aura. Her eyes glossed with tears. "What do you mean?" she asked, her voice thinning to a fragile gasp of air. "Why won't I see the waterfall?"

"Because you can't journey with us any longer. It isn't safe for you in Alaise. Tosya is going to take you with him to stay with the Esten Romska for a while—just until we all travel back to Riaznin together."

"No!" Her fingers tightened around my hands. "I want to be with *you*!"

"Oh, Kira, I want to be with you, too. But think of Sestra Mirna. Can you imagine how would she have felt if I put you in any more danger?" The weight of the words I'd spoken at the sestra's grave pulled at my heart. *I promise to do what you'd do in my place. I'll bring Dasha and Kira back here safely.* "And what about Dasha? You're more important to her than anyone. Even if I regain my power, do you think I can persuade her to leave Valko if she doesn't have *you* to come back to?"

Kira bit her lip and shook her head, her tears streaking to her chin.

"Come." Tosya offered her his open hand. "Good-byes are easier when they're quick. Besides, I have so many Romska songs to sing to you. You're going to love 'The Ballad of the Swarming Gnat.' I wrote that one myself." He winked at her.

She didn't laugh, but she squared her small shoulders and shuffled over to him.

As Tosya rode away with her, she kept glancing back at me with watery eyes and a trembling mouth. Guilt overwhelmed me. I waited until she was out of sight, and then I choked on a dry sob. Anton, who had caught up to us, came over and brought me into his arms. "You made the right choice," he whispered.

I leaned my cheek into the crook of his neck. "Why are the

right choices the hardest?"

He kissed the crown of my head. With one last look at Kira and Tosya, we departed the peaks of the Bayacs and began our descent.

Five days later, we emerged onto flatland. La Forêt Royale—the vast "Royal Forest" separating the capital city from the Bayacs—spread before us. We rode through it at breakneck speed, cutting the remaining two-day journey six hours shorter, our horses finally getting a chance to stretch their legs on the wide, smooth road.

My tailbone ached. My thighs cramped. My hands gripping Raina's reins were numb and calloused. I didn't care. Madame Perle was near. My power was within reach. Genevie, however, looked the opposite of excited. As she rode on horseback, her shoulders hunched over her chest. As she walked across camp, her arms folded tightly across her body.

"Is everything all right?" I asked on the last night of our journey. By tomorrow afternoon, we would finally arrive in Alaise.

"*Oui*," she said, though dark rings had surfaced beneath her eyes. The skin of her face was sallow, despite the warm lantern light of our tent and made the freckles sprayed across her nose and cheeks pale. "I am only growing weary of all the men." She shuddered as the sound of soldiers laughing in the distance traveled to us.

I tried to find the root of her discomfort. Genevie had grown accustomed to those in our regiment, so I suspected her unease had more to do with a man who *wasn't* here, a man she'd likely encounter very soon. "If you're worried about Floquart, he won't recognize you by the time I'm finished." Monsieur de Bonpré was the king's most trusted advisor, and as such, we'd have a difficult time avoiding him. But thanks to the makings of a disguise I'd purchased from a passing merchant today, I prayed Genevie would go unnoticed. Tomorrow she would enter the Esten castle disguised as another Riaznian Auraseer in Anton's delegation.

"I hope you are right," she replied, lying down on the packed-earth floor of our tent while I plastered a doughy poultice of black dye over her hair. She sighed. "I am sorry to be so sullen. I do not wish to take away from your eagerness to meet Madame Perle."

My hand froze along her hairline. "Do you . . . *feel* my eagerness?" How else could she have known? I hadn't spoken about Madame Perle for several days. I hadn't wanted to be insensitive to Genevie's period of mourning for her friends.

She broke into a humored smile that flushed much-needed color to her cheeks. "Your emotions are easy to see, Sonya. I do not need to feel them."

My shoulders fell. "Oh." I gave a weak grin, embarrassed by my surge of disappointment. Had I really thought my aura would awaken so easily?

She watched me for a moment, her finger idly scratching a rough stone on the ground. "Madame Perle will be honored to meet you." Genevie was trying to cheer me up, I realized.

My emotions really were plain to see.

I bit my lip. "You told her about me?"

"Of course. Your story inspired her, too."

My chest fluttered with warmth. I lowered my gaze, spreading more of the poultice behind Genevie's ear. "I'll be honored to meet her, as well." Under the empire, Riaznian sovereign Auraseers had been chosen by seniority to serve our emperors, unlike Madame Perle, who had been chosen because of her level of talent. It must have been awe-inspiring. "I wonder why King Léopold preferred an Auraseer like her, one that can help recall buried memories."

Genevie swiped away a bit of poultice that dropped near her eye. "King Léopold's father suffered from . . . in Esten, we call it *insanité sénile*?"

"Senile insanity?"

She nodded. "A madness caused by memory loss. The king feared he might one day suffer the same fate, so he hoped Madame Perle could help prevent it. None of this is known to the Esten court, of course. King Léopold does not want anyone thinking he might have a weakness. He keeps Madame Perle sequestered, along with his secret."

Any rosiness I'd envisioned regarding Madame Perle's lifestyle in the castle turned to dismal gray. At least I'd been able to leave my room when I'd served Valko as his sovereign Auraseer. "I hope it won't be too difficult to see her," I said, remembering how Genevie had said she knew a secret way into Madame Perle's chambers. "How soon do you think we can manage it?"

My palms itched with another flare of anticipation.

She sighed. "Not straightaway. Once we arrive at the castle, it is the Esten custom for distinguished foreign guests to be bathed and perfumed before we are received by the king. He pretends the custom is to honor his guests, but the truth is he does not want foreigners to sully his court."

I arched a brow, spreading on the last of the poultice behind Genevie's left ear. "King Léopold sounds like a charming man."

She scoffed. "He is a pompous fool, but I can forgive him for that. At least he is not cruel." Her nostrils flared slightly, and her eyes shut, fluttering as she held them closed. "I have learned what I know about the king because Floquart required me to be his spy. I know almost everything that happened at the castle, and when I failed, Floquart . . ." A vein along her brow surfaced, pulsing as she pressed her trembling mouth closed against saying more.

Aching to give her comfort, I moved to squeeze her shoulder but stopped myself as my hand was coated in ashy poultice. "Don't let that man steal another moment of your peace. We'll wear weapons beneath our dresses and stick together, all right? I won't let him trouble you again."

Genevie drew a deep, shaky breath. "*Merci*, Sonya." She took my hand, despite the muddy mess it was. "You are a true friend."

Her words settled deep inside me, a space I held for Pia and Yuliya. I blinked back the moisture collecting in my eyes and finished applying the poultice. Once it had set, I wrapped it in an anchoring cloth for the night and extinguished the lantern.

Genevie fell asleep close beside me. Between the acrid smell of the dye and my impatience to reach the castle, sleep was a long time in coming for me. My thoughts swirled between Genevie and Madame Perle, then, at some point, Sestra Mirna. My grief at losing her tended to surface like this, when my exhaustion stole my ability to lock away my sorrow.

As my pulse slowed and I began to drift off, I imagined meeting Madame Perle, but she had Sestra Mirna's wise eyes and careworn wrinkles. I threw my arms around her and wept against her shoulder . . . and finally fell asleep.

What felt like two short hours later, a small hand covered my mouth. I startled at the petite figure above me. I couldn't make out her face in the darkness. She wasn't Genevie. I heard my friend beside me, her breaths rising and falling in deep slumber. "Kira?" I asked, my mind hazy. What was she doing here?

The girl lowered her mouth to my ear. The bell-tone of her voice, even in its whisper, splintered ice through my veins.

Dasha.

CHAPTER THIRTEEN

"SAVE ME, SONYA!"

I struggled to breathe, even though Dasha had removed her hand from my mouth. "Where's Valko?"

She pulled upright, her dark and wispy hair settling over her shoulders. "I ran away from him." I couldn't see the gray in her eyes. They looked black in the darkness. "He's following me."

My heartbeat crashed. This could be a trap, I realized. I shouldn't go with her. I glanced sidelong at Genevie, but Dasha's aura hadn't awakened her. She must have been sleeping deeply, rest she desperately needed. "All right. Let's go outside." If Valko was indeed coming, I needed to alert Anton. I hastily grabbed my flintlock pistol, after Dasha exited the tent, and threw on my cloak to conceal the weapon.

The crescent moon provided little light, especially past the grand firs of La Forêt Royale. The night air, eerily absent of any breeze, amplified our footsteps. Strange, since my feet barely touched the ground. I felt like I was flying.

Dasha and I glided around pillars of shadowy firs. I'd already forgotten why we'd come out here. Soon she was grinning and running, just out of my reach. I laughed as I tried to catch the fold of her snow-white dress. It blazed in and out of sight, trailing behind her.

Some buried part of my mind begged me to ask, *Aren't you in trouble, Dasha?* But I couldn't stop smiling and chasing. I caught up the hem of my nightgown and ran faster.

She disappeared, but her bright voice still echoed back to me through the forest. "See if you can find me now, Sonya. I dare you!"

More laughter pealed out of me. "I'll sniff you out by your aura!"

"You can't feel my aura," she singsonged.

I pressed onward, craning my head around the endless columns of trees. A massive fir loomed ahead. I slowed when I reached it and peered around its fat, moss-covered girth. Beyond it, the earth recessed into a gully rimmed with fog. Its white puffs frothed and undulated, like a brew in a cauldron.

"Almost here!" Dasha beamed from the opposite bank. She kicked up a swirl of fog with her pointed toe.

I plunged into the gully, but my feet didn't brush the ground. I really *was* flying. The fog swelled to my waist, and I skimmed my fingers across its surface as I sailed through it.

When I came to the middle, a figure cloaked in imperial

red rose up, the fog cleaving around his ice-encrusted crown.

My smallest finger twitched with a current of fear, but my overpowering awe eclipsed it. I would have knelt before him, but my legs went suddenly numb.

Valko's wolf-gray eyes gleamed as he swept nearer. "So you're alive," he said.

Pain blasted through me. Red bloomed over my stomach and drenched my nightgown with blood. I remembered being shot. How I hated him. What he'd done to me. I wasn't flying anymore. I plummeted to the thorny ground. "I'm not so easy to kill."

Valko tilted his head. "Maybe not. But *he* is."

I followed his gaze, and a shock of dread lanced my belly, cutting even deeper than my gunshot wound. "Anton."

The man I loved hung from a rope like the two Esten Aura-seers had, his hands bound behind his back, another frost-laden crown on his head. He didn't thrash, but he was still alive, eyes sharp and alert and tight with fear. For a moment, his aura pierced mine. I gasped, reeling from the jolt of my awakened awareness. Then, just as quickly, the feeling was gone.

"Save me, Sonya." Anton's voice rang desperate and clear, not strangled from the rope's chokehold. Still, I knew he was dying. That certainty was as real as my racing heartbeat, as real as my inability to intervene.

I turned desperate eyes on Dasha. She had power. "Do something! He's your brother."

A thin green snake dipped from the tree and slithered onto the slim shoulder of her dress. "Valko says Anton deserves to die."

"He's wrong. Valko is the one who should die. That's the only way to end the war." I suddenly remembered my pistol and withdrew it with fumbling hands. But when I blinked, it was gone, replaced by the crystal dagger that once belonged to Nadia's mother.

"Sonya, Sonya." Valko clucked his tongue and swaggered closer. "You can't kill me. Dasha won't let you. In fact, she's the one who can kill *you*." His eyes glittered darkly. "How about we stop her breath together?" he asked his sister. "Ready?"

"Always," Dasha replied, though her voice trembled.

I lunged forward, trying to stab Valko, but he grabbed my wrist and twisted my arm back.

"Now!" Valko commanded Dasha.

My body went limp with staggering fatigue. I dropped the dagger.

Valko let go of my arm and deftly caught me around the waist. His other hand braced the back of my head. I couldn't draw air; I was too tired to muster the strength.

"Know this before you die," he told me. "After you, I will kill my brother, and all that was left of your revolution will die with him."

He clamped a hand over my mouth, a final seal of my death.

The white fog rose, enshrouding us. Black stars darkened

my vision. My heart pounded through the length of my dangling body, screaming for air despite my weakness to fight. I needed to sleep.

As if Valko sensed my desire, he lowered me to the ground and cradled me in his arms, smoothing back my hair.

Several feet above him, Anton kicked as the noose tightened around his neck. He ripped apart the rope binding his hands and reached for me. But it was too late. His thrashing slowed. His face purpled. I watched him helplessly through a veil of tears. Neither one of us could save the other.

The frost cleared from Valko's crown just as Anton's fell away and smashed to the ground in icy shards.

A moment before my vision fully blackened, Anton shut his eyes.

And death came for both of us.

CHAPTER FOURTEEN

EVERYTHING WENT BLACK. COLD. MY BODY TWISTED, TAN-
gled in a dark cocoon. I thrashed, desperate to loose myself.
I tore away Valko's cloak, or my own, or whatever was binding me. I felt his body at my side and shoved him hard, then
scrambled to my feet. Air sucked into my lungs with such force
that a fresh wave of dizziness assaulted me.

"Help!" I rasped, clawing my way past the tangible darkness, ripping through its cloth-like walls. I burst into a circle of
trees. "Help me!" My eardrums shuddered with my cry.

"Sonya?" a girl called. Her voice didn't have Dasha's bell-
tone ring.

I jerked around and found Genevie peering out of our tent.
The cloth around her dye poultice had fallen away, exposing the
caked mess of her hair.

"What is wrong?" she asked.

I shook my head, my hands pressed to my temples. I didn't

understand. "Where—where is he?"

"Who?"

Disoriented, I glanced up. The moon's light shone brightly. Nearly round, not crescent.

"I sense no one here besides our regiment," Genevie said.

A hand touched my back. My heart flared, and I spun around. *Anton.* He stood before me, not hanging from a noose. "Everything is all right. You've been dreaming."

"No, we're in danger. Valko and Dasha . . . they were here."

He gently gripped my shoulders and lowered his face to mine. "It was a dream."

I blinked hard. A hoarse sob escaped me. Anton wasn't dead. I fell against his chest, and his arms came around my back.

Four soldiers raced out of their tents, their muskets gripped midbarrel in haste.

"Valko isn't here," Anton said. "Lower your guns."

Their eyes darted to the forest. Their disheveled hair and unbuttoned shirts flapped in the breeze.

"Sonya had a nightmare," Genevie explained.

The men relaxed, though I was still shaken to the core. Perspiration flashed across my breastbone and soaked into the loose neckline of my nightgown.

Anton guided me back to his tent, not the one I shared with Genevie. I stumbled forward on trembling legs. Valko's voice spun on a vicious loop in my mind. *After you, I will kill my brother, and all that was left of your revolution will die with him.*

Anton laid me down on his bedroll and came to rest behind me, holding me in a tight embrace as the worst of my tremors quelled.

"Do you believe dreams can foretell the future?" I asked, my teeth chattering.

"I don't know. Why? What did Valko do in your dream?"

Killed you. Killed me. "Conquered Riaznin." I pictured the ice melting off of Valko's crown while I suffocated and Anton hung from a noose. My fingers clenched around his forearm and anchored him to me.

"Half of our nation must have that same nightmare." He smoothed back my hair. "I know I do. It isn't prophecy, but only our fears that rattle through our heads."

I tried to draw comfort from his words and his calming scent of musk and pine. Maybe he was right.

But maybe he wasn't.

What if my dream had been a warning from Feya—a sign that if I didn't regain my power, Anton and I would die and Free Riaznin would fall? "I need to speak to Madame Perle as soon as we arrive in Alaise," I said. Which would be tomorrow. My heart broke into a wild canter.

"I know you're anxious to see her, but you'll have to be patient for the right time to present itself. As far as King Léopold is concerned, you've joined my delegation as my Auraseer guardian. When he requests me, you'll be expected, too."

I released a slow exhale, tamping down my anticipation. "Of course."

He sighed. "I'm afraid much of our time at the castle won't be pleasant for you, Sonya. The Estens hold little regard for Auraseers."

"I know." I only had to look as far as Genevie to understand that.

He pulled me closer and kissed the nape of my neck. "We have to promise each other to remain strong. I fear the next few days are going to test our relationship."

I shifted around to see him. Moonlight permeated the tent, but not enough for me to see his eyes clearly. "How do you mean?"

His lips feathered across mine. "Our time in the castle will be limited—barely sufficient to obtain an alliance. I won't be able to defeat Esten prejudices, as well. So what I do in Alaise—how I present myself—it will have to be in the best interests of Riaznin . . . which may, at times, be at odds with what's best for you and me."

I began to understand. "You have to conceal our relationship." I wasn't surprised, but a flicker of disappointment chased through me just the same.

He found my hands and threaded our fingers together. His voice dropped to a vulnerable whisper, shuddering warmth across my skin. "Will you remember how much I love you?"

I smiled softly. "Of course." I wasn't about to let a few days in Estengarde rekindle my old insecurities. "But since we are speaking about remaining strong for each other, I should be frank with you, too." I took a long breath. "Genevie is going to help more of her Auraseer friends escape Alaise, and I've promised to help her."

He stiffened. *"What?"*

"It's been her mission from the beginning—why she traveled to Riaznin in the first place, why she came back to Estengarde. Seeing her friends dead in the forest only strengthened her resolve."

"Sonya . . ." The groan Anton released scraped from a deep well inside him. If this had been any other time, if I hadn't still been trembling from the echoes of my nightmare, he might have lost his temper. But when he spoke next, the tender scratch in his voice sounded, above all, concerned. "I can't do what I need to in Alaise if I'm worried for your life. What you're talking not only risks our chances of achieving this alliance, but is also grounds for execution."

"I know that"—I squeezed his hands—"but Genevie is my friend, and Auraseers are my people. I need to do what *I* believe is best, too, even if it's at odds with what is best for you and me."

He fell quiet at his words thrown back at him, although I'd said them as lovingly as possible.

"Trust me." I kissed his mouth, trying to soften its worried edges. "I'll be wise and careful."

His body finally yielded against mine. "I trust you. Trusting

Genevie is harder. How do we know she won't let her emotions blind her?"

I couldn't resist grinning, despite all the toil of the night. "Not every Auraseer began as recklessly as I did."

CHAPTER FIFTEEN

GENEVIE BLANCHED, CLUTCHING HER STOMACH AS WE turned onto the main thoroughfare of Alaise the following afternoon. Its castle appeared in the distance. "Do not think less of me if I vomit."

I rode closer to her. "You're going to be all right; just breathe deeply. I'm right here with you."

She nodded, fanning her face with a hand and dabbing the corners of her newly red-stained mouth. In addition to her black-dyed hair, she'd darkened her brows and eyelashes, dusted light powder over her freckles, and applied rouge to her cheeks. She wore one of my Riaznian sarafans, and the bell-shaped dress helped complete her transformation. She truly looked like a different person. Once the color in her face had returned, I looked back at the castle, doing my best to keep my jaw hinged.

I'd felt a similar sense of wonder when I first set eyes on the palace in Torchev, although this place looked vastly different.

Instead of brightly painted tiles and tall, gold-leafed domes, Alaise's castle spread wide across the land in monochromatic cream stone. Its majesty and staggering size stole the air from my lungs. As we traveled nearer, I counted one hundred and six windows across its front façade, including those wrapping around its four wide towers.

Did any of those windows belong to Madame Perle?

The city dwellers gaped at us as we progressed farther down the road. I couldn't help gaping back. Except for Genevie, the only Estens I'd ever seen were aristocrats and their finely dressed entourages. These peasants wore much simpler clothes, the little ruffles on their collars, puffed sleeves, and mop caps the only embellishments.

"Stop staring," Genevie whispered. "They think you are rude."

"But *they're* staring at me."

"You are Riaznian and riding in the company of a prince they admire. I hear their whispers. Word has spread about Anton's coming."

Anton's icy crown blazed to mind, and a shock of fear gripped my heart. In my dream, his crown had shattered the instant before he died. "They need to stop thinking of Anton as a prince." I eyed the peasants, doubting how well they truly admired him. "He's a governor."

"They do not distinguish the difference," Genevie replied. "Power is power."

The throngs of city dwellers thickened. I held my breath,

tense in case they made a move for Anton, and at the same time bracing myself for the jolt of several hundred auras. He glanced back me, his brows raised in concern. Was he trying to warn me? Did he know he was in danger?

But as his gaze searched my face, I realized he was worried about *me*. An old habit. I'd never done well in large crowds. I nodded reassuringly and tried to relax. No auras would bombard me, I reminded myself. I turned to Genevie. She wasn't so fortunate. "How are you faring?"

Perspiration beaded through the powder on her brow. She flinched and shifted sideways in her saddle. A moment later, a man with a pock-scarred face stepped into the road. "Auraseers," he hissed at us. The gaunt woman beside him spat on the ground.

Genevie's shoulders hitched up in a protective stance. We rode faster, putting more distance between them and us. "I wondered how long it would take the people to realize what we are," she said, glancing in all directions. "Word must have spread about *our* coming, too. You are lucky not to feel their disdain." She winced, as if deflecting a physical blow.

I remembered the near hysteria I'd experienced when traveling to Torchev for the first time. The countless people in the packed streets had assaulted my awareness, their auras thrashing at all my defenses. "I've felt it before. I'm sorry you have to endure it alone."

More heads turned our way, more mouths twisted into snarls. When Anton wasn't looking, a teenaged boy threw a handful of sharp pebbles in front of Raina, trying to make her buck. I yanked her reins, and she sidestepped the hazard just in time.

I stared back at the boy, shocked he would try to hurt a stranger, but he only sneered and picked up a fist-sized rock. I galloped away before he had the chance to hurl it. Genevie kept close, riding alongside me as we wove around people and carts and tried to catch up to the rest of our regiment.

Angry, spiteful faces flashed in my peripheral vision. Then gray eyes. A deadly smile. *Valko.*

I jerked around but didn't see him, only another man with a similar build and the same shade of dark hair. I swallowed, trying to tamp down my panic. But everywhere I looked, the people's smug and hateful expressions were him all over again. Taunting me. Threatening me.

Genevie was right; I *was* lucky not to feel the people's disdain. What I felt on my own was bad enough.

By the time she and I rode up to the gates of the castle's outer curtain wall, my heart hammered and my hands trembled, ready to withdraw the pistol at my thigh if anyone so much as took another step closer.

"Stay calm, Sonya," Genevie said, her eyes on my twitching fingers.

I flexed my hand, abashed that *she* was the one now keeping *me* steady. I needed to pull myself together. Be wise and careful, like I'd promised Anton.

The guards opened the gates. Once they clanged shut

behind us, I blew out a tremulous breath. Hopefully within the castle grounds, we'd be safer.

Our horses were taken to the stables and our cloaks brushed of dust, but we weren't escorted up the curving steps to the main door of the castle. Instead, servants in jackets with long coattails guided us to a side entrance, where they led us across a long, open corridor on the lowest level. Pillar after pillar, I glimpsed the grand courtyard inside, my fear abating, my skin prickling in awe. The castle's opulence gleamed from every corner within.

Three tiers of open-air corridors lined every wall of the inner square, supported by a colonnade of arches on each level. Rimming the top, above the highest level, was a marble balustrade. Women with impossibly cinched waists and satin puffed skirts strolled about, some on the arms of men in silk breeches and waistcoats. Meanwhile, servants milled about on the lower levels and ground floor, pruning evergreen hedges into ornamental masterpieces and scrubbing sections of the abundant cream stone.

When we crossed halfway to the other side of the open corridor, Genevie took a sharp breath and wavered on her feet. I immediately supported her arm. "Where is he?" I asked, knowing at once what had set her off.

"The Nobles' Terrace." She swallowed and turned her head away.

I glanced to the upper balcony. Floquart de Bonpré leaned against the balustrade, conversing with another nobleman. They must have recently emerged from an inner chamber, because that corner had been vacant a moment ago.

I studied the man who had once come as an emissary to Riaznin. Floquart wore a pale-blue velvet waistcoat with long coattails. A matching ribbon tied his white-flocked hair at the nape of his neck. He opened a silver compact, and its lid winked in the afternoon sunlight, then he brought the back of his hand to his nose. He must be inhaling snuff powder off his knuckles.

I switched places with Genevie, so I stood nearer the open side of the corridor. "It's all right," I whispered. "He'll never recognize you."

Our movement drew Floquart's eye. He gripped the balustrade and met my gaze. Even from down here, I could see his face twist into a grimace. My stomach tightened, and dread crawled up my spine. I fought against the impulse to cower and instead lifted my chin.

You've come here for important reasons, Sonya. The alliance. The Auraseers. Your power. Don't allow yourself to be rattled by the likes of Floquart.

Monsieur de Bonpré had never been impressed with me. To him, I was the sovereign Auraseer Valko preferred over marrying King Léopold's favored niece, Madame Delphine Valois—also Floquart's goddaughter. Not only had I offended him, I'd made his long journey to Riaznin obsolete, as no marriage-based alliance had ever formed.

Something moved from the corner of my eye. I gave a little jump, but it was only another group of servants coming to meet us. I composed myself and peered up at Floquart again. He was gone. *Good.* I exhaled, rolling the tension from my shoulders. I hoped to see him as little as possible here.

As the servants guided our group to the other end of the corridor, I took Genevie's hand—for her comfort as much as mine. They led us through a tower and up a twirling staircase to the second story of the castle. There, the male servants passed off Genevie and me to female servants.

Anton turned back and gave us reassuring smiles, though the curve of his mouth was weak. He must have been nervous, too. "I'll see you soon."

I nodded, fighting a ridiculous wave of panic that I might never see him again in this enormous place. His gaze strayed to me another moment before his servants ushered him away. I took a steeling breath and departed in the other direction with Genevie.

On the second level of the castle, she and I were given a shared apartment, adjacent to one of the open corridors over-looking the courtyard. One look inside the room was enough to remind me of the low esteem Auraseers held in Estengarde.

Two narrow, canopy-less beds rested against one wall, with a small oak table nestled in between. Except for a fireplace and two plain chests for clothing, the room held nothing else. No tapestries hung on the walls for warmth. No rugs spread across the stone floor. Still, we had been sleeping on bedrolls and root-ridden earth for weeks. A heated room and an actual mattress were divine by comparison—although a fire had yet to be lit.

Just as I lay on one of the beds and stretched out my limbs, a maid tsked and shooed me off of the clean linens.

"We need to bathe first," Genevie reminded me, her voice low so the maid wouldn't hear her Esten accent.

I glanced at the clean but simple dresses another maid laid on Genevie's bed, while a third maid dropped a sponge in a basin of tepid water (judging by its lack of steam) and abruptly left the room. The others followed. I stared at the closed door. "Are they going to return?"

Genevie started undressing. "No. They would not deign to wash us. Auraseers bathe themselves here, even those in the king's castle."

I huffed and sat on the edge of my bed as I began to unlace my boots. I didn't like being snubbed, even if I preferred bathing on my own. Trying to think of something optimistic, I said, "You don't need to worry about Floquart. He was too busy glaring at me to pay you much heed."

Genevie shivered, now stripped down to her chemise, though I doubted it was from our chilly room. "That does not relieve me, Sonya. If you draw his attention, we are both still at risk."

I chewed at my lip. She had a point. If Floquart suspected me of any offense, he might start digging deeper, and that could lead him to discover Genevie's identity. "Then I'll do my best to be as uninteresting as possible whenever we cross paths." I pulled off my wool socks and stood to remove my outer dress.

"You could *never* be uninteresting." Genevie replied, no teasing undercurrent in her voice, only an edge of concern. She untied the strings of her chemise thoughtfully. "You need to think of a better plan. We both do."

"Agreed." I paced the floor while unbraiding my hair. "We should make some rules for ourselves." Genevie was a traitor in Estengarde, and I was an Auraseer without abilities. I could help protect her, and she could warn me of impending danger. "To begin with, we have to promise to never leave each other alone."

She nodded adamantly.

"Second, we must always remain armed."

She patted the sheath at her thigh. Between us, we had two weapons—my brass pistol and a slim dagger—which we took turns carrying, although Genevie was better at handling the gun than I.

"And third . . ." I paused and pulled my arms out of the sleeves of my chemise. "What if you and I came up with some sort of code to alert each other when we need help?"

Genevie stepped closer. "We can tuck our hair behind one ear, like this." She demonstrated.

"Perfect. One side tucked means we're uncomfortable and need intervention. Two sides means *emergency, urgent assistance required.*"

She nodded again. "*Très bien.* I like this plan."

I grinned, feeling exceptionally clever—until I threw off my chemise and plunged into the bath. "Feya in the skies above!" I gasped. "This water is freezing!"

Genevie suppressed a smile. "Surely it is better than a mountain stream."

"Not by much."

She came over and wrung some water from the sponge. "You are an Auraseer in Alaise now, Sonya." She tossed the sponge at me. I caught it, blinking as it splashed my face. "This is how the king's city welcomes you."

CHAPTER SIXTEEN

THREE HOURS LATER, SERVANTS ESCORTED GENEVIE AND ME to a private dining room branching off King Léopold's apartments. Anticipation built in my chest. Any moment now I would see Anton again. But as we walked inside, I discovered we were the first guests to arrive.

I glanced around and whispered to Genevie, "The room is so small." While fifteen feet long and twelve feet wide was an otherwise respectable size, it seemed out of proportion with the rest of the vast castle, especially since it had been designed for the king.

"Perhaps," she mused. "But it is just the right size to make important guests feel honored by receiving the king's exclusive attention. Common guests are entertained in the castle's main dining room."

I nodded in understanding, though the idea of some

people being treated better than others chafed at the revolutionary in me.

We stepped deeper into the room. Gold wainscoting with rose-shaped embellishments adorned the cream walls. The only other color present, aside from that in the paintings of royal hunts through La Forêt Royale, was pale blue, the same shade Floquart had been wearing earlier. It must have been in the height of fashion, for it shimmered from the curtains, the velvet-cushioned chairs, and the flower-painted porcelain vases.

My gaze fell on the varnished mahogany dining table, only spread with three place settings, despite the ten chairs. "We don't get to eat?" I whispered.

"Or sit at the king's table," Genevie murmured as a servant ushered her to a separate chair in the far corner of the room. I was led to another, situated diagonally opposite her. I sat down with a sigh, my stomach growling and my mood sour. I wondered how long we'd be detained here before Genevie and I could be free to search out Madame Perle and some food for ourselves.

Moments later, Anton entered through the same door we had, a few feet to my left. He met my gaze, and a sweet rush of adrenaline flooded my limbs. He was clean-shaven, washed from all the dust on our journey, and his hair gleamed in dark waves. He'd been given a brocaded, sage-green kaftan to wear that was tailored to his broad shoulders and tapered waist. I gave my loose gown a tug at my shoulder. While I was grateful for fresh clothes, this drab-blue peasant dress was built for someone far more voluptuous than I.

Anton didn't seem to care. His eyes warmed as he looked over me and gave me a private smile.

A delicate gasp sounded directly across from him, followed by a rich and lovely voice. "Anton? No, it cannot be."

The most beautiful girl I had ever seen waltzed in through a second doorway that must have led to the royal apartments. Her creamy silk skin and buttery-blond hair, coiffed in a stack of elaborate curls, perfectly complemented the stone hue of the castle. The lavender gown she wore was distinctively Esten, its skirt puffing out only from the sides of her hips, not the front or back.

She flew around the table and kissed Anton on both cheeks. "Look at you! My first beau, grown into such a dashing man."

My brows jutted upward.

"And you, Delphine!" Anton laughed, stepping back to take her in. "You're so much taller than I remember."

Delphine? This must be the king's niece, Madame Delphine Valois, Valko's almost-bride. She was even lovelier than I'd imagined. I gave another sorry tug on my dress and tucked a loose strand of hair behind my ear. Genevie's eyes widened, and I caught myself. I rapidly untucked the hair and sent her an apologetic look.

"I was only fifteen when you last saw me," Delphine replied to Anton. "I hadn't even reached my bloom."

My gaze shifted between them, impeccably charming together. So Anton was Delphine's first beau? Was she *his* first sweetheart? Heat surged to my cheeks as I imagined them strolling through the castle gardens together and dancing in each other's arms. In my perfect naivety, I'd never considered the possibility that Anton had courted other girls before me.

He caught my eye, and I took a breath and smiled, the tension easing from my stomach. It didn't matter that he and Delphine had once courted. I had been interested in other boys before him, hadn't I?

"Delphine," Anton said, "you must meet my friends, Sonya and Trinette," he said, using the alternate name Genevie had chosen for herself.

Genevie and I rose from our chairs.

"Your Auraseers are *friends*?" Delphine asked, tilting her head. "How refreshing." I scrutinized the surprised tone of her voice. No scorn sharpened its edges. Perhaps Delphine wasn't in agreement with her uncle, the king, about how Auraseers were treated in Estengarde.

"Wait one moment," she said, her blue eyes narrowing as she left Anton's side and stalked closer to me until she was only a few inches away. I held my breath. What did she want? What had I done wrong? "Are you Sonya *Petrova*, the emperor's former sovereign Auraseer?"

My face tingled, surely blooming a deeper shade of red. Floquart de Bonpré must have told Delphine about me—and how Valko chose me over her. "Yes," I squeaked.

She smiled, revealing a row of straight, pearlescent teeth. "Then I must thank you for preventing a most ill-fated match. I hope very soon I may also call you *my* friend."

I shifted on my feet and forced a small grin. I wished I could sense if Delphine was being genuine. She *seemed* genuine, at least.

A large man strode into the room from the inner entrance. Genevie's nostrils flared with a quick breath as her eyes slid up to him. He was at least as tall as Tosya, though he had twice his muscle. His nose was his prominent feature, and the thin bulb on the end was cleft like a chin. "*Zut alors!*" he said, opening his arms as he drank in the sight of Delphine and Anton from across the table. "*Quelle réunion joyeuse!*"

Delphine laughed with a reprimanding shake of her head and swept closer to Anton. "Speak *Riaznian*, Uncle—for your guests' sakes."

This was King Léopold? He hadn't even been heralded into the room. Valko, at his smaller dinners, entered with pomp and flair, preceded by guards and trailed by attendants. But the Esten king had come in alone, a casual swagger in his step.

He circled the table to Delphine, his demeanor severe as he looked down his nose at her. "Do you mean to paint me as a fool?" he asked, switching to Riaznian. "I can speak their language as well as you!"

Delphine didn't blink. "I'm sorry, your accent is so thick I cannot understand the words you are saying."

King Léopold's mouth snapped shut. I exchanged a tense glance with Genevie. If I'd said such a thing to Valko, he would have struck me. The king's eyes warned he might, but then he threw back his head and roared with laughter. "Oh, my dear child, I have missed you!" He cupped Delphine's face in his great hands and planted a kiss on her brow. "Won't you come back and stay with me in this drafty castle?"

Anton turned to Delphine in surprise. "You're no longer living in Alaise?"

King Léopold huffed. "I have to throw celebrations in her honor to lure her back here." He clamped an affectionate hand on Anton's shoulder. "And you, my dauphin, never return to visit unless your madcap brother drives you across my borders, not to mention the Shenglin."

Anton had the grace to look abashed. "Forgive me, Your Majesty. Riaznin has required all of my attention as of late."

The king waved a dismissing hand. "Yes, yes, such a dramatic feud within your family, and now a half-breed Auraseer princess to boot! What a legacy for the illustrious Ozerovs."

Though Anton was a master of controlling his poise, his grin tightened and his fingers flexed.

"We're very fond of Dasha," I said, speaking frankly, though I strived to sound amiable. "She's a lovely girl with great potential." I pushed the other image of Dasha out of mind, the nightmare girl with glowing gray eyes and a green snake on her shoulder.

For the first time since he entered the room, King Léopold's sea-blue eyes fell on me.

My cheeks burned under his scrutiny. I couldn't tell what he was thinking.

Anton stepped forward. "This is Sonya Petrova, sire, former Sovereign Auraseer under Emperor Valko's reign, as well as an invaluable aid to me during the revolution."

King Léopold pursed his lips, his nose wrinkling. I realized who I was to him, a girl who had helped destroy a monarchy. Without another word of acknowledgment, he marched past me and took his seat at the head of the table, which happened to be close to my corner of the room. He clapped his hands at the two servants posted near the outer doorway. "Bring the first course."

As they bowed and left, Delphine and Anton also sat down, she at her uncle's right, and Anton on his left. Genevie and I followed suit in our designated chairs. Situated five feet behind Anton, I fought another flare of frustration at not being admitted to the table, although he had tried to warn me I wouldn't like the way I'd be treated in the king's castle.

I squared my shoulders. *Let it go, Sonya. Soon you'll see Madame Perle. In the meantime, play your part.*

King Léopold spread a napkin over his lap. "I miss the old days when you could come here without your Riaznian Auraseers, my dauphin. To be honest, I'm insulted you brought them with you. Don't you trust me after all these years?"

"It isn't that, sire. I'm a governor on the Duma now and must respect the council's wishes. They insisted that my Auraseers attend me on this journey."

The king sighed and glanced impatiently the doorway where the servants had yet to return with the food. "No doubt you wish me to give you money or military aid for those accursed wars of yours."

Anton cleared his throat and adjusted his position in his seat. "Thank you for bringing those up, sire. That is, in part, why I have come, though my vision is much larger in scope and can benefit you, as well. If Riaznin and Estengarde were to form an alliance—"

"No, no!" King Léopold grumbled. "I am in no mood to discuss politics tonight."

"I understand, Your Majesty, but we are in haste. The wars—"

"—are not Estengarde's wars, my dauphin."

"The Bayacs can't protect your kingdom forever," Anton said as delicately as possible. "We can lend you aid, too, when your time of need comes."

"Enough!" The king slammed his hand on the table.

I flinched along with Delphine. She recovered quickly and laid a hand on Léopold's arm. "You must forgive my uncle," she said to Anton, giving him a peace offering of a smile. "He won't be himself until my ball is over."

The king's expression softened at her touch. "Lavishing you with attention is no small feat, *ma chère*."

"You are too good to me." Delphine patted his arm. How cleverly she doused his anger.

King Léopold stretched out his arms, pushing his cuffs back a little, as the first course of the meal was presented: fresh oysters and bread stuffed with a pâté of layered meat and cheese. Genevie unclasped her hands and settled back in her chair, which told me the food must have already improved the king's mood.

"Is there a special occasion for this ball, aside from Delphine's return?" Anton asked, laboring to make simple conversation since politics were off the table for now. "Did you finally move away to the sea?" He looked to Delphine. "You often wished to reside there."

"She has been away at university in Chauvigné," the king replied. "Apparently, the royal tutors in Alaise are not good enough for her."

Delphine let the jibe pass with a little slap on her uncle's hand. "The occasion is my birthday," she answered Anton. "Please tell me you haven't forgotten the day. You made my fifteenth quite memorable." My toes curled in my shoes, watching Delphine's sea-blue eyes, the same shade as the king's, linger on Anton as she took a demure sip of wine.

I couldn't see Anton's face—he was sitting with his back to me—but the tips of his ears flamed red. A nervous chuckle bubbled from his throat, and he took a long drink. "So you must be eighteen, then, in what, two days?"

He remembers her birthday.

He remembers the kiss.

Before I could dwell on it another moment, Floquart de Bonpré strolled into the king's private dining room with the ease of a frequent guest.

Ice shot up my spine. Genevie went rigid, and her face

leeched of color. Floquart spared her a quick glance, then, with a perfunctory bow to King Léopold, rounded the table and took a chair beside Delphine, even though there wasn't another place setting for him. Delphine's shoulders tensed, and she shifted slightly away.

"What have I missed?" Floquart said, beckoning a servant with a flick of his fingers. Within seconds, a goblet of white wine was pressed in his hand. "Has another Ozerov proposed an alliance to Riaznin?"

"The dauphin tried," King Léopold mumbled, his lips wet from slurping an oyster.

"Really, Uncle, you must not put off everything." Delphine pierced a bite of stuffed bread onto her fork. "Some matters are more important than my birthday."

"Such as the execution," Floquart piped in. "I still say we should not delay." The king groaned and threw his napkin on the table.

"What execution?" Delphine looked between them. *"Whose?"*

"Why, the rebellious Auraseers, of course. All fifteen of them." Floquart swirled the wine in his goblet, his eyes sliding toward me. He didn't notice Genevie's reaction in the far corner of the room behind him. She'd moved to the edge of her chair and gripped the seat with her hands. "Surely you've heard how some have been trying to escape while you were away at university, dearest Delphine."

His goddaughter's chest fell, and she set down her fork.

"Must they really be executed?" She turned imploring eyes on the king.

Floquart scoffed, staring askance at her. "Of course they must be executed. What else do you think will prevent every other Auraseer in Alaise from thinking they can also flee their masters?" He shook his head. "Honestly, what have you learned all this time you were away? Am I sponsoring your education for nothing?"

Delphine's nostrils flared. Her gaze was riveted to her plate. "I never asked you to sponsor it."

"Auraseers are *property.*" Floquart tapped his jeweled finger on the table to drive in his point. "A slave class in Estengarde. When the bottom of society suddenly believes it doesn't have to answer to the upper classes, the scales of our social structure—which have held Estengarde in balance for centuries—are thrown into disarray." His voice started rising. "If an example isn't made of these Auraseers, we will soon have a much larger problem on our hands. Other people in the lower classes will start demanding more esteem that they have done nothing to merit, not to mention a decrease in taxes." His heated words bounced off the walls. "We have only to look across our borders to Riaznin to see the disastrous experiment of 'equality among all people.'"

The room went quiet. Servants hovered at the door with silver platters, unsure whether or not to present the second course. Delphine held her neck stiff, refusing to look at Floquart. Anton hadn't taken a bite of his food, and his knife and fork were clenched tight in each hand. Across from me, Genevie sat hunched, slightly rocking. Even King Léopold had the decency to look taken aback by Floquart for offending his guest. As for me, I was ready to grab a serving knife and flay Floquart like a fish.

Anton finally broke the silence. "I must say, I agree with King Léopold, Monsieur de Bonpré; I'm in no mood to discuss politics tonight." He laid down his cutlery. "Would you please excuse me, Your Majesty? After my long journey, I am more weary than hungry."

"Yes, of course, my dauphin." The king waved him off, his good humor having returned. "We'll discuss the friendship between Estengarde and Riaznin the day after Delphine's ball."

"Thank you, sire." He scooted his chair back, then hesitated, his jaw working as he labored to keep his temper in check. "Until then, might I also request that you share any intelligence you receive regarding the wars in Riaznin? I have scouts, but they aren't free to cross your borders to bring me any news."

"Yes, yes." King Léopold gave him another shooing motion. "Though I doubt you will find any such correspondence comforting."

Anton stood and offered a clipped bow.

Anxious to leave, I rose with him. But when Genevie did the same, she swayed on her feet and almost stumbled into a tall vase before she managed to right herself. Too late, I noticed her hair was tucked behind both ears.

I inwardly cursed myself and hurried around the table.

Sliding my arm under hers, I scrambled to make an excuse. "We're all overtired, I'm afraid."

Anton rushed to help me and took Genevie's other elbow. She buried her head in my shoulder. As we led her to the exit, Floquart's gaze narrowed, regarding her intently. "The day after the ball is also the perfect day for the execution," he remarked. Genevie's knees gave out. Anton and I held her steady. "You wouldn't want your subjects to think entertainment is more important than the order of this kingdom." He glanced at the king, crossing one leg over the other. "Shall we set the date, then, Your Majesty?"

King Léopold grumbled and spooned up the soup he had just been served. "Very well, Floquart, so long as you promise to stop badgering me."

"You have my word, sire." Floquart raised his goblet to his lips. As he swallowed, he met my eyes, taking no pains to wipe the smug grin off his mouth. "Three days and our rebellious Auraseers hang."

CHAPTER SEVENTEEN

"You should be resting," I whispered to Genevie. It was after midnight. Our backs glided along the shadowy wall as we crept down the open corridor on the second level of the castle keep. The light of the waning moon spilled past the colonnade of arches that faced the grand courtyard, its beams almost reaching us. "If you drew me a map, I could find Madame Perle's room myself."

"This castle has eighty-five staircases, Sonya. It is not so simple to sketch. Besides, we promised not to separate."

I hadn't forgotten, but I hated to tax Genevie any further. Her eyes were puffy from the tears she'd shed after we left the king's dinner. Being in the same room as Floquart had been difficult enough without learning her Auraseer friends were scheduled to be executed. I pressed a hand to my churning stomach. If I had my power, I could free them. *Please, Feya, let Madame Perle be able to help me.* "I only need to know the staircase that leads to the secret passageway."

"The stairs *are* the secret passageway. And you must navigate many to keep your movements hidden. No more than half are in use at any given time, depending on what is happening in the castle."

"We can't bribe the guards to let us visit Madame Perle during the day?"

"They would not dare to cross the king, not with so many Auraseers trying to escape. Madame Perle is His Majesty's precious commodity. Her talents are afforded only to him."

We froze as two servants crossed the courtyard below. Once they left the grounds, Genevie peered around an archway column.

She gasped and ducked back.

"What is it?" As far as I could see, the grounds below were vacant. But then Floquart walked out from an inner chamber across the castle keep.

He strolled from one end of the open corridor to the other, his hand gliding along the balustrades between archways as he scanned the keep in all directions. I clenched my jaw. I loathed him more than ever after watching Genevie suffer tonight.

She trembled beside me, pressed with her back against the shadowed wall, and wrapped her cloak tighter across her shoulders.

At last, Floquart entered another room.

Genevie released a heavy exhale and dug her hands in her hair. "I cannot let him affect me like this. But what if he knows I am here? What if he is searching for me?" Her words tumbled from her mouth. "In the dining room, his emotions were suspicious. He will discover who I am if I keep acting like a coward."

"You're not a coward. Returning to this castle, where you knew he would be, took exceeding bravery."

"I did not think it would be so difficult. But his aura, Sonya . . ." A tiny whimper escaped her. "Feeling it brings back all the torment."

I rubbed her arm. "He will never hold power over you again, I swear it."

"How am I going to help my friends when I am so paralyzed by fear? I thought we would only have to escort them out of Alaise, not free them from prison." Her voice cracked. "They are going to die if I fail them."

I hugged her, trying to offer comfort, but I found myself also leaning on her for support. I couldn't fail, either. I shuddered, remembering the mottled and slack faces of the hung Auraseers in the forest, and my gut lurched with guilt and horror. "You're not alone in this. Somehow we're going to free them, and right now our best chance of doing that begins with finding Madame Perle. If I can regain my power, this will be simple."

I pulled away and forced a reassuring smile, but my knees quavered. Terrible memories assaulted me and paraded my mistakes: an innocent girl badly injured when I'd tried to break up a fight, Terezia Dyomin slitting her own throat with a crystal dagger, Valko breaking past my hold to shoot me during the convent battle.

"Come on." I sucked in a steeling breath. I had to take this chance no matter the danger. Riaznin needed me, too. Dasha did. I was useless to help unless I walked away from Alaise whole again. "Let's hurry while the grounds are clear."

We darted from the castle keep to the adjoining castle proper—a large cluster of towers and wings at the head of the courtyard, which, according to Genevie, included the royal theater, several drawing rooms, the grand hall, and a massive ballroom, as well as the king's apartments and Madame Perle's chambers. The architect who had built this castle must have been a touch mad, for in addition to the eighty-five staircases Genevie had spoken of, I spied countless pinnacles, turrets, belfries, chimneys, and serpentine balustrades. Genevie said newer servants were always getting lost in the mazelike corridors of the castle proper, nothing like the orderly structure of the castle keep surrounding the courtyard.

We snuck through several towers, zigzagging hallways, and winding staircases. Our progress didn't make any sense, except that we slowly converged toward the center tower.

"Please tell me we're getting close," I panted when we arrived on a rooftop. My legs quaked, and my lungs were on fire.

She motioned me over to crouch beside her. "We are here."

Together, we peered over a ledge to a balcony below. Genevie cast down a rope ladder already attached to the roof. "Madame Perle is a friend to all Auraseers," she explained. "This is how we enter."

She climbed down first, and I followed. Glancing around us one last time to make sure no one was watching—Genevie's awareness only stretched so far—she stepped up to Madame Perle's closed balcony door. "Ready?"

I nodded and swallowed my thundering heartbeat. My palms ached with anticipation.

She rapped seven times on the door, the first three knocks loud and rapid-fire, the last four intermittent and soft. A code, I realized, though no one answered it.

"Maybe she's sleeping," I mused.

Genevie frowned. "Madame Perle always wakes when she senses another Auraseer. Nighttime is our only chance to visit."

"Do *you* feel her in there?"

Her teeth tugged on her lower lip. "I am not sure."

She knocked one more time, then tried the handle. The door wasn't fully shut, so the lock didn't hold. With a creak that sounded cacophonous in the otherwise thick silence, the door swung open. I expected moonlight to shaft inside and illuminate the darkened quarters, but they were already lit by a circle of gold, shining brightest around a radiating candle. It perched on a table painted with creeping vines and pastel flowers.

In the dark recesses of the room, a beautiful bed with a brocade canopy caught my eye. But Madame Perle wasn't in the bed. I pivoted, searching for her.

She was nowhere to be seen.

Genevie clutched my hand with icy fingers. "We are not alone," she whispered.

My heart stuttered. "Madame Perle?"

"Someone else."

Dread coiled my nerves. Catching up the hem of my dress, I unsheathed my dagger. Genevie and I had swapped weapons earlier.

"Careful, Sonya. We don't know who—"

Something rattled near a tall wardrobe. I whirled and swiped at the air.

"*S'il te plaît, arrête! Je suis Delphine Valois.*"

My blade hand froze. "Delphine?"

She slowly stepped out from the shadows, walked into the ring of candlelight, and lowered the hood of her cloak. "Forgive me for hiding, but I didn't know whom you were—entering from the balcony, no less." She stared down the end of my dagger, her gaze gradually rising to me.

I released the breath I'd been holding and sheathed my weapon. "Please excuse me, but, as an Auraseer, I don't feel safe in this castle." I rolled back my shoulders and strived to compose myself. "We were looking for Madame Perle. She's a friend to Ge . . ." I pressed my lips together. "To Trinette."

Delphine nodded and sadly glanced around the room. "She's a friend to me, too. I'd also hoped to find her here. But I fear the worst has happened." She clucked her tongue. "What is my uncle thinking? He relies on Madame Perle."

"You believe she's imprisoned with the others?" Panic scorched my nerves.

"It must be the only explanation. I've never known Madame Perle to leave this tower."

Genevie dropped into a chair, her hand covering her mouth.

I couldn't move for several moments. "No . . . Madame Perle can't be imprisoned." The imprisoned Auraseers were scheduled to die. *How can I help them now?* "We need her." When Delphine frowned, I hastily added, "All the Auraseers do. She's been a friend when friends are hard to come by, especially for us."

"Yes." Delphine sighed. "She has been the same to me."

I found myself mirroring Genevie's narrowed gaze on the king's niece. What did a royal know of scarce friendships? Delphine wasn't like Anton or Valko, who had been raised away from palace life and children their own age.

She lifted her chin against our accusatory stares. "I do not pretend to understand the hardships you have faced, but I have my own. Because of the great esteem I hold with the king, others try to use me for it." She glanced down, fidgeting with the rings on her fingers. "True friends—those who don't want something in return—have been precious and rare."

I checked for Genevie's reaction. She must have observed Delphine during her years in the castle. She would know if her story was fabricated to gain our pity. At the very least, she'd be able to sense Delphine's sincerity. After a long moment, Genevie finally offered her a nod of empathy, though she didn't speak a word. Her Esten accent would have surfaced otherwise.

I took a measured breath and a tentative step toward Delphine. Hopefulness sheared through my despair. "Will you help us?" I asked. "If you spoke to King Léopold—"

She recoiled and walked outside the glowing ring. "You're just like the others who believe I can lower taxes or grant titles or improve trade routes just by one whisper to the king." With a humorless laugh, she added, "All I can persuade my uncle to do is buy me a new wardrobe each season. He doesn't even pay for my education because it takes me away from him."

"I'm sorry," I said, trying to be sensitive and patient, though my heart pounded with urgency. In only three days the Auraseers would be executed if we didn't intervene. "I'm not trying to take advantage of your position. I understand what it's like to have a measure of power, and then have others try to use you for it." Valko and Feliks blazed to mind. "But won't you consider at least *trying* to persuade your uncle, especially if it could save the life of your friend?"

The whites of Delphine's eyes shone against the darkness. I yearned to know what she was feeling, if she was receptive at all to my plea. Did she understand she was our only hope?

I snuck another glance at Genevie, but her pensive and almost-strained gaze told me nothing of Delphine's intentions. Maybe the king's niece had learned to hide her emotions from Auraseers the same way Anton had.

Delphine brushed past me and plucked her candle from the table. Before she reached the door, she swiveled back to me, her cloak rustling over her dress. "I *will* speak to the king. I would have done so without your impassioned speech. But you are wrong to think having the king's ear means anything in Estengarde. My dear uncle is a puppet. Monsieur de Bonpré is the monster who truly rules this kingdom."

CHAPTER EIGHTEEN

THE NEXT DAY I ASKED EVERY SERVANT IN MY PATH TO TELL Madame Valois I'd like to speak with her, since they were disinclined to show me which of the castle's four hundred and forty rooms belonged to the king's niece. Delphine didn't seek me out. I prayed she was busy imploring her uncle and godfather to save Madame Perle or stall the execution. Perhaps her influence was at least enough to grant me a visit to the dungeons. One visit might be long enough for Madame Perle to crack me open and release my power.

My gut squirmed with doubts again. What if I remained broken? I needed an alternate plan in case I couldn't be Estengarde's *grande voyant* and Riaznin's Sovereign Auraseer. But as the hours ticked by, I couldn't think of anything, not even a way to help Anton achieve the alliance we'd traveled here for. Feliks's ultimatum gnawed at the back of my mind. We had little more than three weeks before we reached the deadline he gave me.

With nothing more to do but anxiously bide our time until Delphine's ball tomorrow, Genevie and I spent the day with Anton in his vast guest chambers. His great bed with red feather plumes atop the canopy took up only a small fraction of the space. The rest of the room was filled with tastefully arranged groupings of velvet and mahogany furniture. The room I shared with Genevie was a closet by comparison.

Seated at a desk, Anton dipped his quill in an inkwell, busying himself by drafting the alliance treaty. I stood at a nearby window, nervously picking at my nails. He kept sending me sympathetic glances. I'd broken the news to him this morning about Madame Perle.

"*Une amande* needs an *E* in the middle," Genevie said, pointing out a passage on his paper, "or else you are talking about an *almond* and not making *amends*."

Anton gave a self-deprecating groan and scratched out the word. "Perhaps you should write the treaty, or I might walk away from Estengarde with a stuffed picnic basket and nothing more."

She drew up a chair. "You write it as best you can, and I will help you refine the language in a clean draft."

I drifted closer, watching them for a moment. My pulse quickened as another solution sprang to mind. "What if you negotiated the imprisoned Auraseers' lives as one of the terms in your alliance treaty? Perhaps the king will be satisfied if they are banished to Riaznin."

Anton sighed and reached out to clasp my hand. "We can't solve another nation's injustices when we haven't even conquered our own," he said gently. I remembered what he'd told me in his tent a few days ago: *I won't be able to defeat Esten prejudices, as well.*

Genevie looked up at me. "Even if the king is persuadable, banishing the Auraseers to another nation would never satisfy Floquart." Her arms folded over her stomach when she said his name. "He will say banishment insults the king's regime and diminishes the people's faith that the monarchy can handle its own problems." I noticed for the first time that her Riaznian speech was no longer broken, like when she first came to the convent. Her time spent traveling with our regiment had improved her vocabulary. "Floquart will make sure all the Auraseers die."

Anton shook his head in bewilderment. "Is it only me, or does Floquart's hatred for Auraseers seem personal?"

"I know that to be true." Genevie's eyes darkened. "He is the kind of man who strives for excellence and superiority, but he only feels that way when he is crushing others to the ground."

"And Auraseers have an ability that he can never attain," I added grimly.

She nodded, her gaze lowering. "That is enough for us to merit his contempt."

Just as I despaired I might never meet Madame Perle and

regain my power—because how else could we stop a man like Floquart?— someone knocked on the door. The three of us exchanged a look. We weren't expecting any visitors.

Anton rose, crossed the room, and opened the door halfway. After some murmuring with whoever was there, he turned to me. "It's for you."

I analyzed his expression. His brows weren't lowered in warning, only furrowed with curiosity. Could Delphine be the visitor?

Anticipation spiked through me. I hurried over on light feet and swung the door wider. My chest fell. It was only a maid in a mop cap.

Her narrowed gaze scraped over me, and she wrinkled her ruddy nose. "Auraseer Petrova?" When I nodded, she reached beneath her shawl and removed a sealed note. In broken Riaznian, she said, "I promise to Madame Valois I give this to only you." She passed the note with a pinched frown, as if it was against her better judgment.

I thanked her and shut the door, not giving her another opportunity to sneer. I wouldn't let Esten prejudice bother me in this moment. "Delphine must have spoken with her uncle," I said, grinning at Anton and Genevie.

Genevie crossed to where I stood near Anton. "What does it say?"

I broke the seal and unfolded the message, hurriedly scanning its contents.

My shoulders wilted, but at the same time, hope kindled

inside me. "Nothing about any conversations with the king, but Delphine *has* discovered where Madame Perle is—and it's not the dungeons with the other Auraseers. King Léopold has her sequestered in a room directly adjacent to his chambers."

"Why?" Genevie asked.

"Apparently she was caught trying to help the other Auraseers escape, so the king had her moved to a more secure location."

"Of course." Genevie's brows pulled together. "Madame Perle is too valuable to the king to be executed or even imprisoned somewhere filthy."

"Do you know any secret entrances into the king's chambers?" Anton asked Genevie.

She gave a sorry shake of her head.

He scratched his jaw and started pacing. I was surprised to find him so anxious to plot with us. He wasn't exactly thrilled when he'd found out Genevie and I had been sneaking around the castle last night. I braced myself, knowing he would hate what I planned to do next.

I held out the note for him and Genevie to read. "Delphine claims she can help me into the king's chambers on the night of the ball. I think she wants me to free Madame Perle."

Anton's jaw stiffened. "No."

"No?" My defenses sparked, even though I'd predicted his reaction.

"Go and visit Madame Perle, but leave any freeing to Delphine. The king won't punish her if she's caught. And if *you're* caught for being there, you can say Delphine brought you."

"But—"

Someone knocked on the door again, and Genevie startled.

"Floquart?" I asked, all my nerves at attention.

"No." She placed a hand on her chest and took a steadying breath. "I am sorry. Your quarreling distracted my senses."

Anton glanced at me, and I folded my arms. He sighed and opened the door, this time wide enough for all three of us to see who was standing there—another servant, this one male and more finely dressed than the first. On a silver platter, he presented a large envelope, then snapped his heels together and said, *"Pour Monseigneur Anton Ozerov."*

Anton took the letter and closed the door. "The king's seal," Genevie said as Anton ran his thumb over the embossed lion and crown symbol.

He opened it. Inside were two letters, one in Riaznian and one in Esten. He read the first aloud:

"'The intelligence you requested, my dauphin.'"

The second letter Anton passed to Genevie. "You can translate it better."

She swallowed, a little self-conscious, and then straightened her back. "It is dated two weeks ago," she began.

Anton nodded. "The time it would take a courier to travel here."

Genevie continued:

"'Unto His Majesty, the King of Estengarde,

I bring more news regarding the wars in Riaznin. The

infantry and cavalry belonging to the former emperor, Valko Ozerov, are converging on Torchev. From a separate direction, the Shenglin army is also approaching. If both forces continue at the pace they are traveling, they should arrive at the capital in five or six weeks' time. We have reason to believe they are now working together. The former emperor was recently seen meeting with the Shenglin commanding general, Jin Pao. Gifts were exchanged. But rest assured, Your Majesty, no foreign soldiers have yet to breach our borders.

Your loyal subject,

Ambassador Bertrand'"

A rush of dizziness assaulted me. I turned desperate eyes on Anton. His face was ashen. "Valko was supposed to ask Jin Pao to retreat," I said weakly.

Genevie looked between us. "Pardon?"

"It was Valko's plan when I . . ." *When I agreed to help him.* Valko was going to take me to meet Jin Pao last spring. The general was an old acquaintance of his, from Valko's years of hiding near the Shenglin border. Using my power of persuasion, I'd intended to compel Jin Pao to call off the invasion, but I'd come to my senses and broken my fleeting agreement with Valko. I could never trust him or take an action that would place him back in power again. Now Valko had persuaded Jin Pao on his own, perhaps with Dasha's help, and for a different and darker purpose. With the strength of Shengli's formidable army, Valko could wipe out Free Riaznin's troops and our crumbling democracy, once and for all.

I sucked in a long breath, fighting to slow my racing heart-beat. "Valko has formed an alliance with the Shenglin."

The silence in the room grew so thick it seemed to pulse like a living thing.

My legs went weak, ready to buckle. How could Valko do this to Riaznin? He never wanted peace with Shengli. When I'd been his sovereign Auraseer, he'd plotted to invade their nation and expand his empire. But after the revolution and his abdication, the Shenglin attacked Riaznin first while the fledgling democracy was forming.

Anton turned aside and cursed, dragging a hand over his face. I found the nearest chair and clutched it for support.

Genevie watched us with worried eyes. "Everything is not lost. You still have hope if you can forge an alliance between Free Riaznin and Estengarde." Her words sounded less like comforting statements and more like desperate questions.

I didn't know how to answer. I'd never imagined this com-plication. Free Riaznin's chances at winning the wars—*one* war now, us against Valko *and* Shengli—were more remote than ever. We desperately needed the Esten alliance. And my power.

Anton flexed his jaw and grabbed the draft of the alliance treaty from his desk. He strode for the door. "I'm going to find the king and settle this. I need to get back to Torchev."

CHAPTER NINETEEN

"I NEED YOU TO TEACH ME HOW TO BLOCK OUT AN AURA-seer," I said to Anton that night. The candle in my hand flickered as I shut his bedroom door behind me.

He hadn't been sleeping, either. As I entered, I'd caught him pacing near a tall window in his untucked shirt and trousers. A few glowing candles in the room illuminated the ends of his hair. It was disheveled like he'd been tugging his fingers through it for hours. Anton had requested another audience with King Léopold, and I'd searched for Delphine again, but the king sent a message reiterating he would not meet with Anton until the day after the ball, and the servants said Delphine couldn't admit me to wherever she was in this enormous castle. "You want me to do *what*?" Anton asked me.

I realized how strange my request had sounded. "I know I'm already blocking aura, but when I get my power back"—I forced myself to say *when*—"I'll become vulnerable to Dasha again. We have to assume she's doing Valko's bidding now." My stomach pinched, and Anton rubbed a hand over his face. "I need to start training so I can be prepared for her."

"Sonya . . ." He crossed the room to me, his brows lifted. He smoothed my unbound hair behind my shoulders, his touch gentle, his eyes loving. "Do you really want your power back?" His forehead creased. "*That* power?"

The way he asked it, the tender scratch of his voice, made me consider the question without my defenses flaring. In truth, I didn't miss the tremulous instability and dark temptations that came hand in hand with my power to bend emotions. But . . . "How else can I save Dasha?" Or Anton from his brother. Or the people of Riaznin. Or the Esten Auraseers.

"Sonya," he said again, the barest whisper. I heard his sympathy. I felt it as he stroked my cheek with the back of his hand. But I couldn't feel it inside me, where I ached to know his aura once more.

I stepped around him, blinking back my forming tears. I wouldn't cry now. Crying wouldn't help anyone. "During the battle at the convent, Dasha was able to manipulate the auras of over one hundred people, including us," I said, refocusing myself. "You almost broke her hold. I felt it. And Valko broke *my* hold when he shot me, so I know it's possible. I think the key must be calming every emotion, like you used to do so I couldn't tell what you were feeling. Teach me how you did that."

Anton ran a hand through his hair, mussing it even more. "I'm not sure where to begin," he said, moving to sit on a nearby couch. "Training myself to subdue my emotions took over a year before I moved back to the palace." His rebellion against Valko had involved careful planning, including learning to dodge the awareness of his brother's sovereign Auraseer—*me*, and before me, Izolda.

"You breathe differently when you're actively blocking someone," I prompted, setting my candle on an end table before I sat beside him. "And you pretend to make eye contact, but your gaze is a little off, like this." I scooted closer, curling up on my knees so he could see me better in candlelight, while I lowered my eyes to the upper bridge of his nose. "Is that the basic trick of it?"

He gave me an amused look. "Blocking an Auraseer requires more than just steady breathing and skewed eye contact."

"You also meditate," I supplied, clasping my hands in my lap, determined to be an exemplary student. "I remember sensing your body relaxing, but I don't know how you did it."

"You have to empty your mind. Think of nothing."

I stared at him blankly. "But that's impossible."

He broke into a soft chuckle, his gaze warm, like that might be the most endearing thing I'd ever said. "Truthfully, Sonya, I don't think meditation is in your nature."

"No, no, I can do this." I sat up taller and tried to exude calm. "I'll think of nothing," I instructed myself. I picked at my fingernails, waiting for nothingness to come. But too many somethings got in the way. *Kira.* Was she safe with Tosya and the Esten Romska? *Dasha.* Even if I could save her, could I reverse the damage Valko must have done by influencing her? *Genevie.* Was she sleeping soundly or having a nightmare about Floquart? *Nadia.* Had she found any Riaznian Auraseers, or was she alone at the convent? I scratched my arm. "How long does it take to think of nothing?"

Anton bit down on a smile. "Try focusing on your heartbeat and your breathing. Don't try to *control* your breath, but notice how your chest expands and contracts with it. Every time your mind wanders, bring it back with your breath."

I squared my shoulders. Clenched my hands. Nodded. *Focus, Sonya.*

"You're all tense. *Relax.*" He reached over and shook my body loose. I moved into a cross-legged position on the couch. "Now close your eyes."

"But I won't be able to close my eyes if we're ambushed."

"Which is why you should savor the opportunity now."

I huffed but humored him. Eyes closed, I concentrated on all that was happening inside me. My stomach gurgled. I should have eaten more supper. My legs ached, still sore from the long ride to Estengarde. The muscles in my back pulled with tension, growing tighter every hour we were forced to delay in this castle. "Listening to my body isn't helping," I complained. "It's still making me think."

"Separate your body from your emotions. Try not to quantify what every fluctuation inside you means. Just acknowledge it. Make peace with it. A sneeze is nothing more than a sneeze, for example. It doesn't mean you're catching a cold."

My head hurt as I struggled not to struggle. All I felt was frustration. "I can do this," I told myself, balling my hands into fists.

"You can't *force* yourself to meditate. You just have to meditate." Anton kissed my neck.

"Not helping," I said, keenly aware of how my belly tingled at his touch.

He drew me into his arms, reclining on the couch with me. "You should go to sleep, my love. You're not going to learn how to block aura in the middle of the night when you're exhausted."

I fidgeted, trying to relax. He was right, of course. Idly, I rubbed the threads of a torn seam in his shirt, but my gaze trapped on my candle. I let its flame sear spots in my vision. "I can't fail," I murmured, and I meant more than blocking Dasha. First I had to regain my power through Madame Perle—tomorrow.

Anton's lips pressed warmth on my head. "*We* can't fail," he amended. His fingers flexed as he tightened his hold around me. He might have felt a similar foreboding because he said, "Please tell me I have no choice but to kill my brother . . . assuming he doesn't kill me first. I'll do my best to imprison him again, but I fear when we meet, it will be on the battlefield. I don't see how else this war will end unless one of us dies."

I folded my ankles around his. "If Valko wins, it will mean the deaths of thousands of people. It will mean Riaznin's death. He'll crush our last fragments of identity and our freedom. He'll oppress and abuse, worse than ever before. He won't risk another uprising." I tucked closer to him. "You have no choice. If you face him in battle, you need to finish him. He won't suffer his pride to surrender again."

All of our talk rode on the thinnest thread of hope. The reality was that Anton and I had a much greater chance of dying at Valko's hands.

Anton's sluggish heartbeat thumped against my ear. "Will Dasha forgive me if I kill him?" he asked.

I didn't answer. I didn't know. Dasha was only seven years old and very impressionable. She had been growing to love and trust Anton before being abducted, but now she was likely loyal to Valko. I feared the image of her that often surfaced to mind: Dasha wearing a princess's crown made of ice and seated on a throne beside Valko, her gray eyes as cold and merciless as his.

"I have one memory with my brother, from when we were children." The quiet rumble of Anton's voice vibrated through his chest. "I used to not remember anything from the time before we were separated, but this moment came back to me the other day. I don't know why."

"What do you remember?"

"Teaching him to fish. Or at least trying to. Our mother gave us the poles, but our father could never spare the time to take us to the Azanel River. We were forbidden to go outside the palace grounds, so Valko and I snuck down to the pond in the gardens. I managed to bait our hooks and showed him what I thought was the best way to cast the line." Anton shook with a silent laugh. "We caught everything from our shirts to the reeds until Valko's hook finally sank into the water. Almost instantly, the line tugged, and I helped him pull in a fat carp. The servants found us then and gave us a good scolding—the fish were ornamental and not to be eaten, and we might have drowned, for that matter—but it was worth it to see Valko's beaming smile." Anton had been stroking my arm, but his hand paused, as if he was lost in the memory. "I'd feel easier now if I'd forgotten that. How is it that joy can bring such sorrow?"

"Joy means that you have loved," I whispered. "It means the pain is worth that love in the end."

He held me closer. The breeze rustled on the windowpanes, the grandfather clock ticked in time with the pulse in my wrist, and Anton's scent of musk and pine came stronger with my nose pressed against him. I wondered what moments from my own childhood I might remember with Madame Perle's help tomorrow night. And if the remembering would bring me joy or sorrow.

CHAPTER TWENTY

WHEN I RETURNED TO THE ROOM I SHARED WITH GENEVIE early the next morning, I found a taffeta-covered basket outside our door. Inside were ball gowns for us. I suspected they were gifts from Delphine—her apology for not allowing me to see her yesterday.

With nothing more to do to pass the maddening hours until the ball began, Genevie and I took our time getting ready. The dress I wore was a shade between coral and red, its delicate gold-and-green lace dripping at my plunging neckline and the ends of my three-quarter sleeves. The skirt alone must have been made from at least thirty yards of silk. Its front panels folded back from the center, revealing swaths of green gossamer beneath. I didn't have any jewelry, so I removed the velvet ribbons from my shoes and tied one around my neck, the bow at my nape. The other Genevie wrapped around my hair, which she'd done up in a coif of braids and curls.

I swiveled a little, admiring the flared hips of the dress. The Esten style was starting to grow on me. "Is dancing with Auraseers frowned upon in Estengarde?"

"Everything regarding Auraseers is frowned upon in Estengarde," Genevie replied. Her voice was more than sardonic; it was distressed. The brief fantasy I'd entertained of dancing with Anton shattered. All my worries came rushing back—above all, in this moment, her.

While she looked beautiful in her tiered lavender gown, with her black hair teased into a nest of curls, Genevie's skin was pallid and her brows drawn tight. "I think I am going to be sick," she said, clutching her stomach.

I grabbed an empty bedpan and rushed it over to her. "You really don't need to come tonight."

She vehemently shook her head. "That will make Floquart even more suspicious. Besides, I do not want to be alone."

I fought a wave of guilt for leaving her last night. I could tell by her drooping eyes that she'd slept fitfully.

"I will be fine, Sonya," she said, her knuckles white as she gripped the bedpan. She lurched a little, then swallowed the impulse to retch. "*Both* of Anton's Auraseers will be expected in the ballroom. I just need a moment."

It was much longer than a moment before Genevie felt well enough to accompany me. I gave a servant a note to pass to Anton, explaining we would be late.

When we finally approached the ballroom's open doors, the swirl of shimmering gowns and rich candlelight was already ablaze within. The music of a harpsichord, string quartet, and flute traipsed in time to an Esten minuet. Tension I'd unwittingly been carrying released as I reminded myself none of the auras in this crowded space would have the power to overwhelm me. Being amid throngs of people had always been breeding grounds for panic attacks in the past. That was one less thing I had to worry about tonight. Genevie, however, didn't have that luxury.

"Are you sure you're all right?" I asked, watching her wobble on her feet.

"Yes, you can let go of my arm now." She lifted her chin, her face still slightly green. "I feel perfectly fine."

Hesitantly, I released her, and we entered the ballroom together. Eggshell pigments of pink and green dominated the walls and ceiling, and shimmering gold roses wove their way through the trim work. Golden statues of the Esten goddess Gwenaëlle, with her arms twined over her head, held up scores of candles throughout the room. Noblemen and -women danced the minuet, walking forward in pairs in a cycling parade, their arms extended and hands barely touching.

I spied Delphine in the formation, already midway on her journey back to the end of the line. She wore easily the most gorgeous dress in the ballroom—a creamy golden silk masterpiece with a diamond-encrusted stomacher. Jewels glittered from her throat, her ears, and coifed hair. When the king wished for his dearest relative to have a happy birthday, he clearly spared no expense.

Delphine found her partner again—Anton. He looked just as stunning, if not extravagant, in his knee-length coat, long vest, and matching breeches. The dark-gold fabric gleamed in the candlelight. He took Delphine's outstretched hand, continuing the dance, and smiled warmly at her.

My cheeks burned hot. "Shall we get a drink?" I asked Genevie. Without waiting for her answer, I headed for the least crowded banquet table. I leaned against it and exhaled.

Pull yourself together, Sonya.

Anton and Delphine were old friends, nothing more. I trusted him, and I was grateful for the help she would be offering me . . . whenever she could spare a moment to leave the room. Which would be difficult as this ball inevitably placed her in the center of attention.

A servant poured Genevie and me two long-stemmed glasses of a frothy white wine. I took a sip and coughed as my mouth fizzed and nose burned. "Your wine has bubbles," I complained to the servant as I wiped my mouth clean.

"It is champagne, mademoiselle." He looked down his nose at me.

"The bubbles are the point," Genevie added with a grin.

I frowned, watching her take a sip.

"*Les Auraseers de Riaznin,*" a nearby woman said. I heard the sneer in her voice before I turned to see it on her powdered face. She leaned into the nobleman beside her and spread her fan to conceal her mouth, though when she spoke again it was just as loudly and now in Riaznian. "Who let them into this party?"

The nobleman wrinkled his nose. "*Les animaux de vermine.*"

I didn't know what that meant, but it didn't sound friendly. Until this couple, no one had taken special notice of us in the ballroom, but their words were a stone in a large pond of prejudice. With a ripple effect, their animosity spread, and we caught other people's attention. They turned, whispered, and pointed. They spat more words in Esten I couldn't understand that made Genevie's shoulders curl and head lower. I fought the impulse to demand the nobles leave us alone; it would only draw more scrutiny when we needed to be inconspicuous.

I took a gentle hold of Genevie's arm and pulled her toward the other end of the ballroom, where no one was yet looking at us. I tried to catch Delphine's eye as we passed by, but she was too absorbed with Anton.

Genevie and I situated ourselves near a few tall potted plants against the far ballroom wall. "People should not complain if we stay out of the way over here," she said. "As long as we don't dance or eat the food—"

"Or appear like we're enjoying ourselves?" I finished for her.

She nodded and tugged the sleeve of her gown. "We should not have dressed in such finery. I know better. I suppose for one night I wanted to feel . . . like the rest of them." As the minuet ended she watched a group of Esten girls our age who laughed with bright smiles and gathered with their circle of friends. "Their auras are light and free. I doubt they have ever felt true suffering."

I gently touched her arm. "I wish you hadn't suffered at all,

Genevie, but you're stronger than any of those girls because of it."

"Am I?" She gave a rueful laugh and rubbed her hand across her stomach as she scanned the room. "Have you seen him yet?"

I knew whom she meant. "No."

"He is out there. I feel him like a sickness inside me."

"Do you think—?"

Her brow twitched, and she startled back a step. Her eyes roamed faster. "The feeling is stronger." She grasped my hand. "*Aide-moi!* He is coming."

I whirled to follow her trapped gaze. Floquart was fifteen feet away, just emerging from a group of noblemen, and walking straight for us.

My spine went rigid. Genevie's grip tightened, smashing the bones in my fingers. Floquart hadn't seen her up close in the king's dining room. But if he came any nearer, he would. He'd see right past her disguise.

"Trinette," I said loudly, "hurry and present Governor Ozerov our report before the next dance."

At the opening I gave her, Genevie fled, granting Floquart a wide berth as she darted around him.

He arched a brow, watching her go, and his footsteps slowed as he ambled closer to me. "I take it Anton is still safe from any threats in the castle," he said, one corner of his mouth curled in mockery. "Don't you think it's a little overmuch that he brought *two* Auraseers to Estengarde?"

I shrugged. "During wartime one can never be too care-ful, even this far across the Bayacs," I replied, striving to be as indifferent as possible, so he wouldn't suspect anything off about Genevie.

Another song struck up, this one a waltz. For one terri-ble moment, I feared Floquart had approached me to dance. Instead, he turned around to share my view of the ballroom. Of course he wouldn't ask me to dance. I was a lowly Auraseer. But then why was he conversing with me at all?

Energy scattered across my skin, almost like aura. Perhaps it was—so fleeting, though, I couldn't trap it. All it left me with was a feeling of deep foreboding.

"I must tell you," Floquart said, "when I heard Anton was coming, I didn't take the news well. I wasn't keen on the idea of allying with a weaker nation."

I bit down on a caustic remark. Riaznin was over four times the size of Estengarde, and more than three times its popula-tion, even though the civil war had divided us.

"But in light of the fact that your former emperor has joined forces with the Shenglin," he continued, "perhaps Anton was right and the Bayacs may not protect Estengarde for much longer."

I eyed Floquart warily. His words rang with false humility. I braced myself for whatever point he was driving at. Surely it would be derogatory.

"Is King Léopold as pleased as he looks?" he asked.

"Pardon?"

Floquart gestured to where the king sat on his throne, his

fingers tapping to the strains of the orchestra while he smiled at his niece and Anton. Of course I couldn't sense the king's aura, but by all appearances he seemed untroubled by the fact that he'd ordered many Auraseers to their deaths tomorrow.

"Anton is doing his job well," I replied, treading carefully. I didn't know what Floquart was trying to bait me by saying. "He's keeping the king in good spirits before they meet tomorrow. Pleasing Delphine means pleasing her uncle, after all."

Floquart tilted his head in acquiescence and pulled a silver compact from his pocket. He sprinkled snuff powder on his knuckles. "Did you know Anton and Delphine were once betrothed, back when his father, Emperor Izia, was alive?"

My stomach dropped. *Betrothed* rang in my ears, clashing with the music and the din of conversation all around us. I glanced at Anton and Delphine as they swayed in the one-two-three rhythm of the waltz. Behind her radiant smile, I imagined the ache of a lost future with him. "He never told me," I murmured.

"I suppose he never needed to." Floquart snorted the powder and blinked twice. "The arrangement ended when Izia died and Valko became emperor."

Realization settled across my prickling mind. Now I understood the zealous desire Valko had once harbored to marry Delphine and ally Riaznin to Estengarde. She'd been Anton's sweetheart, and Valko was desperate to have everything his brother might lay claim to—his throne, as well as his intended bride.

"King Léopold, however, is still fond of Anton"—Floquart raised his chin—"so I'm sure another arrangement can be reinstated."

"What do you mean?"

His mouth pursed, almost smirking, as he waited for me to catch on.

My lungs constricted. My breaths came shallow. "Riaznin doesn't need a marriage to seal an alliance like we did before. We're a democracy now. Anton won't govern forever, and he's only one member of the Duma."

Floquart lifted a shoulder. "You'll find King Léopold quite the traditionalist when it comes to these matters, regardless of the ever-changing whims of your government."

"But . . . other pacts can be made to forge an alliance. Riaznin can offer Estengarde more borderland or build up better trade routes between our nations. Perhaps an Esten ambassador could serve as an advisor to the Duma."

Floquart's cunning eyes narrowed on me. "You're very concerned about this, aren't you? One might think you have feelings for the former prince."

I felt my blood rising. "Is that why you're telling me all this?"

"You have a knack for interfering with alliances," he replied coolly, "as well as playing with the hearts of men in power." I swallowed, remembering how he'd once caught me tangled in a passionate kiss with Valko. Of course, Floquart hadn't stayed long enough to see Valko bash my head into the wall.

"Is this my warning, then?" I asked, standing taller so I

could meet the contempt in his gaze head-on. "Or are you threatening me?"

"I'm *watching* you." He slid his compact back inside his pocket and crossed his arms. "Do you know what the dungeon guards told me?"

"Of course not."

"The Auraseers whisper of a *grande voyante*. Does that mean anything to you?"

My heartbeats slowed to heavy thuds. I looked away from him and shook my head, suddenly dizzy. The couples on the dance floor were only streaks of color and flashing faces.

"Apparently, this person inspired the ridiculous notion of freedom in the Auraseers. They were planning to run to Riaznin, which leads me to believe this 'grand seer' lives there."

My cheeks were on fire. I could barely find my voice. "Perhaps they're referring to the former emperor's half sister."

"Yes, I've heard of the child that travels with Valko. There are even rumors of a rare ability she possesses to persuade others to her way of thinking . . . or *feeling*, I suppose. You Auraseers work with emotions, after all."

I nodded weakly.

"I don't believe Dasha is the *grande voyante*."

"Why?" I couldn't help asking.

"Ambassador Bertrand sent something along with his letter of intelligence from Riaznin—I'm sure Anton shared it with you." Floquart batted his hand at me. "King Léopold hasn't had a moment to read it yet, but I have."

"The letter?"

"No, the book."

Dread mushroomed inside me.

"*Sovereign Auraseer* by Tosya Pashkov."

My pulse thrashed in my ears. "That poet has a vivid imagination."

"Evidently." Floquart's brow arched at a severe angle. "So, again, Auraseer Petrova, I am watching you."

"There you are, Floquart!" Delphine's lively voice shattered the intensity of Floquart's glare. As he turned to her, I let myself exhale. Black spots dotted across my vision.

"What are you two chatting about all the way over here?" Delphine asked, taking both of our hands. "Aren't you going to dance with your goddaughter on her birthday?" Her sea-blue eyes riveted on Floquart at the same time as something cold and hard scraped into my palm from hers.

"Of course." Floquart grinned, looking amiable and unruffled. "I was only waiting for my chance. Until now you've had a very devoted partner."

She laughed like he'd said the most flattering thing. "Luckily for you, he is busy talking with my uncle at the moment." I stole a glance at the king's throne. Anton was providing the distraction he'd promised me. "Hurry before he steals me away again."

Floquart chuckled—the sound was odd, coming from him—and bowed his head to oblige her.

Delphine released my hand, and I tucked my closed fist

into the folds of my dress. Floquart missed the movement, but he gave me another tight-eyed look of warning before he strolled away with her.

As Delphine guided him deep into the throngs of people on the other side of the ballroom, the orchestra began playing another waltz.

I waited until Floquart was out of sight, then pulled out my hand and uncurled my fingers.

Genevie snuck back over to me. "What did he say?" she asked.

I inhaled a sharp breath. "I'll tell you later. We have to act quickly. Delphine isn't coming with us." I prayed she could detain Floquart for as long as possible. We needed enough time to meet with Madame Perle.

"How do you know she isn't?"

I showed Genevie what was in my hand. "Because she gave me a key."

CHAPTER TWENTY-ONE

"Wait, Sonya!" Genevie hissed. She caught my arm and pulled me behind a thick pillar. "Auras are close. Probably guards."

"How many?" I crouched beside her.

"Two, I think."

Candles on a brass stand flickered from a draft wending its way through the corridor that led to the king's apartments. The guards must have been stationed outside his doors.

A distant bell chimed the quarter hour. "Five more minutes," I whispered, unrolling the small strip of paper in my hand. It was a note Delphine had wrapped around the teeth of the key.

Don't go inside until twenty minutes after the hour.

We didn't know why Delphine had warned us to delay. Maybe at that designated time the guards Genevie was sensing would change patrol, and we'd have an opportunity to slip inside.

As we settled into more comfortable positions, Genevie asked, "So you do not think Floquart suspects me?"

I shook my head. "Whatever you felt from his aura must have been directed at me." I'd filled her in on my unsettling conversation with him during the several minutes it took us to arrive in this wing of the castle proper.

"I am not sure." Genevie bit down on her lip. "When he looked at me, his aura made my throat squeeze like he was wrapping a chain around my neck."

A chill branched up my spine as I remembered Valko's dark possessiveness. "I know that feeling."

"Do not underestimate him, Sonya. He is more dangerous than you think." Hesitantly, she touched the end of her flared sleeve. With a quick breath, she ripped it back.

"What are you doing?"

"I want to show you something." She leaned out from the shadows and into the candlelight and angled her upper arm to me. There, on the pale underside of her flesh, she revealed a rash of angry scratches, some sharp, some ragged. They were old, healed over to some extent, but never faded. In various places, the skin puckered where certain wounds must have been reopened and sliced over again.

I couldn't remove my shocked gaze. "Floquart did this to you?"

"Can't you see his mark?"

In the pit of her arm, where it would have hurt most to be nicked by a knife, I found the small, sharp lines of a letter *F*.

My hand pressed over my nose and mouth. "Oh, Genevie . . ." She'd suffered even more than I'd imagined.

"This was just him toying with me. He has done much worse. If we are caught, Floquart will make sure you pay with your life."

Footsteps pounded toward us from the corridor. We shrank back behind the pillar. The two guards ran past us, shouting in Esten. My brow wrinkled as I watched them race down the nearest flight of stairs. What was that about?

"We must hurry!" Genevie grabbed my arm.

We sprinted for the king's chambers. As we approached the doors, Genevie and I halted at the corridor window. A bright orange light drew our gaze—a pair of curtains were on fire in the tower directly across from us. It must have been Delphine's doing. Perhaps she'd bribed a servant to commit arson. Knowing something of the complex castle layout, I was sure it would take the servants several minutes just to reach the fire.

"Go inside, Sonya." Genevie nudged me. "I will keep watch here and warn you when the fire is put out."

Warmth radiated through my chest as I took in her face, framed by undulating amber light. In that moment, I realized I'd come to love Genevie as deeply as I'd loved Pia and Yuliya. I wanted her to have happiness and true freedom. I wanted her friends to have the same. I would do anything to help her gain that peace. "Thank you." I embraced her. "I won't fail you."

She squeezed me back, then gave me a gentle shove. "Go!"

I nodded and spun for the doors. Fit the key in the lock. Turned it over. Placed my hand on the latch.

My heart danced across my rib cage. All my anticipation over the last long weeks culminated. Every nerve was on end.

Madame Perle was finally within reach.

I shut the door behind me, and the abundant coral-red silk of my gown swished at my ankles. I could barely see into the darkened room, but it must have been vast from the way my footsteps echoed off the walls and ceiling. Moonlight bled through the seams and edges of the curtains at the windows, and my eyes adjusted to the dimness just in time to prevent me from colliding into a small table.

Turning around, I spied a four-poster bed with a tall canopy along with other expected furnishings, but not what—or whom—I was looking for. "Hello?" I said, my voice breathy. Why was I being so tentative? I didn't have time to be skittish. "Hello?" I called again.

"You're Riaznian," she said.

I yelped and spun toward the left wall. Another door was there. Open, but not lit from within. A woman faced me. The shape of her trailing dress was all I could make out of her in the darkness. "Madame Perle?"

"What is Genevie doing outside the door?" she asked, continuing to speak my language. "She was one of the few who succeeded in escaping Alaise." Her voice sounded papery and gnarled with age, but also sharp with authority. My skin prickled in gooseflesh. "Genevie brought me here so I could meet with you and help the other Auraseers," I replied.

The scrape and soft whooshing of a match strike sounded just before its tiny flame pierced my vision. It cast a faint ring of illumination around Madame Perle as she lit a candle. My heart pounded as she closed the twenty feet between us. Why did all my instincts scream to run? Then I realized—*I'm afraid she won't be able to help me.*

We sized each other up. She wore a velvet robe over a linen nightgown. Her hair was unbound and abundantly gray with streaks of brown and blond. Her eyebrows had a strong arch, which made her look severe, but something about her eyes and the many careworn lines of her face reminded me of Sestra Mirna.

"*La grande seer?*" Madame Perle said, her mouth creased in a deep frown. "Why are you drawn behind a veil?"

Powerful yearning throbbed at the back of my throat. "Can you even feel it? My aura?"

She tilted her head, regarding me intently.

And nodded.

A sob broke from my chest. My legs buckled. I fell to my knees, and my dress bloomed wide. Tears burned down my face.

Up until this moment, I'd feared my aura was lost forever. That somehow I lived while it was dead. But now relief took such fierce hold of me I began to quake.

I have aura.

The sacred breath of energy inside me still existed. The cradle of my emotions. The force that pulsed them from my body.

Madame Perle knelt before me, the light of her candle dancing beneath the bones of her cheeks and brows.

"Make me feel again," I pleaded. "I can't help anyone like this. You sense me, but I don't emit aura to any other Auraseer. I've been blind to my awareness since I was shot."

Lines branched from the corners of her eyes. I couldn't discern her expression. Pity? Worry? Helplessness? "What did Genevie tell you I can do?" she asked.

"Release my suppressed memories through the emotions that evoke them," I said in a rush, swiping away the last of my tears. "I was separated from my family as a child, you see. But I don't remember them. I can't even recall my parents' faces. I might have shut away my memories to protect my heart. And if that's true, maybe I shut away my abilities in order to guard my aura when I almost died. So Genevie thinks—*I* think—well, I hope, that is . . ." Heat flooded my cheeks. Was any of this rambling making sense? *Relax, Sonya. Breathe.* "I hope there's a connection between the two—that my buried memories and my trapped abilities are stuck in the same place inside me— and when you free one, you will free the other." I pressed my mouth together and gnawed at the corner of my lip. Saying all this aloud made my postulating and my plan to become whole again suddenly seem ridiculous.

Madame Perle gave a long sigh that rattled through her chest. My muscles bunched. Was she reluctant or overwhelmed?

Or was I asking something impossible?

"You can help me . . . can't you?"

"Remember things, yes. But your Auraseer abilities . . ." She rubbed her fingers over her mouth. "How long do we have until the guards return?"

"Twenty minutes maybe. Thirty, if we're lucky."

She set her jaw. "Then we must make haste."

Relief poured out of me on a heavy breath. I pushed to my feet and helped her up, leading her toward the outer door.

"No." She pulled back. "We will do this in my room."

"But this is your chance to escape."

"I am not running away. I'm an old woman. I would not survive the journey."

"But—"

"The Auraseers still need me in Alaise. Not all of them are brave enough to leave here." I stared at her, amazed she would choose to stay. "I am like a mother to them," she added, her somber voice reflecting the weight of that responsibility.

I finally understood. She was like Sestra Mirna, who wouldn't abandon the convent while there were girls left to care for, even during wartime. Even if those girls were only Nadia and me. My eyes burned with a surprising rush of gratitude . . . and loss. I wished I'd appreciated the sestra more. Recognized what she'd sacrificed for me. For all of us.

"Come quickly," Madame Perle said, motioning to her room.

I followed her, and she shut her door behind us. She set her candle on a tea table and lit two sconces on the wall. I joined her on a small divan, and she positioned me so I sat facing her.

"We have only just met," she said, "but you must place your complete trust in me in order for this to work. There can be no resistance on your part."

"All right." I rolled back my shoulders. Resistance was in my nature, but I needed to surrender myself. A difficult task when I didn't know exactly what she was about to do. "Genevie says you'll feel my aura so deeply that you'll fall into a trance."

"And you will, too."

My brows shot up. "I will?"

"As long as you don't resist me. Your trance is necessary for you to recall your memories. All I can do is guide you by relaying how they feel. Your mind must do the rest."

I rubbed my palms against my skirt, suddenly feeling unprepared.

"You must trust yourself, too, *grande voyant*. You are capable. I feel your strength. When I speak to you during the trance, you will not hear my words, but you must follow what you feel."

I had no idea how to do this. "All right."

"Give me your hand," she said. I obliged. She clasped it so her fingers stretched over my inner wrist and rested against my beating pulse. She shook my arm back and forth, then pursed her lips. "You are resisting me. You must relax." I loosened, letting her movements jostle my upper body. Next, with her free hand, she pressed a tender spot behind my shoulder. "Are you ready?"

My gut squirmed. "Yes."

"Your buried memories may be beautiful or harrowing." Madame Perle's gaze trapped me with its intensity, yet her voice exuded calm. "Are you willing to face them?"

The words Sestra Mirna had once lovingly spoken to me rang through my mind: *Be careful with your heart, child.* But I couldn't be. Not this time. I only had this one chance with King Léopold's Auraseer. *Surrender, Sonya.* My words now. My conviction. "Yes."

She swiftly pulled my arm. My head rocked forward. "Sleep," she said.

A great whoosh of darkness swooped over my vision.

Bitterness filled my mouth, and my chest flowered in pain. The blackness around me took form, shadow separating from shadow. Images surfaced, first transparent then opaque. They fanned over each other in rapid succession. The letter *F* scarred onto flesh. Anton and Delphine dancing in the ballroom. Two Auraseers hanging from nooses. Kira weeping inconsolably.

I wanted to look away. My body jerked. A soothing hand patted my back.

Surrender, surrender, surrender.

The pain clawed deeper inside me, burrowing for my heart. More images unfolded.

Freshly turned earth. A new grave. Sestra Mirna slumping in a chair. Blood on her handkerchief and blood on my dress, a wide bloom across my belly. A crack of gunfire. Valko's triumphant face. Dasha's hands in my hands. One hundred violent auras trapped inside her shaking body. The deepest look of hurt in Anton's eyes. A crystal dagger dragged across Terezia Dyomin's throat. Nadia's hood cast back, revealing the burn scars I gave her. My hand on top of Valko's hand. Driving a blade into an assassin's chest. Pia's heart-shaped face, bruised and bleeding. Yuliya, pale and lifeless. The convent on fire.

Shame bled through every space of my body. I tasted salty tears, but didn't hear myself crying.

The images flickered faster. All I could see now were faces. Each convent girl who hated me. Romska tribespeople. Sestra Mirna. Another woman. Sestra Mirna. The woman again, her eyes hazel. Sestra Mirna. The woman.

Dizziness seized me. Tension pounded through my head. Everything—everyone—came at me too fast. It was too much to take in. Too hard to breathe. To feel. It had to stop.

Stop!

"Shh, Sonya. Relax. Trust yourself." Madame Perle's voice. Distant. Tinny. I felt her hand on my back again, a gentle but steadying pressure. "We've caught a loop in your emotions. An important memory is trapped here. Now open your mind. What is waiting for you? Would you like to . . . ?" Her words faded and the last image I saw—the image of the woman—appeared again.

She held still, like I'd painted her on canvas. Her hair was tied back in a kerchief, but a long, dark-blond braid spilled out from beneath it and trailed over the front of her shoulder.

My body flashed hot and cold. Air trickled inside me, then out again.

Who was this woman?

Did I want to know?

I had a choice, I realized. My eyelids fluttered. The woman would bring me more pain, that was certain. I could wake up now. End this. But warmth skipped across my chest. Maybe she could offer me something more.

I took a step toward her, and our surroundings transformed. We were in a small house with a tile stove. Herbs dried from the rafters above us. Hazy sunlight filtered in through a window.

As I drew closer, shame and sorrow bled into me. "Oh, Sonya." The woman cradled my cheek in her hand. "Will you ever understand why I had to let you go?"

It was like staring into a mirror, both of us the same height, though she looked a few years older. Her chin was shorter, her nose thinner. "Mama?" I asked.

I shrank smaller, my hands slight in size as they clutched her apron. I was a child now, gazing up at her, my anguish raw and suffocating. Why did I feel so sad? Papa had told me I was going on a journey with the Romska. We would see the endless Ilvinov Ocean, the grassy plains near Grishina, and the great ice caps of the Bayac Mountains. "Why can't you come with me?" I asked.

Mama sat on her rocking chair and pulled me into her lap. "I wish I could, dear heart."

Racking pain wove into my bones and threatened to break them. "Did I do something bad? Is that why Papa is making me leave?"

"Hush, hush. You can't help what you are."

I *was* bad, then. Always losing control. But my brother provoked me. He got me into trouble on purpose. "If I have to go, why does Dominik get to stay?"

"Oh, child, don't you see? Dominik doesn't have to hide like you do."

My shoulders drooped. My parents were ashamed of me. I'd always known it. I never got to go with Papa to the crowded market or with Mama to do her washing at the well with the other village women. My brother said I was spoiled, guarded like a princess. But Dominik had friends. He could go wherever he pleased.

I tucked closer against my mother, anchored in her arms. She smelled like sage and apples from our kitchen. "Maybe after I'm gone for a while, I can come back," I said hopefully.

She crushed me tighter against her chest. Tears slipped down the bridge of my nose. None of this made sense, except one truth: it was my fault I had to leave. "No," she replied. "You must never come back. Wicked people will try to put you in a cage."

What did that matter? I already lived in a cage. "Then I'll break free and find you."

My mother's sigh split down me like a jagged knife. "My

stubborn little girl. What can I say to make you mind your mama?" She smoothed my hair. "If you ever come back here, Papa and I will suffer, too. The wicked people will kill us."

"What?" I gasped, drawing away to stare at her large eyes.

"You wouldn't want that, would you, dear heart?"

"Of course not. Don't talk about such things." I buried my head against her chest.

She patted my back and rocked me back and forth. "Then forget me, Sonya. Forget my love, if it saves you."

"How can I?"

"What more could I have done for you? How was it possible to teach you anything?"

I turned around, frowning at my mother's stern and altered voice. But she was gone. The house, too. I stood in the convent infirmary, looking into Sestra Mirna's weary eyes. Lines of concern bridged between her brows. Her remorse made my bones ache. The scent of acrid ashes filled my nostrils. The lingering smell of the convent fire.

"I prayed for you, Sonya, after you left the convent and were taken to the palace," she said, though now I was lying in the infirmary and the light coming from the windows was no longer bleary with winter and smoke. My gut throbbed from my gunshot wound. The stitches under my bandages pulled tight. "I prayed for you, even after I buried what was left of your sister Auraseers. You were obstinate and wild, but I never gave up hope that you might find yourself."

"I did find myself," I replied, but I was back in the rocking chair with my mother.

She touched my cheek. Then Sestra Mirna touched my cheek. Their faces kept interchanging. "That is all I wished for, child. I do care for you. I do care for you," one woman echoed the other. Dust shimmered like embers above them. "I always have. I always have"—their voices blended—"even if you haven't had the skill to decipher it."

With a sharp intake of breath, I bolted upright. Perspiration flashed across my face, neck, and breastbone. Trembling uncontrollably, I glanced around me with wild eyes. My mother was gone. Sestra Mirna, too. An aching hole gaped in my chest.

I twisted to face Madame Perle. Her cheeks were flushed with exertion, her eyes alert but heavy. "Do it again!" I grasped her arm. "Please, I have to go back." The image of my mother's face was already fragile and cracking apart. I couldn't forget her, despite what she'd made me promise.

"Your body pulled you out of the trance," Madame Perle said. "This is all you can handle for one day."

My mouth opened and closed. "We don't have another day."

"Look at yourself, *grande voyant*. *Feel* yourself. You are in distress."

Nausea burned in my stomach. Beads of sweat dripped down the nape of my neck. My head split in pain, and I squinted so I didn't see double. "It doesn't matter. Nothing's *changed* inside me. My aura, my power . . ." My hand splayed across my chest. "It's still trapped."

Madame Perle turned her palms up. "All I can give you is memories."

"Please, I beg you, do it again!"

She twitched and looked toward the door. "Genevie."

I heard nothing for a few seconds, then a creak came from the king's chamber. Rushing footsteps grew near, and Madame Perle's door swung open. Genevie braced her hand on the doorframe, her eyes wide with fright. "Sonya, the fire is out! We have to go!"

I couldn't. I wasn't ready. "But the guards still have to walk back."

"They're almost here. I felt them. We must leave at once!"

My heart thundered against my ribs. I met Madame Perle's gaze. "Come with us."

Her wrinkles set in stiff lines. "I told you, I cannot. I will not."

"But the Auraseers will die tomorrow. How can I help them the way I am? I need more time with you."

"I have given you enough. Only *you* can bring your aura out from hiding."

"I've tried," I said desperately. "I don't know how."

Genevie grabbed my arm and pulled me away. Madame Perle rose to watch us leave, her expression plaintive but resolute.

My hopes shattered as we fled her room and the king's

chambers and frantically locked the outer door. "I'm so sorry, Genevie," I said as we ran down the corridor. I'd failed her and her friends.

She tugged me behind the same pillar we'd hidden behind earlier and put a finger over her lips. The guards strode past us to resume their post.

We waited a tense minute, then scrambled away through the castle proper's maze of towers and staircases. We stumbled against each other, the protruding hips of our dresses bumping. Genevie wasn't leading us back to the ballroom, but to our bedroom, it seemed. My head throbbed. All my nerves felt raw and exposed. What was I supposed to do with what Madame Perle revealed to me? Memories of my mother and Sestra Mirna couldn't change the course of the future, only break my heart.

Genevie and I came to a twenty-yard mezzanine, open on one side to a foyer below. She went rigid beside me, waiting. Perhaps she sensed more guards on patrol. I faintly heard their footsteps echoing up from the foyer, but they were out of sight. We needed to take our chance. Hitching up my skirt, I ran forward.

"No, Sonya, stop!" Genevie hissed. Terror laced her voice.

I skidded to a halt on the marble floor and glanced back at her. Her shaking hand rose to her hair. Fumbled to grip it. Tucked a lock behind her ear.

Dread gaped inside me. I spun around. It took me a moment

to see where he was—standing halfway across the mezzanine. Lurking in the shadows of a wide column. Only ten feet away from me.

He stepped out into the light of the chandeliers, his hands clasped behind his silver waistcoat. His easy manner belied the predatory gleam in his eye.

Floquart de Bonpré.

CHAPTER TWENTY-TWO

"Run, Sonya!" Genevie shouted.

Floquart smirked. "No one is running." He withdrew a small flintlock pistol from behind his back.

Genevie gasped. All my muscles seized.

Floquart walked forward and glanced over the length of Genevie's body. "Did you think posing as a Riaznian lady would hide you from me? I would recognize you from a mile away, now that I see the shape of you so clearly." His eyes lingered on the tight bodice and low neckline of her dress. "I've searched for you everywhere, you know."

"You sent a bounty hunter, you mean." Genevie's voice trembled, although she spoke defiant words.

"They're the most effective. At any rate, I'm glad you've come home."

"You are *not* my home," she said. "You are no longer my master."

He clucked his tongue. "Auraseers are imprisoned when they talk like that. Even worse, they are executed. I don't wish for you to die, Genevie, whatever you may think. You are valuable to me."

I scoffed. "Yes, for you to abuse and to brand. She is a citizen of Riaznin now." A lie, but it wouldn't take much for Anton to make it a truth. "You have no claim on her anymore."

Floquart halted, his eyes sharpening on me. "It seems wherever we meet, Auraseer Petrova, you stand between me and my purpose."

"If that involves torturing other people, then I do not apologize."

His face contorted in a snarl. "Did my warning to you in the ballroom mean nothing? You went missing soon after we spoke."

My fingers twitched over my dress pocket. I still needed to return the king's key to Delphine. "Anton dismissed us for the night."

"And so you felt free to roam the castle?"

"I do not answer to you."

He took three more strides, and I sucked in my breath. He was close enough to touch me. That was more disturbing than his pistol pointed at my chest.

"You won't shoot." I held myself stone still. "How would you justify your actions to Anton and your king?"

"Quite simply, Sovereign Auraseer." I flinched at the way he said my former title—the title Tosya had given me again in his book—like it was an abomination. "I'll start by saying I heard the strangest report this evening. The curtains in a guest room caught fire, yet they were in a tower that has been unoccupied for months—a tower in view of the corridor leading to the king's chambers. Now, why would you go there except to free Madame Perle?"

My knees locked. "I don't know what you're talking about."

"I suppose you had no other Auraseer left to rescue in this castle."

Genevie made a noise of despair. She stumbled a few steps closer, her flared eyes narrowing on Floquart. "What have you done? They were not to be executed until tomorrow!"

"Oh, Genevie," he chided, "always jumping to the worst conclusions. They are still alive, my dear. King Léopold has released them into my custody. We discussed the matter further and agreed that an execution wasn't necessary as long as the Auraseers were guarded more diligently and received proper punishment. While His Majesty doesn't want to be troubled by that, I have the resources at my estate and could happily oblige."

Genevie paled and mouthed, *No.* I couldn't feel her aura, but I understood the horror behind her expression. Living with Floquart was worse than a death sentence. She knew from experience.

"Turn out your pockets," he commanded me.

"Pardon?"

He inched closer. "Ever since Madame Perle has been sequestered in the king's chambers, His Majesty has kept his key with him at all times. He became quite agitated at the ball once he realized he'd lost it."

"I don't know anything about a key." I strived to keep my voice steady. "We never made an attempt to free Madame Perle. Check the king's chambers for yourself. I'm sure you'll find her there."

One corner of Floquart's mouth curved upward. "Do you think I'll believe you so easily? Your magic of persuasion won't work on me, Sovereign Auraseer. You'll find me too unfeeling a subject to be moved upon. Now turn out your pockets. I know the key is in your possession. It will be my proof to the king that you are guilty."

My heart raced in double time. I couldn't make myself remove the key. If Floquart arrested me, I couldn't prevent him from seizing Genevie. How could I stop him, regardless? If I reached for my own pistol, holstered at my thigh, he'd shoot me on the spot.

Floquart growled, impatient, and caught hold of my arm. "Give me the key!" he spat in my ear.

Grabbing at my skirt, he searched for it himself. I struggled against him. His pistol hand wrapped around me, trying to force me still while he clawed at my dress.

"Stop!" I pushed him, but I couldn't break free from his grip. The barrel of his pistol jabbed against my ribs. Adrenaline pumped through me. He couldn't find the opening of my pocket, so he tore away a fistful of fabric.

Genevie raced over with her unsheathed dagger. She raised

the blade, but froze when Floquart turned his gun on her.

"No!" I twisted and elbowed him in the gut to throw off his aim.

The key shook loose and clanged onto the marble floor.

Floquart glanced down. Genevie swiped her dagger across his arm. He hissed, and the pistol fumbled from his grip.

I shoved him hard. Dropped for the gun. His foot connected with my stomach. I doubled over, tensed into a tight ball and gasped for breath.

A loud crack of gunfire split the air.

My head jerked up. Floquart's eyes flew wide. He made a stifled noise of pain.

I looked to Genevie, my mouth parting in shock. She held his pistol.

Blood dripped from Floquart's chest. He staggered to the balustrade for support. He couldn't catch its low ledge.

He toppled over headfirst, plummeting in a flash of silver silk.

CHAPTER TWENTY-THREE

I RACED TO THE EDGE OF THE BALUSTRADE, UNABLE TO STOP myself from staring down, despite the horror I knew I would see. I swallowed a surge of nausea and clutched my already weak stomach. Thirty feet below, Floquart's body splayed out in unnatural angles, his joints turned every wrong way. Dark blood pooled from his head into the cracks of the fractured stones.

"Is he dead?" Genevie asked, strangely calm.

"Yes," I croaked.

Her arm fell. She dropped the pistol. It clattered to her feet unceremoniously. Without looking at me, or at the ledge where Floquart fell, she turned and walked away, tripping once on the hem of her dress.

"*Arrêtez-la!*" a man shouted from one of the staircases above.

Guards pounded into the foyer below, drawn to the noise of gunfire and Floquart's prostrate body. Their eyes rose to the mezzanine—to where I stood. *"Saisissez-la!"* One of them pointed at me.

I stumbled backward and shook my head. Genevie spun around, her eyes round with worry. *"Elle est innocente!"* she cried to the guards and rushed back to place herself in front of me. *"Je suis coupable."* She rapped her fist on her chest. *"Appréhendez-moi."*

I ducked and grabbed the key on the marble, then shoved it down the front of my bodice.

Heartbeats later, four guards flooded in from both sides of the mezzanine. We couldn't escape them.

I stood and clutched Genevie's arm, pulling her protectively to my side. I'd lost Yuliya. I'd lost Pia. I wouldn't let them take her.

A guard shouted something and aimed his musket at my head.

Genevie barked a flurry of words at him—at all of them. Gone was the girl who skulked in corners, the girl who trembled every time Floquart's name was mentioned. Now her shoulders were squared and fierceness lined every edge of her body. She'd stalled the guards and come to some sort of agreement with them. Turning to me, her eyes softened with resignation, sorrow, and love. It felt like a farewell. "You must let them arrest me, Sonya, or they will kill us both."

My throat closed around my voice, but I forced out words on a weak breath. "You'll die if they take you." She had killed a high noble of the Esten court.

She held my gaze. A calm smile graced her lips. "I will die with no regrets."

The guards swarmed us. Two grabbed her and yanked her arms behind her back. The others seized me.

They dragged us away in separate directions. Genevie didn't fight them, but I thrashed and shouted for her. Above us, guests emerged and stared down from the curving staircases, shock and curiosity written plainly across their powdered faces.

"Sonya?" At the sound of Anton's voice, my heart leapt. Desperately, I searched for him and found him leaning out of a tower window on my left. "Let her go!" he demanded. "Where are you taking her?" He couldn't see Genevie. She was already out of sight.

The guards continued to wrangle me away. Anton couldn't stop them. More important, he couldn't save Genevie.

Neither could I.

✳❨❁❩✳

The guards brought me back to my bedroom. I made a noise of sheer frustration as they slammed me inside. Their low murmurs resonated just beyond the door. They must be standing sentinel in case I tried to escape.

I paced and dug my hands through my hair. What could I do to help Genevie now? I desperately needed my power, but how could I bring it out from hiding, like Madame Perle had said?

I sifted through my newly revealed memories.

I tried to understand what I couldn't discern as a child.

The shame I'd felt in the presence of my mother belonged to her, not to me. I'd misplaced her emotions for my own. I'd thought myself undeserving of her love. But she *did* love me. Deeply. Her guilt came from having to send me away.

"Mama," I whispered on the thinnest, aching breath. I felt the warmth of being tucked against her chest, the gentle pressure of her hand smoothing my hair. Peace and sorrow threaded together, weaving their way around my heart. I wished I could have thanked her, embraced her one last time.

I took a long breath and paced the other way, my thoughts turning to Sestra Mirna. Why was she so tangled up in the memory of my mother? The sestra had been a strict and unrelenting woman who gave only sparse words of affection, if she gave them at all. But Madame Perle had unearthed the words from her that meant the most to me.

I do care for you. I always have, even if you haven't had the skill to decipher it.

Sestra Mirna had loved me, too.

Tears flowered behind my eyes. Realizing that both the sestra and my mother loved me was a beautiful and unexpected gift, but I had to compose myself and think. Their love was also a key to freeing my aura.

I walked the length of my small room several more times, but no matter how much I dwelled on the memories, my Auraseer awareness remained locked inside me. I couldn't compel the guards to free me, or the king to release Genevie, or Esten-garde to ally with Riaznin. Shame and guilt tore into me with the same racking, sharp, and bone-deep pain that my mother felt when she had to let me go. I sat on the edge of my bed and buried my head in my hands.

Within the hour, there was a knock on the door. Delphine stepped inside. She still wore her diamond-encrusted ball gown. She shut the door behind her and leaned against it. Pressing her lips together, she took in my ripped dress and mussed hair. "The guards told me your Auraseer friend killed my godfather," she said softly.

"It wasn't premeditated, I promise you. Floquart held me at gunpoint. There was a struggle and . . . Genevie gained control of the pistol. She was only trying to save me. "

"I believe you."

I released a heavy breath. "But the Esten court won't, will they?"

Delphine rubbed her arms, as if suddenly cold. Her eyes sagged in the corners, and she shook her head. "I came for the king's key," she said. "If the guards find it in here, you will be in more trouble."

Numbly, I knelt and reached under my bed. I'd tucked the key between the slats of my frame and mattress. Standing up again, I passed it to her.

She turned the key over twice and bit her lip. "So Madame Perle—"

"I gave her the chance to escape, but she refused. She said she needed to remain in Alaise to assist the other Auraseers."

Delphine closed her eyes, her brows hitching in pain. "That sounds like her, stubborn and selfless." She sniffed and slid the key in her pocket. "I shouldn't have helped you. Your friend wouldn't be imprisoned right now if I hadn't interfered."

I took a tentative step forward. "Is there nothing you can say to persuade your uncle to let her go?" I tried speaking as gently as possible, but Delphine stiffened. "You're in a higher position than any woman in Estengarde," I added, "regardless of your title. The king would listen to you if you truly implored him. Other people would, too. You're respected here. Women do their hair like you. Girls dress like you. Why do you think the nobles try to befriend you for your influence with the king?"

Delphine's nostrils flared. "Because they have no qualms about using another person for their gain."

"Or they believe in your strength. They think you can make a difference."

She folded her arms and glanced away. "You don't know what life is really like here. And you cannot judge my ability to make a difference when you've known me less than a week."

"But Anton knows you, and I know him. He wouldn't have given any measure of his heart to someone with no moral courage."

Delphine's sea-blue eyes dropped to her hands.

I took a breath of cautious hope. *Now* she was listening.

"What if you spent your whole life fighting to change the wrongs of the world—like Anton has, like I know he will until his dying day—but, in the end, none of it changed anything?" My voice quavered, sobered by that very real possibility. "Does that mean you shouldn't have tried with every ounce of your strength?"

She raised her chin. "I'm sorry, Sonya, but you are wrong about me. I don't have any power to save your friend." Her lower lip trembled. "I can't save any of them."

My shoulders fell as despair closed around me. But then I wondered how much moral courage *I* had? Had *I* exhausted every ounce of my strength trying to fulfill my mission here? I may have failed the Auraseers of Estengarde, but I'd also come to help Anton win an alliance. I had to do my best. "Before Flo-quart died," I said, clumsily changing the subject, "he told me you and Anton were once betrothed."

Delphine's gaze snapped back up to me, her cheeks flushing red. "Yes, but none of that matters now. His feelings aren't what they were. When we danced tonight, he told me he holds *you* in affection." She swallowed and gave me a conciliatory smile.

Warmth welled inside me. My love for Anton radiated through my chest, and I struggled to stay focused. I couldn't dwell on what I had to let go. "Floquart said the king wouldn't settle for anything less than a marriage-based alliance," I continued, forcing myself to keep eye contact with her. "You must realize our nation won't survive the war without Estengarde's help, just as Estengarde needs Riaznin."

Delphine frowned. "I have no desire to come between you and Anton."

"That's very noble of you, but you have to think of the greater good. And I know you two could be happy together." As much as I hated to say the words, I believed them. Delphine and Anton had both been raised to hold sway in society, and they were well matched in intellect. She would easily gain the people's respect in Riaznin. In all ways, she would be the perfect bride, the perfect wife. She had no history of being impulsive or reckless, only polished and reliable.

Delphine tilted her head and studied my face. Could she see how much I loved Anton, too? "Marrying Anton relies on more than my willingness," she said.

"I know." I tucked a loose hair behind my ear with a trembling hand. "That's why I need you to tell him something for me, in case I don't see him again. Tell him I said to do what's best for Riaznin. Tell him I give him my blessing."

Delphine considered me for a long moment. "Are you sure?"

I nodded, holding my posture resolute, even though my legs wobbled.

She reached behind her and placed her hand on the latch of my door, then met my eyes again. "I will also tell my uncle that you are innocent."

I offered her a small smile, but no hope kindled inside me. Despite my earlier professions that Delphine had the ability to persuade the king, I despaired.

I was only a lowly Auraseer in Estengarde. Though, in truth, I was even less than that.

I was only Sonya Petrova. Not a *grande voyant*. Not a sovereign Auraseer.

I was only a powerless and frightened girl.

CHAPTER TWENTY-FOUR

THREE GUARDS ENTERED MY ROOM LATE IN THE MORNING THE next day. I stood on shaky legs from where I'd been sitting on the edge of my bed. I had changed out of my ball gown and into my simple sarafan, anticipating this moment. The king must have decided I was complicit in Floquart's murder.

While two of the guards came and took hold of each of my arms, the third guard started rifling through my belongings: another sarafan, a shift to wear beneath it, a coat, and a hair comb. He must have been searching for the king's key. Delphine had it, of course, though she may as well have left it with me. I'd been found guilty regardless.

The guard looked under my bed and pulled out my traveling bag and water flask. "*C'est ici,*" he said to the others, then stuffed my belongings inside.

I wrinkled my brows. "What are you doing?"

None of the guards answered. Either they didn't speak

Riaznian or they refused to talk to me.

They escorted me out of my room and brought my bag with them. They didn't take me to the lower levels of the castle proper, where the dungeons must be, but outside the castle keep to the royal stables. All nine soldiers from our Riaznian regiment were there, already mounted on their horses. "What's going on?" I asked, shivering in the brisk autumn air. My own mare, Raina, was also saddled and waiting for me.

Konstantin, the largest Riaznian soldier, nudged his horse forward and replied, "We were told we needed to take you away at once." I couldn't tell whether his voice held sympathy or embarrassment when he added, "King Léopold said you are no longer welcome in Estengarde."

I stared at him, trying to process what he'd told me. Instead of imprisonment and possible execution, my punishment was to be driven out? "What about Genevie?"

"We were told she must answer to the Esten court for her crimes."

My heart sank. How could I leave without her? But what choice did I have? In addition to the three Esten guards who'd led me out here, at least a dozen others now surrounded us.

Delphine approached tentatively, her arms laden with several glossy pelts. "I brought you furs for your journey. The Bayacs can be treacherous if the frosts come early."

I glanced from her to the stables, where Anton's stallion, Oriel, poked his head out from a stall. He wasn't wearing a bridle. My hands went limp at my sides.

Anton chose the alliance.

I tried to summon happiness, or at the very least satisfaction. This was the decision I'd wanted him to make—duty above desire. Free Riaznin had hope now. So why did I feel so lost inside?

"Is Anton coming to say good-bye?" I asked Delphine, striving to keep my voice strong as my throat constricted. He must have been planning to travel back to Riaznin after he married her and sealed the pact between nations. Knowing Anton, that would be as swiftly as possible. A confrontation with his brother was inevitable.

She lifted a shoulder, her lovely sea-blue eyes filled with a sorrow that seemed genuine. "I don't know," she replied, adjusting her violet shawl. I passed your message to him last night. I haven't seen him since. I was told he spent most of this morning with my uncle."

"Have you spoken to the king since then?"

"Yes."

"What did he say about Anton? Does he know I'm being sent away?"

Delphine nodded, averting her gaze. She draped the furs on a nearby barrel. "Apparently, Anton negotiated a parting gift for you." She brushed a loose curl off her face. Her hair was still done up in the same coif from last night, though it now looked like a wilted flower. "You know my uncle; he doesn't like to be bothered by anything controversial." She gave a humorless laugh. "I think he was secretly relieved that the matter was taken out of his hands, especially since Floquart is no longer around to manage it."

I wasn't following. "What did Anton negotiate?"

"The release of the imprisoned Auraseers, those who were recently taken into Floquart's custody. The king has agreed to banish them to Riaznin. Your regiment has been tasked to take them with you." Delphine waited for my response, fidgeting with the fringe of her shawl. I couldn't find any words. My skin tingled with a flush of adrenaline. "So, you see," she said, "you didn't need me to persuade my uncle, after all."

I couldn't draw breath. I stared at her in disbelief. Anton had ensured the Auraseers' release—for *me*? I hadn't thought it was possible for me to love him even more, but I did. I didn't have room inside myself to contain the ache of it. How could I leave him here to marry someone else? "But did you talk to the king about Genevie?"

Delphine's posture drooped. "I tried, Sonya. I'm sure Anton did, too."

Heaviness pulled at my limbs. Genevie's heart was pure. She didn't deserve to be sentenced by a prejudiced Esten court, no matter what she had done. She would die now. I knew it. I'd feared for her life when she'd asked to travel with me to Estengarde. Why had I said yes? "Will you tell Anton thank you for me?" I bit my lip so Delphine wouldn't see it tremble. I understood now why he hadn't come to say good-bye. That would only make our farewell harder. We had to accept what was necessary for the greater good of Free Riaznin.

She nodded. "I wish I could do more for your friend."

I met her gaze, wondering if her words were sincere or empty. "I wish you could, too." I wished *I* could.

The Esten soldiers escorted us away from King Léopold's castle, permitting none in our small regiment to remain behind with Anton. I tried not to worry. Surely the king had soldiers to spare for when the time came that Anton would travel back to Riaznin with his new bride. My eyes blurred hot, and my throat constricted. Anguish racked every bone in my body at being separated from him and Genevie, but as our party detoured to Floquart's estate in Alaise, some of my pain lifted. The fifteen Esten Auraseers stood near the gate, waiting for us. Their faces were haggard and their clothes filthy from their time in the dungeons, but their eyes lit with hope.

A deep feeling of kinship warmed my chest. These were my sisters, though I'd never met them. Auraseers like me. Rare and precious and terribly misunderstood. They deserved kindness and compassion. I resolved to give it to them. I would return to Riaznin as its sovereign Auraseer, even without my power. I would strive to make my nation a safe home.

The Esten Auraseers couldn't stop staring at me. They whispered among each other in their language and, when the gate opened, they nudged forward one of their own, a middle-aged woman with strawberry hair. She drew a long breath as she approached, and I dismounted so I could greet her properly.

"I am Lara," she said, dipping into a low curtsy.

I returned her shy smile and curtsied back so she would understand there was no rank divide between us. "I am Sonya."

Her grin widened. She turned back to the others and nodded. "*La grande voyant!*"

At their ripple of excited murmurs, my cheeks flushed with heat. I rubbed the back of my neck, waiting for their expressions to shift to confusion and disappointment once they'd had another moment to search for my aura.

"I am the most fluent in Riaznian," Lara continued. "So if you ever wish to say anything to the others, you can tell me and I will relay your message."

I snuck another glance at the girls and women. No one was frowning yet. "Thank you."

"No, thank *you*—for all you have done for us."

The heat in my face spread to my ears. Lara's gratitude was misplaced. It was Anton who had negotiated the Esten Auraseers' release, and Genevie who had encouraged them to leave their masters in the first place. "I've done nothing."

"That isn't true." Lara's green eyes softened. "What you did in your nation has inspired us. And your hope bolsters ours with courage."

"My hope?" I hadn't mentioned any hope.

"It is stronger than your sorrow." She tentatively placed a hand on my shoulder. "Our hearts hurt for Genevie, too."

My scalp prickled. Lara was speaking about my emotions—emotions I hadn't told her I was feeling.

Dizziness rocked me, and I stumbled closer to Raina,

bracing myself against her side. There was a very real possibility I might faint. "Do you mean to say . . . are all of you . . . ?" I drew a shaky breath and scanned the other Esten Auraseers. I couldn't sense them for myself. "You *all* feel my aura? I'm *emitting* it?"

Lara gave a gentle and bemused laugh. "Of course. Your pulse radiates strongly."

My gaze tunneled on her. "And it's really coming from *me*?" I stole a glance over my shoulder, but the regiment soldiers were several yards away.

Lara tilted her head, like she wondered if I was unwell. "Yes."

White spots flashed in my vision. My heart froze, then gave a hard pound.

My power . . . it was returning.

CHAPTER TWENTY-FIVE

I SPENT THAT EVENING AND THE NEXT DAY STRAINING TO FEEL aura. If I was emitting it, why couldn't I sense it in others? My awareness was still thick with an impenetrable black void. If any of my actual abilities were present, I would have ridden back to Alaise to try to free Genevie. But dark clouds loomed over the Bayacs. An early frost was coming, a month shy of winter. If our regiment and the Esten Auraseers didn't hurry, the snow would come to the mountaintops and impede our journey. With another heart-heavy sigh for Genevie, I left the city with the others and embarked for La Forêt Royale on the first stretch of our journey.

I walked most of the way, giving the girls and women turns riding Raina. They hadn't been provided horses of their own. We pressed ourselves to exhaustion in the days that followed, trying to beat the elements. Despite our best efforts, as we reached the peaks of the Bayacs, winter came. A tease of snowflakes at first, kisses melting against our noses and fingers. But then the wind howled and the sky unleashed a torrent. Icy downpour lashed at our skin and split our lips and made us shiver to the bone.

At every fork in the mountain pass, I searched for the first marker of the Esten Romska settlement—the rope of painted beads strung around a tree branch that Tosya had shown me. I'd promised to meet up with him so he and Kira could travel back to Riaznin with our regiment. But every tree was coated in ice and snow, masking any signs. Foreboding drummed inside me like a second, racing heartbeat. Now that we were outside the protections of Alaise, fear of Valko seized hold of me again. I wondered, at times, if my almost palpable dread could be my awareness returning, but the other Auraseers didn't mention any worries besides the freezing temperatures.

As our party trudged forward, we could find no decent shelter; only craggy trees grew at these heights. With the wind raging wildly, we couldn't stake our tents, so we tied our horses under an overhanging rock and huddled wherever we could along level spots of ground. The teeth of the blizzard bit sharp through our coats and blankets.

I felt in my saddlebag for the paltry remains of my food: half a hard biscuit and a three slices of salted venison. With trembling fingers, I passed two slices to the Auraseers nearby me and split what was left of my biscuit with Lara. The soldiers of our regiment had as little as I did. We'd all been sharing with the Auraseers, who hadn't been given any provisions when they'd been banished, other than a few musty blankets.

We were going to starve if we didn't freeze first.

The storm didn't let up by morning. Knowing we couldn't last much longer, exposed on the crest of this mountain like this, we stumbled through the deep snow, walking our horses down the other side of the mountain for better shelter.

Every hour only brought us another quarter mile forward. We kept our heads ducked against the vicious winds, and I wrapped a scarf around my head and a blanket over my coat. My feet were blocks of ice. When I feared my toes might fall off from numbness, Konstantin, who had taken charge in Anton's absence, finally found a rocky ravine, wide enough for two horses to stand abreast, but long enough for all of us. The ravine walls weren't tall, only ten feet or so, but if we ducked low, they blocked the worst of the wind.

I tended to Raina, pulling her down to lie beside me and rubbing warmth into her coat. She'd been eating a little snow in lieu of water. I tried to get her to swallow more, but she refused. I dug under the icy ground and clawed up roots and a few shrubs, which she chomped up greedily. Knowing that wasn't enough, I gave her the last slice of my salted venison. She licked and chewed it for a while, then spit it out as I'd suspected she would. Hopefully it had still offered her some nutrients.

"You'll be all right, girl," I murmured, pressing my head to her brow. I wished I could reach into her aura and make her feel comfortable. Nothing I'd done so far seemed sufficient to help. With a soft nicker, Raina finally rose and returned to the other horses. They stood close together at the end of the ravine and tried to gather heat, their necks wrapped over one another. My shoulders sagged, and I burrowed my arms into my cloak.

"Do not feel guilty," Lara said past chapped lips and chattering teeth. She had been watching me quietly all this while. "Your horse has great affection for you, but she is trying to survive. She will be safer with the others."

But the horses' warm huddle wasn't enough to help all of them. That night, one of them died. An hour later, Lara warned the soldiers that a second horse, a lovely sorrel mare, was rapidly weakening. We tried to get her to eat more snow. We threw blankets over her and made her walk our narrow confines to warm her blood. But she staggered about and finally buckled to the ground. Heartbroken, I laid her head in my lap and whispered comforting words while death stole her away.

I drew an icy breath that exhaled in a cloud of frost. *We're going to die out here.*

The soldiers dragged both carcasses out of the ravine. They debated whether or not they should cut them up for meat. I couldn't listen. I gazed up, trying to see the stars, wondering if they still shone or if they'd died out, too. Only darkness and bitter snowfall reigned.

The next morning—when the soldiers were about to butcher the dead horses and I sat with my knees to my chest, my head buried in my hands, my whole body in cramps from cringing— Konstantin raced into the ravine, a wide smile on his face. "We're saved!" he cried, roughly wiping away his tears. "They've come!" He shouted above the howling wind. "They have shelter, food." His voice hitched on a sob. My eyes glistened to see such a large man—one of the sternest and toughest in our regiment—break down with relief. But I didn't understand. *Who had saved us?*

He moved aside as a small group of people entered the mouth of the ravine. They had deep olive skin and were bundled tightly in furs. At the back of the group, a young girl stepped forward. A fur hood covered her hair, and a scarf was drawn across her mouth. When she pulled it away, I gasped. "Kira."

She grinned and tugged on the coat of the tall person standing behind her. "You see, Tosya?" she said. "I told you I sensed Sonya's aura."

CHAPTER TWENTY-SIX

As THE ESTEN ROMSKA LED US TO THEIR SETTLEMENT, TOSYA explained how they'd found our regiment. He'd told the nomads we'd be returning soon, so they had been watching for us. Two tribesmen had seen our tracks in the snow, but the blizzard blew away most of the evidence. When Kira found out, she'd insisted on helping the rescue party find us by searching for our auras.

"I wish you could have seen her," Tosya said. Fat snowflakes fell between us as he placed his fisted hands on his hips. *"I'm the only one who can sense the soldiers!"* he squeaked in a voice pitched three times higher than Kira's. *"I'm coming!"*

I winced. "What a terrible impression." I looked down at Kira, where she walked beside me. "If I were you, I'd be deeply offended."

She giggled. "I liked it."

"Why, thank you." Tosya preened and flourished a bow for

her. "Would you like to hear my impression of Sonya?" Kira nodded and clapped, already applauding him. I braced myself as Tosya cleared his throat. After a dramatic pause, he tossed his head back and threw his arms wide. "I have aura!" he exclaimed in a breathy voice and twirled around twice. "I have feelings that pulse feelings!"

I made a valiant effort to scowl at him, but when he started leaping through the snow like a drunken ballerina, I snorted despite myself. "You're the cruelest of friends."

He chuckled. "I'm just trying to keep you warm. Laughter is better than a campfire, I always say."

I rolled my eyes and blew on my frigid hands. "I'll take the campfire, thanks."

He clomped back to me and mussed my hair like we were children again. "I really *am* happy for you, you know. I didn't believe Kira at first."

"I sensed your aura before anyone else's," she added, a skip in her step.

"We were within a hundred yards of the ravine," Tosya continued, "but we couldn't see it past the blizzard. Without Kira, we never would have gone in that direction."

I grinned and kissed the top of the girl's head. "I'm very grateful to you."

She tucked her mittened hand inside mine. "And I'm happy you feel like you again."

We came to another ravine, even narrower than the one we'd been camping in. My breath frosted on the air as I told

Tosya all that had happened in King Léopold's castle, ending with Floquart's death, Genevie's arrest, the Esten Auraseers' banishment, as well as Anton's decision to forge a marriage-based alliance with Estengarde.

"But you never talked with him before you left?" Tosya asked. "Even if Anton was despondent, it's out of character for him to not say good-bye. What if he's being detained against his will?"

I shrugged away the suggestion, also trying to dismiss the ever-present ache in my chest. "Anton came to Estengarde for an alliance. He *chose* to stay behind to see its terms through." *He chose to marry Delphine.* "I'm sure he'll explain more when we meet him in Torchev." At least to Tosya he would. I didn't know how I'd manage to be near Anton and his new bride without my heart breaking. "He's bound to travel there in haste with Estengarde's army." And face Valko. And probably die if my power remained dormant. I shivered with a bone-deep coldness, a fear I couldn't shake.

The ravine opened to a network of caves, one designated as a stable for the horses. As some of the Romska tended to them, we walked onward through a wending tunnel until it reached a vast cavern. Snow sprinkled through a few open spaces in the ceiling and shimmered in beams of wintry light. Other holes pocked the far wall and served as natural windows. Campfires flickered in the more ventilated areas, wafting only the faintest smoke.

A tall woman with wise, hooded eyes and bow-shaped lips

came to meet us. Thick braids dangled to her waist, and fine wrinkles branched from the corners of her eyes. I recognized her as Ula, the chieftain of the mountain tribes. We'd never met, but Motshan, who was chieftain over Tosya's tribe, had told me stories about his cousin.

Ula was a fierce nomad who had saved her people from slaughter a few years ago when King Léopold turned a blind eye to anyone who decided to kill the Romska in Estengarde— a necessary measure, some claimed, to thin out their growing numbers. While other Esten tribes perished, Ula's tribe found places to hide and thrive in the Bayacs. She was revered like a queen among the Romska.

I dipped into a bow, and Ula removed one of her many beaded necklaces, placing it over my head. "Tosya tells me you are our kin, an Auraseer, rare and blessed among your kind."

I nodded humbly, knowing the tribespeople believed powerful Auraseers descended from the Romska. Dasha was evidence of that truth. While the dowager empress was Dasha's mother, Motshan, not Emperor Izia, was her father.

"Then I welcome you and your company to take rest here from your journey."

❧⚜☙

I sat between Tosya and Kira that evening as we warmed ourselves by the glorious heat of a campfire. "I think it began when she taught the children to play Bear in the Cave," Tosya said, telling me how Kira had won over the hearts of the tribespeople these past few weeks. "Then she started asking the grown-ups to take turns being the bear. *I* was the first bear—and the best bear." He bared his teeth and swiped clawed fingers at her.

Kira laughed and knocked his hand away. "You had the best growl, but you weren't very fast. It took you forever to tag us."

As they chatted merrily, my attention wavered to where some of the Esten Auraseers were sitting at another campfire, twenty feet away. With their bellies full, clothes dry, and bodies warm, every girl and woman seemed to be in a congenial mood. Some rested their heads on one another's shoulders. Others combed knots from their friends' hair. I kneaded the folds of my skirt, desperate to feel what they did, that deeper kinship, the way Auraseers' auras reverberated in and out of one another in synchronized energy.

"I think we can agree that Enzo was the worst bear," Tosya went on. "Remember when his—"

"Why do they make you so sad?" Kira asked me, cutting Tosya off.

My cheeks warmed, and I glanced away from the other Auraseers. "Oh, it's nothing. I just miss sensing aura. It's hard that all of you can feel it except me."

"Or me." Tosya raised a finger. "I haven't sprouted any aura feelers in your absence."

I rolled my eyes and gave him a playful shove. He chuckled, drawing an arm around me. "Tell me again about what happened with this Madame Perle."

I took a deep breath and described the memories she'd helped me recall.

"And you think they were the catalyst for your aura to start emitting?"

"Well, it didn't happen right away, or else Genevie would have told me." My throat tightened at the mention of her name. I prayed she hadn't been executed already. "But I don't know what else would have sparked the change in me."

"All right, let's analyze the memories, then. If we can figure out how they helped you, maybe we can nudge you along in that direction and your abilities will wake up." He leaned his elbows on his knees. "I'm interested in the part when the voices of your mother and Sestra Mirna blended and their faces interchanged. What do you make of that?"

I thought back to the biggest revelation I'd had since meeting with Madame Perle. "My mother and Sestra Mirna loved me. I hadn't really known that when each of them was alive."

Tosya nodded thoughtfully. "Anything else they have in common?"

The three of us fell into silent contemplation as we gazed into the popping embers. Then Kira sat up taller. "They're both mothers. Well, kind of." She tucked her chestnut hair behind her protruding ears. "Sestra Mirna was a better mother than *mine*, anyway."

Tosya wagged his finger at her. "Have I told you what a brilliant girl you are?" She smiled and ducked her head. "I think Kira has nailed why your two memories wove together, Sonya. You've lost other people in your life, but your mother and Sestra

Mirna were both mother figures to you. Their deaths must have left a deeper print—something you haven't been able to cope with yet."

"How do you mean?" I asked. I'd never sustained any false hope that my mother was still alive, and Sestra Mirna had died before my very eyes.

"Well, you blocked the last memory of your mother for over eleven years, so it stands to reason that you haven't emotionally come to terms with the loss of her."

My brows wrinkled. Of course I hadn't come to terms with it. Any child of a dead parent might say the same. "I'm not sure I'm following your epiphany."

Tosya patted my knee. "You never properly grieved for your mother, Sonya."

I blinked at him. He was right. My mother had died while I'd lived with the Riaznian Romska. When the authorities had discovered my parents hid their Auraseer child from the empire, they were both executed. "I was told she and my father were buried in Bovallen, but I never got to see their graves. The caravans I traveled with didn't journey that far."

"You mean you never got to go to your mother's funeral?" Kira asked. I nodded sadly. Her eyes shimmered and she rested her head against my arm. "I didn't get to go to Sestra Mirna's funeral, either."

Tosya scratched his chin. "Perhaps there's something else you can do to honor your mother's memory. Sestra Mirna's, too, since she's tangled up in all of this."

"But we gave Sestra Mirna her burial rites before we left for Estengarde," I replied.

"You and Nadia prepared her body and prayed to Feya for her soul, but you never shared any stories about her or gave any sort of tribute to her life. And you haven't spoken of her much since then—at least when I've been around."

As I considered him, my gaze idly strayed to one of the openings in the ceiling. A steady stream of snow sifted inside from the raging blizzard. It wouldn't be letting up any time soon, which meant we could spare a little time to give my mother and Sestra Mirna the memorials they deserved.

I turned to Kira and gave her hand a gentle squeeze. "Do you think Sestra Mirna would have liked us to pay a special tribute to her?"

She thought about it for a moment, chewing on her lower lip. "If Sestra Mirna were here, she'd be mad and embarrassed. She'd tell us to stop. But I think she'd also secretly like it. I'd feel her aura smiling inside."

"Would you like to help me?"

Her grin revealed the little gap between her front teeth. "Yes."

✥❧☙✥

The next morning, the Romska wore white to honor the dead and also dressed me and Kira in that color of purity and protection. Many of them wanted to attend the memorial, so Ula let us use the main cavern. There weren't enough white clothes to share for the Esten Auraseers, who also desired to take part in our mourning, so the Romska lent them white beads and scarves.

Kira and I painted *Mirna Sorokina* and *Alena Petrova* on large stones to stand in place of our loved ones' graves. I set smaller rocks by my mother's to represent my father and brother, whom I still didn't remember, but also wanted to acknowledge.

We spoke little during our preparations, but never separated in the hours leading up to the memorial. The peace I felt around Kira was an almost like aura, a nearly palpable comfort. I hoped she felt some of my strength in return. All my energy focused on holding my emotions together so I wouldn't fall apart. Though maybe the point of this day was to *let* myself fall apart. To break the shell around the wounded child in me. To properly grieve, as Tosya had said.

Kira didn't wish to be the first to speak, so at midday I stood in front of the gathered people. I brushed my thumb against the sprigs of two holly berry bouquets in my hands and tried to find words to express what Sestra Mirna and my mother meant to me. Tosya gave me a nod of encouragement, and I inhaled a deep breath.

"I knew Sestra Mirna for only a year before she passed away," I began, "but in that time I witnessed her fierce dedication to the Auraseers at the convent in Ormina. Each woman and girl was precious to her."

My gaze fell to my wrist, where I'd worn a black ribbon of mourning after the Auraseers had died in the convent fire.

"For a long time I was sure Sestra Mirna hated me because of the poor choices I'd made. I was blinded by my own self-loathing, so I couldn't sense the genuine concern she had for me." I swallowed, remembering the feel of Sestra Mirna's strong but weathered hand on my cheek. "It wasn't until I was at the brink of death that I finally allowed myself to receive her love. Once I did, the convent became a home to me."

Looking up, I found several Esten Auraseers were sniffing and wiping the corners of their eyes. How strange it felt to be among so many grieving people and not feel like I was going to buckle under the weight of their emotions. I gave them each a little smile like they were helping me bear my sorrow. I hadn't yet admitted to them that I'd lost my ability. I wanted to be the person who could still give them hope.

"When she was younger, Sestra Mirna lost the love of her life." My voice broke as thoughts of Anton overwhelmed me. I closed my eyes, and I was back in the secluded dining room of the convent, dancing in his arms to music of the breeze against the windowpanes. "That could have filled the sestra with bitter resentment, but she chose to channel her heartbreak into serving others." I blew out a shaky breath and squared my shoulders. "I want to do the same." I touched two fingers to my forehead then my heart. "Feya bless you in Paradise, Sestra Mirna."

I placed her bouquet of holly on her memorial stone, then looked up at Kira. Her tears fell in time with mine. She rose from where she sat on the cavern floor by Tosya and walked over to my side, her head lowered. "Can you stand by me?" she whispered. More tears slipped down her cheeks, coming faster now. I wished I could alleviate her suffering. While she was forced to feel everyone's emotions here, I only had to contend with my own.

"Of course." I took her small hand. In her other one, she held another bouquet.

Behind the Romska and Esten Auraseers, the soldiers from our regiment, who had also come to know Kira, gave her supportive smiles from the back of our gathering.

"Sestra Mirna tucked me into bed every night," Kira said, her tears now relentless and collecting under her chin. "She told me it was fine that I cried more than the other girls." Her voice strained higher as she fought to keep speaking. "She didn't throw away my favorite blanket, even when it started to fall apart. She told me I was a good girl. She said Dasha needed me . . . but I needed her, too." Kira hiccupped and tried to breathe through her weeping.

I brought her closer and leaned her head against my torso, my heart aching for her. This was as much a memorial to Dasha as it was for Sestra Mirna. Kira had lost them both.

"On Feya's Holy Day, I wanted to help Sestra Mirna bake a cake," she continued. "I accidentally poured in salt instead of sugar. I thought she would scold me—her aura burned so hot—but when she tasted the batter, she started laughing." Kira released the smallest giggle and wiped her nose. "We baked the cake anyway, and Sestra Mirna let me spread on the glaze. She said it would please Feya." Kira's trembling smile faltered with a sob. "I love you, Sestra Mirna. I miss you."

She wept for another moment, her face bright red. Then she let go of my hand and set her bouquet next to mine by Sestra Mirna's memorial stone. Once she finished, she rushed over to Tosya, who took her into his lap.

One last bouquet remained in my hand. I lingered at the front of the gathering and scrubbed tears from my cheeks. How could I follow Kira's pure and heartfelt words? I wished I had stories to tell about my mother. I wished I had a treasure trove of memories to choose from. All I could say was everything I knew about her, even though it was little.

"My mother was beautiful," I said. "She had a gentle voice. She was brave, too. She could have given me to the empire the moment she learned I was an Auraseer, but instead she kept me for as long as possible, seven years, then placed me in the care of the Riaznian Romska. Because of her sacrifice—because of her love for me—she died." My voice quavered, and I inhaled deeply through my nose and forced myself to stand tall. "I want to make Riaznin a place where injustices like that don't happen, where Auraseers and their families have safety and liberty and peace."

I closed my eyes and pictured my mother in her rocking chair. I felt the tendrils of her deep affection enshrouded by her sorrow, fear, and shame. "I'm sorry you suffered for me, Mama"—I crouched and laid down the final bouquet—"but I thank you for giving me my life."

Some emotion in me must have conveyed that the memorial

was over, because a moment later, the Esten Auraseers rose and came to where I stood, taking turns giving me embraces. As I held each of them tightly, flickers of a new kind of grief stole inside me. All I wanted was to be a child again in my mother's arms, to tell her I'd never forget her. I wanted to turn back time and tend Sestra Mirna back to health with the same selfless devotion she'd given me.

I glanced at Kira a few feet away, also surrounded by loving friends. She must have also ached to be with the woman who had raised her like her own daughter—the woman she had paid such a tender tribute to today. Now Kira was motherless like I had been most of my life. Like Dasha now was, too.

Poor Dasha. She probably didn't even know Sestra Mirna was gone. She'd be heartbroken when she found out.

And dangerous.

I knew firsthand what volatile emotions could do with her level of power.

Dasha needed constancy in her life. Someone who understood her. Unconditional love and female companionship. Valko could give her none of that. He'd only twist her mind and teach her hatred.

As the last few Auraseers and tribes people offered their condolences, Kira smiled feebly, her gaze straying to the cavern like she was searching for someone. I felt for her so deeply I could almost sense the aura she was remembering, the other person who wasn't here. I grieved for Dasha, too.

Kira's words from the memorial rang through my mind. The

girls desperately needed each other. Dasha had been born in the convent, and Kira had lived there since she was four years old. Dasha's tie to Kira was stronger than her tie to her brothers, whom she'd only met a few months ago.

Dasha needed to come home.

I stared at the candles that a group of Romska women lit by the stones for Sestra Mirna and my mother. Their bright flames burned spots in my vision. Even so, I felt like a blindfold was suddenly removed from my eyes. The way ahead became perfectly clear.

I couldn't be Sonya the Sovereign Auraseer anymore. I didn't want to be tempted by that kind of power. It was too unstable to offer anyone lasting salvation. Feya had blessed me with my enhanced ability long enough to compel Valko to abdicate and ignite this revolution, but everything else I'd done with my gift had been a step backward for the good of Riaznin. At least my experience helped me understand Dasha. No one else knew what it was like to be overwhelmed and terrified and emboldened by bending another person's emotions. No one else knew how it felt to be manipulated by Valko for that gift.

I may not be able to reach inside Dasha's aura and compel her to leave him. I may not even be able to sense what she was feeling anymore, but she could sense *me*. She'd feel my love and understanding.

Maybe I couldn't save Riaznin with my power, but I *could* help a little girl. I could give her back her sister and her home.

I broke away from the others and searched the main cavern

for Tosya. At some point, he'd drifted away with Ula and Konstantin. I wanted to tell him what I'd resolved to do.

He was still with the chieftain and soldier when I found him standing near the far wall. Their heads bent together by the light of one of the cavern windows. Ula held a letter in her hands. Konstantin's jaw muscle tensed as he looked at it. Tosya stood with a rigid back. "What's happening?" I asked, approaching them.

Ula glanced up and released a heavy sigh. "There was an avalanche not far from here. One of our tribesmen discovered a man and his horse buried in the rubble."

"He was a courier," Konstantin added. "This letter, addressed to King Léopold, was found in his satchel. It's a report about the war in Riaznin."

Dread dropped like acid in my stomach. "What does it say?"

Tosya placed a hand on my shoulder, as if to brace me. "Valko's troops and the Shenglin army have razed the city of Orelchelm. This letter was dated ten days ago, which means—"

"They've already arrived in Torchev," I finished, my voice barely rasping past the sudden dryness in my throat. Orelchelm was only a one-day march from the capital.

Tosya nodded, his brown eyes flat, grave, and almost hopeless. "And if Valko takes Torchev, he'll win the war."

CHAPTER TWENTY-SEVEN

"I STILL THINK YOU SHOULD STAY WITH THE ESTEN ROMSKA," Tosya said the next morning, hastily packing provisions in his saddlebag. The snow had let up enough to allow traveling again. He planned to ride back with the soldiers to Riaznin. At the border, the soldiers would take the road to Torchev to assist the critical battle happening there, and Tosya would take the road to Ormina to warn the Riaznian Romska of the culminating danger and extend Ula's offer of protection if they desired refuge in the Bayacs of Estengarde. "There's nothing you can do to help in Torchev."

His words stung. *If I only had my power* . . . For months, that had been my endless refrain. But the reality was I didn't have it. I had felt no sparks of awareness after the memorial, either. I was in the same state as before, emitting aura but not sensing it. Far from manipulating it.

"We've been over this," I replied, folding up my bedroll. "I *can* help. I'm going to find a way to free Dasha. She needs me."

Tosya groaned and ran his hands through his hair. "You'll be a walking target. Dasha will be able to bend your emotions now that you're giving off aura. And she'll be able to track you."

"I'll practice meditation on the journey there. Anton taught me how to go about it."

"Anton would hate the idea of you going to Torchev during a siege."

"Well, it's good that he isn't here, then." I winced as soon as the words were out of my mouth. What a foolish thing to say. How I desperately wished Anton were here. "I need to leave with our regiment now. I can't delay and wait to travel with Anton and the Esten army. It's already an eight-day journey to Torchev, and that's only if the weather holds and we ride at breakneck speed. We'll be lucky if Feliks can defend the capital until then. If Valko takes the palace, it will be next to impossible for me to get to Dasha."

"Feliks is another problem you need to consider. How do you plan to hide from him?"

"I won't hide. I'll tell him the alliance with Estengarde has been secured."

"An alliance that has come too late to do any good. Feliks will want you to intervene with your power—all the people will. They'll think you've come to deliver them."

"Then I'll admit I still don't have it. Or maybe I'll pretend I do. Maybe that can get me close to Dasha."

Tosya squeezed the bridge of his nose. "Sonya, a million

things could go wrong with this plan—your death at the very top of that list."

"Don't you see I have to take that risk for Dasha's sake?" I tied a securing knot around my bedroll, then looked up at him with pleading eyes. "Please support me, Tosya. I know you'd risk your life for me. It's what we do for family. It's what Sestra Mirna would want me to do."

He turned a pained expression on me. "Of course I'd risk my life for you, but this is different. You're responsible now for more people than Dasha. The Esten Auraseers look to you as their *grande voyant*."

"I've already spoken with Lara, and she's explained to the others what I have to do. They'll be safe with Ula's tribe." In a rare gesture of friendship toward the non-tribespeople, Ula had promised to let the Esten Auraseers remain here until the early freeze thawed. Then they would guide the women and girls back to the convent in Ormina. While I wished I could have taken them myself, traveling out of the way to Ormina before going to Torchev would have added an extra four days to my journey— and that was by horse, which the Esten Auraseers didn't have.

Tosya huffed, fastening the buckles of his saddlebag. "Well, the other Auraseers may understand, but Kira doesn't. She hasn't talked to me all morning. Now she's hiding somewhere."

I sighed and pushed to my feet. "I'll find her."

I searched, but couldn't locate Kira until I went to the cave stables to tie my pack and gear onto Raina. A smaller pack was already clumsily strapped on, and Kira was sitting in the saddle, her mouth pressed in a hard line.

I put my hands on my hips. "You're not coming."

"You need an Auraseer to warn you if there's danger."

"You're a child."

"*I'm* the one who found you in the storm. I *saved* you."

"That's different. We're not traveling into another storm; we're entering a war zone."

Kira slumped and stuck out her lower lip. "I just want to go back to the convent. Tosya can take me. He's not going to Torchev."

I leaned on one leg and folded my arms.

"Please, Sonya. I've already been here for weeks." Her doe eyes tugged at all my defenses. "I want to go home."

Why did she have to remind me of *me*? At this moment, Kira's stubbornness was very Sonya. This whole conversation was an echo of the one I'd just had with Tosya, except the roles were reversed. "Fine," I relented. "You can stay with me until we cross the border of Estengarde. But once we set foot in Riaznin, you and Tosya are taking the road to Ormina." I supposed having Kira already at the convent would help me persuade Dasha to leave Valko.

She bounced in the saddle, and Raina whinnied. "Thank you, Sonya."

"You should thank Ula, too, for keeping you safe all this time." I needed to thank her, as well. "Hurry." I held up my arms to help Kira off the horse. "We need to leave soon."

We found Ula with the other nomads in the main cavern.

They bustled about, ladling up last bowls of soup for the soldiers and helping them pack their belongings. Kira gave Ula a
big hug, and Ula bent to kiss her brow. I wasn't sure if I should
hug the chieftain, too, but when I expressed my gratitude and
started to dip into a bow, Ula raised me by my chin and brought
me into her arms. My nose stung with a surprising swell of
emotions. I wished I'd held Sestra Mirna like this, though she
had never been one for embraces.

Ula pulled away and removed another of her beaded necklaces. "Tosya has told me about Dasha, my cousin Motshan's
daughter. Give her this for me." She passed me the necklace.
"Bring her back to safety."

"I'll do everything in my power," I promised. A power that
was limited to emitting aura. I prayed to Feya it would be
enough.

Konstantin motioned to me. We needed to leave. I nodded, but then Lara hastened over and took my hand. "The other
Auraseers and I have something to show you before you go. It
won't take long."

My curiosity tinged with wariness. What was this about?
"All right."

She led me across the main cavern to where the Auraseers
were gathered. Each woman and girl kissed me on both cheeks
and whispered words of farewell in Esten. Then Lara guided
me a few more feet to the memorial stones for my mother and
Sestra Mirna. "We thought we should pay tribute to one more
person," she explained.

The Auraseers stepped away and revealed a third stone with *Genevie* painted on it in flowing script. My eyes immediately blurred with tears. One of the younger girls passed me a bouquet of holly. I tried to say thank you, but my throat ran dry. She nodded in understanding. I looked at the others, who appeared to be waiting for me.

Heartsore, I knelt by Genevie's stone. I didn't want to face what I knew must be true: she was dead by now. "You were courageous and noble," I began, then fell quiet for several moments we didn't have. I hated to be rushed. I needed to give Genevie better than this—a garden dedicated to her at the convent, not just a rock I was leaving behind. I remembered what she had once told me, and now I gave her back the words. "You were a true friend."

CHAPTER TWENTY-EIGHT

"Doesn't the air smell different?" I asked no one in particular, my eyes closed as I breathed in deeply.

Late in the afternoon, five days later, we passed through the great watchtowers at the base of the western Bayacs. Despite my aching muscles from the arduous ride and the urgency I felt to rescue Dasha in Torchev—still a three-day journey away—I tipped my head back and released a sigh that shot warmth from my head to my fingertips.

We were in Riaznin. We were home.

"It smells like rain," Konstantin grumbled, but when I peeked at him, he was grinning, too. We'd left winter behind us in the frosty peaks of the Bayacs, and now a lush valley with golden fields spread out before us, dotted with trees brandishing every autumn color. Even the thunderclouds looming above couldn't diminish the beauty. "We need to find a thicket and make camp before we're all drenched."

We rode a little farther until Konstantin found a wooded area to his liking. As the soldiers and Tosya began staking our tents, Kira and I gathered everyone's flasks and walked down to a stream to fill them up. She'd been clinging to me like a shadow. Tomorrow morning, she and Tosya would part ways with the rest of us and take the road to Ormina.

"I can sense what you're feeling." Kira frowned in disapproval as I bent over the bank of the stream and cupped water into my hand to drink.

"I didn't know you were testing me right now." Ever since we'd left the Romska caves, Kira had been helping me train so I'd be better prepared to meet Dasha. Blocking my emotions through meditation was still extremely difficult, but I was making progress. "You need to taste this," I said, reveling in the perfect tang of minerals on my tongue. "There's something divine about Riaznian water."

She folded her arms. "See if you can drink it again without feeling so happy."

"Oh, Kira." I laughed and splashed her. "Enjoy this moment with me. Smell those pines! Aren't they sharper than Esten pines?"

"They shouldn't make you feel anything—or think about anything."

My smile faltered. I leaned my elbow on my knee and studied the pinch of desperation at the edge of Kira's pursed mouth. "I *am* going to bring Dasha home," I promised. *Feya, let my words be true.*

Kira's chin wobbled. "This is the last day I can help you." Raindrops started falling and flecked moisture on her sunburned cheeks. "What if you're still not ready?"

"I will be." *I have to be.* "Look, I'll practice with you one more time, if it makes you feel better." In truth, it would make me feel better, too. My brief joy upon setting foot in Riaznin was swiftly plummeting, replaced by my encroaching fears. I had to master meditation if I hoped to be immune to Dasha's power. I had nothing else to fall back on.

Kira cracked a grin, then pressed her lips together, growing serious. "All right. Stick your whole arm in the water, and I'll tell you what you're feeling. It better be nothing," she warned.

I arched a brow. "My whole arm?"

"I *could* ask you to jump in."

I held up my hands. "I'll take the arm."

I rotated my belt a little, moving back my holster so the pistol I'd taken to wearing wouldn't get wet. Kira screwed up her face in concentration, ready to sense any whiff of emotion. I pushed up my sleeve and strived to even out my breathing. Water was just water. Coldness was coldness. They weren't attached to my feelings.

I slowly plunged my hand in. As soon as the water reached my elbow, Kira sucked in a sharp breath.

"Really?" I slumped back on my knees. "I swear I felt nothing that time."

She glanced around us and started shaking. "Sonya . . ." Her voice strained to whisper. "I remember this feeling." Tears streaked to her jawline. "The bounty hunter." She whimpered. "He's here."

My heart stopped. Then slammed against my ribs.

"Kira, run. Now!" In a burst of adrenaline, I launched for her. Grabbed her hand. Raced back toward our camp.

Feverish panic lanced my nerves. How was the bounty hunter here? Anton's soldiers should have taken him back to Isker.

Footsteps pounded nearer on the woodland mulch behind us. Kira and I made it past the first cluster of trees, then he yanked her from my wet grasp.

She released a muffled scream. I whirled around and froze, staring into the Esten bounty hunter's merciless eyes. His filthy hand strapped across Kira's mouth. A jagged knife bore down against the throbbing pulse of her neck. Any more pressure and he would draw blood.

I held my breath, didn't move, didn't shout for help. I kept my eye on that blade. "Genevie isn't with us," I blurted. "She's back in Estengarde—with Floquart." I smoothed the tremor from my voice, hoping he wouldn't hear my lie. "So you have no more bounty to claim."

"*Peu importe.*" His yellow teeth flashed as he gave a low chuckle. Kira shuddered but didn't dare struggle under his knife. "Someone else has offered me *another* bounty." His oily grin split wider. "This bounty is for you, Sovereign Auraseer."

CHAPTER TWENTY-NINE

RAIN SOAKED MY SARAFAN AND KIRA'S BLOUSE AND SKIRT AS the bounty hunter marched us through the stream so we wouldn't leave tracks. Our coats, cloaks, and other provisions were back at camp, but we weren't allowed to return for them. It took me several minutes to tear a scrap of my sleeve away without the bounty hunter noticing, even longer to find the right moment to snag it on a shrub. Hopefully Tosya would discover it and lead the soldiers to our rescue. My only other hope was the dagger sheathed on my right thigh. I kept myself to the opposite side of the bounty hunter, praying he wouldn't notice the shape of the hilt under my waterlogged skirt. He'd already confiscated my brass pistol and shoved it in the back waistband of his trousers.

Once his fierce demeanor relaxed a bit and he wasn't hovering so close to Kira, I dared to ask, "Who offered a reward for me?" He put a finger over his lips and raised his knife to Kira's neck again. I winced and resolved to keep my mouth shut.

Near sundown, the woodland grew sparser and opened up to a muddy road, a vast field, and a manor house. Past the deafening sheets of rain, the bounty hunter shouted, "We will take shelter there!" He pointed at the house and cast wary eyes about the surrounding field. "Stay low and hurry!" He motioned at us with his knife and barked, "*On y va!*"

We sprinted to the brick walls along the perimeter of the estate grounds. They had been blasted to rubble in several places, and the towering gates no longer hung on their hinges but lay prostrate in the overgrown pathway. As we trampled over them, I read the rusted name of the house, which had been wrought onto the iron: *Trusochelm Manor.*

My pulse quickened. I thought through the map of Riaznin in my mind. We must be near the village of Montpanon, which meant this was *the* Trusochelm Manor, where Anton had been raised in secret. Now it lay desolate and ruined. Half of the left wing looked like it seen the end of a battering ram. All the windows were broken, and the gardens had been overrun with prickly weeds and tall grass, every bit of vegetation dead on the verge of winter in the valley.

The rainfall quieted as we stepped inside the house. Kira's little sobs and gasps for air echoed against the warped floors and mildewing walls. I recalled what I knew of the manor's history: As soon as Emperor Izia died and Anton moved away from here, King Léopold had retracted his protection on this house. The Esten soldiers had then raided it during the border wars.

Seeing Anton's childhood home so forlorn and abandoned amplified my piercing despair. Would I ever see him again? Would I be able to get to Dasha? Who would stop Valko? What would become of Riaznin and everyone I loved?

"We will stay here until it stops raining," the bounty hunter announced, leading me and Kira into what must have once been a bedroom, though it had no furnishings, only peeling, faded-yellow wallpaper.

He pulled some rope from his pack and tied Kira's hands and feet together. Her red and puffy eyes released a fresh stream of tears. When the bounty hunter came to where I sat next and yanked my legs out straight to tie up my ankles, the sheath at my thigh thumped against the floor. I cringed. He glared and opened his hand, beckoning with his fingers. Reluctantly, I removed the dagger and passed it to him.

After binding my wrists and feet, he left the room with my dagger and returned a minute later. I had no idea what he'd done with it. I watched him carefully as he removed his dripping coat. He had at least three more knives—one at his belt, one at his shoulder, and one peeking out of his boot. The jagged blade still remained in his hand, and it never stayed still. Whether from restlessness or dominance, he kept spinning it around his fingers.

I shivered in my drenched clothes. "Who offered the

bounty?" I asked, chancing to speak again now that he had me and Kira secure.

He grinned and slicked his blond hair back. "A man named Feliks."

A shock of icy cold hit my stomach. Today was four days past the six-week deadline Feliks had given me, but I hadn't been overly concerned about him since Torchev had fallen under attack. I'd guessed he'd be too occupied with defending the capital to bother about me. "But General Kaverin is in Torchev with the Duma," I said. "How did you—?"

"He was in Isker where I was imprisoned a few weeks ago. Feliks had heard rumors of a foreigner who was hunting an Auraseer, and he came to meet me. He said I had a useful talent." The bounty hunter puffed out his chest. "He'd already wasted too much time searching for this one." He sat next to Kira and tapped the flat of his blade on her shoulder. She shuddered and closed her eyes. "Said she had run away."

I flexed my hands against my bindings and strived to remain calm. If I reacted, he might torment Kira even more. "I thought you said this bounty was on *my* head."

"It is, Sovereign Auraseer." He tossed his knife to his other hand and twirled it with equal dexterity. "But the child is a welcome bonus. I am sure Feliks will pay me for both of you."

Hatred blazed a trail of fire through my body. No doubt Feliks would. He had threatened Kira before, and he would do it again to try to make me compliant. "I was already returning to Torchev," I replied. "None of this is necessary."

The bounty hunter shrugged. *"N'importe quoi.* It does not matter what is necessary, only that I am paid." He combed his knife through a lock of Kira's hair. "If you give me any trouble," he told me, "I'll kill the child and take the greater bounty."

I swallowed hard. Kira rocked slightly, her head curled toward her chest and her nose dripping. Her relentless tears didn't help.

I had to find a way for us to escape, despite the bounty hunter's warning. Once Feliks realized I was worthless to him, who knew what would become of Kira in the battle zone of Torchev?

I narrowed my gaze on our captor. "Stop threatening Kira, and we'll go peacefully with you."

He cocked a half smile and rubbed the scar cutting through the mangy beard on his chin. Instead of replying to me, he stood and grabbed Kira by the hair, dragging her a few feet away to the corner of the room.

"Stop!" I struggled against my bonds as she screamed and thrashed.

The bounty hunter sat beside her. She startled as he drove the sharp tip of his knife into the narrow floor space between them. He wedged back into the corner and sprawled out his legs, crossing one foot over the other. "You should get some sleep now, Sovereign Auraseer," he said to me. "We all should."

❦❧

I pretended to doze off as the minutes slowly turned to hours with every *drip-drip-drip* from the leaky ceiling. Sometimes I rolled over, like I was adjusting to a more comfortable position, when in reality I was searching for something sharp to cut my ropes. A splintered piece of wood. The edge of a crumbling brick. Anything.

The temperature fell, and the rain outside turned to snow. Through the only window in the room, I watched it fall in fat, twirling flakes. Gradually the sky began to lighten in its crawl toward morning and faintly illuminated the floor. That's when I saw hope wink at me from ten feet away. A finger-length shard of glass lay just beneath the window.

I stole a glance at the bounty hunter. His chest rose and fell evenly. His breath whistled through his nostrils. He'd fallen asleep an hour ago after also feigning to rest. Miraculously, Kira was also sleeping, despite being so nearby him.

Ever so quietly, I turned over and rolled toward the glass. My damp dress twisted around my legs with each painstaking tumble. When I was a few inches away, the bounty hunter gave a loud snort. I froze, my heart thundering. He made a few more grumbles and huffs, then the cadence of his breath steadied. I blew out a slow exhale and reached behind me, with my hands bound, for the glass.

I sawed the ropes around my wrists first. The work was sluggish and messy. I bit down on a small cry more than once as I nicked my fingers, but I finally severed a length. From there

I was able to untangle the rest. The dawn outside continued to brighten. I had to hurry. Soon the light might wake up the bounty hunter.

I set to work on my ankles. With my hands now free, the rope rent apart faster, but just as I went to cut through the last fiber, I pressed too hard and the glass shattered into tiny pieces. The bounty hunter stirred. I silently cursed and picked up one of the sharp slivers. More light came in the room. I hacked at the rope. The last piece split.

I yanked off my bindings and quietly pulled into a crouched position as I stared at my captor. My pistol, still tucked into the back waistband of his trousers, was impossible to get to. Maybe I could withdraw one of his knives without waking him. No, too risky. I needed to find my dagger.

I stood and tiptoed out of the room, taking care to reroute my steps whenever the floor creaked. I crept down a corridor into what might have once been a dining room and searched under a few pieces of rubble near a crumbling wall. Nothing. I checked the next room, an open space with a chain dangling from the ceiling, missing its chandelier. The room was empty, even of debris, but I noticed some heavily buckled floorboards near the side wall. I rushed over and tugged at the planks. One was loose. My chest expanded as I saw what lay beneath on a bed of rotted wood shavings. My dagger.

I pulled the plank away. Gripped the hilt. Rose to my feet. Then my breath caught in my throat.

I dropped the dagger, and it whooshed back onto the mulch.

I didn't reach for it. I stood, completely rigid, my fingers spread wide. My heart somersaulted. I couldn't think. Didn't understand. Only knew one staggering truth.

I was feeling aura.

CHAPTER THIRTY

EACH PULSE OF AURA CRASHED INTO MY AWARENESS LIKE claps of thunder. Completely at odds with the silent snowfall outside. The sensation was so foreign after all these months that I couldn't comprehend the emotions pounding into me. I just knew it was energy. Other than mine. Connected to life. Another heart beating. Another pair of lungs breathing. They quickened my pulse and expelled my breath. I panted and gasped fog into the frigid air.

The aura came from outside. I knew because when I looked past the broken glass of a window, it blazed stronger and spread like fire through my veins.

Half of me filled with dread, wondering who was out there; the other part of me threatened to cry with happiness. I could see again. With my keenest sense. I was emerging from water to breathe after an endless spell of drowning.

I picked up my dagger. The tightening knots in my stomach

compelled me to do so. But then I left the room. I found the front door. I drifted outside, drawn to the pulse beating through me like a siren call. *I can feel you, I can feel you,* I wanted to tell it. *Don't go away.* I couldn't lose this feeling.

Snow laced over my hair, my face, and damp clothes. Dimly, I realized my dress was frosting to ice. I didn't care. Blood dripped from the cuts in my fingers, but the sting didn't reach me. I stumbled through the overgrown grass, searching. The sun crested the horizon, cutting through the clouds, and the world transformed to a glittering blanket of white. Between the beauty and the breathtaking sense wide-awake inside me, it was easy to ignore the darkness coiling through my limbs and deep inside my belly.

You know this feeling.

You know this person.

You know him, Sonya.

I halted, my hand clenching over my heart.

No, it couldn't be him. Riaznin was at war. The battle for the crown was happening now. In Torchev. Days away from Montpanon. He couldn't be here.

He couldn't.

Run, Sonya.

Run!

I took a step backward. Tightened my grip on my dagger. Swiveled to turn. But then I saw him. Walking over the fallen gates. Onto the estate grounds. Only twenty feet away.

Valko held the lead of his black stallion's reins and draped it over a tree branch. He wore a long coat of silver fox fur and a matching, vaulted hat. A short, dark beard framed his jaw, and the color, along with his furs, brought out his striking gray eyes. Eyes that clawed at me, taking in the sight of me, my tangled hair, my muddy half-frozen dress. How I wanted to look strong. Like he hadn't broken me and shot me for dead. Like he hadn't torn away the part of me that made me feel the most *me*. But now I felt it again. Aura. It trembled through my legs and jolted through my fingers and swarmed me with a dark desire to kill.

Valko's desire.

He walked a few steps closer. The snow crunched beneath his boots. I resisted the impulse to flee. I held my dagger at the ready, while he hadn't withdrawn any weapon. I might have a desperate chance to kill him before he killed me. *That's his intention, Sonya, not yours*, my mind tried to reason. Still, I stood my ground.

"You look different," he said, the edges of his new mustache lifting with an intrigued grin. "Thinner, perhaps. A few more freckles across your nose. None the worse off for taking a lead ball, are you?"

He was stalling, I realized. Being cautious. *He still thinks I have power.* I didn't. Not the kind he thought. While the black snake of his aura coiled inside me, I couldn't forge a bridge between us—that deepest connection that allowed me the ability to bend his emotions—though I shook, straining to try. I shouldn't want this power. I'd resolved to let my desire for it go. But now I inwardly begged for it. I desperately needed it.

I pushed back my shoulders, trying to exude a presence of command, trying to pretend I was the same Sonya that thrust a legion of auras inside him during the One Day War, that compelled him to remove his crown, that nearly persuaded him to shoot himself during the convent battle, the Sonya Valko hadn't been able to tame, the Sonya he'd failed to kill.

"Did you come all this way for me?" I asked, tilting my head like I was a predator studying a small prey thrown in my cage. I suppressed the stricken part of me that wanted to cry, *How did you awaken my Auraseer ability when nothing else could?* Instead, I fed off of Valko's pride and used it to strengthen my voice and demeanor. He needed to believe I was masterful. He would rush forward and kill me if he knew I couldn't threaten him. "I'm flattered. I didn't realize I was of more concern to you than taking the capital of Riaznin."

Valko broke into a warm chuckle that scratched up my spine with his genuine amusement. "Oh, Sonya, I have missed your fire. You may be renowned throughout Torchev—the sovereign Auraseer who betrayed her emperor with magnificent power—but I didn't come here for you." His eyes traveled over me, and my throat squeezed with hatred. His *and* mine. "Still, it's a stroke of providence to find you at Anton's former home." He arched an unimpressed brow at the manor. "Now I can tidy up all my affairs in one day."

I frowned at him through the veil of falling snow. "You came for Anton?"

Before Valko could reply, his soldiers entered the estate

grounds on horseback, at least twelve men. I startled when I saw them. I hadn't felt their auras. I still couldn't when I tried. Some rode over the fallen gates; some leapt over the crumbling walls. They wore the red and gold of Imperial Riaznin. At one nod from Valko, they fanned out to circle the house.

Clasping his hands behind his back, Valko advanced another two steps toward me. My legs tensed. "My army and the Shenglin have Torchev well under control. We've nearly won the battle. What better time to surprise Anton far away from the capital." His aura itched deep inside me in a place I'd have to draw blood to scratch. "You see, I've come to realize I won't achieve a true victory until this revolution is pulled from the roots. I have to conquer the man who incited it in the first place. Otherwise, another rebellion will grow and Anton will always threaten my reign. Even Dasha understands." His eyes flashed to the manor. "Not just yet, little princess."

I whipped around, my heart seizing. *Dasha.* She stood beside the house, less than fifteen feet from me and peered into one of the windows missing all its glass. Her hands gripped the sill, like she was about to crawl inside.

I rocked, off-kilter on my feet. Although I hadn't been able to sense the soldiers, when I focused on Dasha, I could feel her aura. But my awareness was unstable. It flickered in and out, like a flame dancing on the last length of a wick.

Dasha pulled away and turned to me. I couldn't see her face well in the shadows of the house, but a red cape fastened around her bird-boned shoulders, its hood fallen back. No furs lined her clothing. They must have scalded her with death, like they'd once burned me. Half of her hair was done up in a braided crown, and the rest hung in loose wisps about her shoulders. Valko had fashioned her into a fairy-tale princess, just as he'd once made me his exquisite sovereign Auraseer.

Dasha's guardedness, almost deadliness, prickled across the back of my neck. Who knew what lies Valko had told her about me? Likely he'd convinced her that I needed to die, too. She had the power to make that happen. I should know. With one burst of my temper, I'd caused Terezia Dyomin to slit her throat.

Calm yourself, Sonya. Don't let Dasha grasp your emotions. If she could catch them, she could change them.

"What's happening inside the house?" Valko asked his sister. "Are the others still sleeping?"

She tucked her hands behind her back and nodded. A snatch of her aura scuttled across my awareness and curled my shoulders toward my chest. But the sensation was so fleeting I couldn't decipher the emotion.

Don't think, Sonya. Be cold. Don't worry about Dasha's feelings.

Feya, how am I going to save her?

I'd never had to focus my thoughts while contending with another person's aura.

Valko held out his hand. "Come, little snowflake. Don't be

nervous. I'll stand by your side. We need to take care of Sonya before we deal with Anton."

He was cunning, as always. He never said *kill*. His aura pulsed a strain of sorrow that lifted my chin rather than pulled at my heart. He made murder feel necessary, righteous.

Dasha plodded forward, lifting her puffed wool skirt so it didn't drag in the snow. As she stepped into the wintry light, my concentration broke. Her gray eyes were bloodshot, and her skin, naturally olive from her Romska blood, had grown star-tlingly pale since I'd last seen her.

I turned an accusatory stare on Valko. Every bone in my body threatened to crack under the pressure of my hatred for him. He could pretend he treated Dasha like a princess, but he was clearly overexerting her and burning her strength to ashes. What had he made her do to help him achieve a victory in this war?

She pressed next to him, and he wrapped an arm around her shoulder. "I know you're tired," he murmured. "After today, you can rest, I promise."

She peeked at me, then shuddered and looked away.

"What is it?" Valko asked her.

"You were right," she said quietly, but her bell-tone voice amplified her words. "Sonya's hate for you is strong."

"I tried to prepare you." His brows drew together with artful sorrow. "Remember, she almost killed me at the convent. It's a miracle I pulled the gun away from my head before it fired."

"What providence that you aimed it at *me*," I bit out.

He grinned, but his aura rode an eerily calm wave. I knew what he was doing, concealing his emotions, both to manipulate Dasha and keep them out of my reach so I couldn't alter them. I wished I could. "Sonya's intentions are no different today," he said. "See how she holds her dagger, while I haven't made any move to harm her?"

Despite his baiting, I didn't lower my blade from my defensive stance. "I'm trying to protect myself," I explained to Dasha. "You must know Valko means to kill me. You must *feel* it. Did you ever have misgivings about him? Uncomfortable feelings he taught you to ignore? He isn't kind. He isn't good, Dasha. Don't let him fool you."

"He's my brother." Snowflakes caught in her dark lashes. "He loves me."

"Anton is your brother, too," I said, "and he would never force you to use your power."

Her aura fluttered with uncertainty.

"I've never forced Dasha to do anything." Valko broadened his chest. "She *wants* to help me."

"If that's true, you shouldn't let her," I snapped. "Can't you see how she's suffering?" Even now, Dasha gripped a strand of her hair, ready to pull it out, an old habit of dealing with stress.

"How cruel you are." Valko frowned at me. "All I see is a beautiful little girl. She will be the jewel of Riaznin."

"Is that what he tells you, Dasha? He'll lock you in a cage.

He won't trust you with other people." My heart pounded with so much urgency I couldn't quell my desperation—or any of my emotions. "You need to come with me and make sure Valko doesn't interfere. The convent is your home. Kira misses you. We all do."

Kira. Dasha's aura sparked at her name, but dread spiraled through my belly. How was I going to save her, too? I glanced at the soldiers, closing in tighter around the house. Were they going to storm inside? Surely the bounty hunter was awake by now. Strangely, I felt grateful to him. With any luck, he was hatching a plan to save me and Kira, if only to collect his money.

"The palace is Dasha's home." Valko tightened his grip on his sister's quivering shoulder. Her fear, anger, and panic trembled through me, rushing to the surface, ready to burst. "She's an Ozerov princess. She belongs with me. Who can understand her more than family?"

"I'm the one who understands you, Dasha. Don't listen to him. I'm the one who is truly like you—the only one." I reached for her, but she squirmed back.

"You're *not* like me," she blurted. "Something has happened to you."

"What do you mean?" Valko confronted her, his brows drawing low.

She wrapped her arms around herself and ducked her head. "Sonya's aura is different. She isn't strong like me anymore."

My stomach dropped. Valko's gray eyes riveted to me and

slit into gleams of silver. "Your power is gone?"

I tried to look formidable, but my cheeks flooded with heat.

Valko's teeth glinted with his slowly spreading smile.

He knows he can kill me now.

I whirled and bolted for the house.

The calm current of Valko's aura snapped into a riptide.

He growled and chased after me, his footfalls fast. The horses whinnied. "Stand your ground, men!" he shouted.

I stole a glance behind me. Valko was only five feet away. He'd withdrawn a knife.

Feya, help me. I wasn't a fighter. I wasn't trained for this.

"Dasha, stop her!" Valko commanded his sister.

Panic gripped me in a chokehold. Blood pounded through my ears. I couldn't keep my fear at bay. Dasha would be able to seize it, use it.

I tripped and fell on a broken beam under the snow.

Valko made a noise of exertion and sprang to stab me.

I rolled to the side. His blade struck the ground. Just as quickly, his knife rose again and arced for me.

I kicked his leg to throw off his aim. As he stumbled back, I jumped to my feet. He spun to face me. A vein throbbed in his forehead.

Panting, I swiped my dagger at his torso. He thrust his knife toward my neck.

"No, don't!" Dasha screamed and raced to catch up to us.

My muscles locked. My franticness heightened to paralysis.

I stared into Valko's eyes, mere inches from mine. He stood just as rigidly, just as conflicted. Our heavy breaths crystallized on the air between us.

"Why do you hate each other?" Dasha cried. "Why can't you be friends?"

Why can't I? Her words took root inside me. Compassion sent a rush of warmth through my limbs. Memories flooded to mind. Valko confessing his vulnerabilities. Crying in my arms. Smiling like a lost boy who'd found one true friend.

He pitied me, too. I felt it in the oddest mind-prickling sensation, like gazing into a fractured reflection. What was *he* recalling about me? Did he remember how awestruck I was when we'd first met? How flattered I'd been by his gifts and attention? How reckless, passionate, and impulsive I once was, just like him? Hadn't he helped me feel free and special? Until I'd met Valko, all my life I'd felt trapped and strange.

Why was I so ready to end his life?

The tension inside me unraveled. My arm fell. The dagger thudded softly in the snow.

Dasha stared up at her brother, her large gray eyes the mirror of his. "Please give me your knife. Sonya doesn't want to hurt you anymore. Be nice to her." She opened her hand and waited.

Valko looked from her to me, his brows twitching. He slowly lowered his knife. Seven inches from her palm. Five inches. Two.

Thoughts chafed at the back of my mind and clashed with my sympathy for him.

This is your chance, Sonya. Kill him.

No, I couldn't.

If he dies, Free Riaznin wins this war, no matter what happens in Torchev. The empire can't triumph with no emperor to take the throne.

No, Valko was only a misguided soul. I could help him see reason. He deserved a second chance.

He'll kill you. And when he finds Anton, he will kill him, too. You've given Valko a hundred chances. His heart will never change.

Dasha took her brother's knife away. She picked mine up from the ground.

Grab your dagger, Sonya!

No, I couldn't hurt Valko.

Dasha walked a few paces from us and threw both blades out of reach, a little over fifteen feet away. They sunk into the ankle-deep snow.

You can still run, still reach your weapon.

No, I needed to leave it alone.

Dasha is changing your emotions. You have to fight back. You have to break her hold.

I closed my eyes. Tried to sever the strings of my anxiety. Sought a shelter within myself where Dasha couldn't reach me.

Beads of sweat rolled down the back of my neck. I restrained a shiver as they met the cold air. I couldn't let myself feel anything. It didn't matter that my heart raced. It didn't matter that my lungs pinched off my breath. I imagined myself a blank space. A sea with no waves. A desert with no water. A glacier in an endless winter.

I opened my eyes and forced myself to look away from Valko. I pushed out my compassion for him, as well as my desire to kill. I turned to Dasha. She was my priority. But I couldn't let my desperation to save her overwhelm me or she could bend those emotions, as well.

I stepped toward her. Inhaled a steadying breath. In through my nose. Out through my mouth. "Dasha, I need you to listen to me."

She startled to see me moving and speaking and freed from her influence. "Stay back!"

"Your Majesty?" one of the soldiers called, disturbed to see Valko languidly standing by while Dasha shouted at me.

I ignored him and focused on her. "I love you," I said, speaking the words genuinely, but not letting them burn through my chest. "So many people do. I wish you would let me show you. Do you remember how Anton taught you to release your pain? He lifted you in his arms and told you to cast stones over the palace balcony. One for your worries, one for your heartache, and one for your anger."

"Be quiet!" She clapped her hands over her ears. "Anton was tricking me so I would like him. Valko says—"

"Nothing Valko says matters. He's the one who has tricked you. He's using you, just like he once used me. What about Sestra Mirna? She loved you like a mother."

Dasha blinked and her lip quivered against a sudden stab of pain. I realized too late I'd released the feeling, and she'd absorbed it. "Why are you so sad when you say her name?" she asked, her bell-tone wavering.

My shoulders fell. I strived to compose myself. "Sestra Mirna became very sick, Dasha. She passed away a few weeks ago. I'm so sorry."

Her head twitched twice in a shake of denial, and she pressed her hands over her mouth. A ragged whine escaped her.

"She thought of you every day. We tried so hard to find you. We marked maps where you'd been. Sestra Mirna wanted you safe and back home—away from him." I threw a sharp glance at Valko. A shudder ran through his arm, and a spark lit through his aura.

"Your Majesty," the soldier called again, this time with more urgency.

"What about Kira?" I walked closer to Dasha and spoke faster, louder, fighting to keep her attention. "She loves you like a sister. Don't you want to be with her again?"

Longing pulsed through Dasha. She snuck a glance at the manor house.

She knows Kira is inside. Can she sense she isn't safe?

The soldier lifted his musket. Aimed it at one of the windows. The other soldiers did the same. Every window was targeted. They were going to blindly shoot inside. I prayed Kira was lying flat on the floor. "Shall we fire, My Lord Emperor?"

Valko's mouth tensed to open just as Dasha screamed, "No!"

My heart thundered erratically. I couldn't take another step. I was too afraid. The soldiers' auras trickled inside of me as my awareness broadened. I could finally sense each man. They were just as fearful and halted, scarcely drawing breath.

"No one does anything unless I say so!" Dasha warned. "I'm in charge now."

The tendons in my neck cramped. I struggled to speak. A few feet away, Valko radiated a different energy. His apprehension waned, replaced by a growing confidence. I latched on to his steadiness. I found my beating heart, my flowing blood, my own feelings. We turned to each other. And broke Dasha's hold at the same time.

"Kill her!" Valko shouted to his men and pointed at me.

I jolted a step backward, but none of his soldiers obeyed him.

He trained a vicious gaze on his sister. "Dasha," he said, feigning patience, "let them go."

She shrank away and stubbornly shook her head.

His calm fractured. "Dasha—!"

She gasped. Her hand flew to the base of her throat. She looked past us to the field beyond the estate grounds. "Other people are coming," she said.

My heart drummed faster. I cast my awareness in that direction, but I couldn't sense as far as she did—or see anyone.

Valko scrutinized her. "Are you telling the truth?" I

wondered the same thing. Maybe this was a ploy to distract him.

Before she could answer, a horse whinnied in the distance, and a crack of musket fire split the air. One of Valko's soldiers cried out and clutched his arm. Dasha and I jerked as his pain ricocheted through us. The shock severed her hold on the others.

The remaining soldiers stirred, one by one, and turned their horses toward the field.

Valko broadened his shoulders. His eyes darkened with resolve. "Charge!" he commanded. His shout cut through the muffling snowfall.

The soldiers galloped out of the estate grounds. At the same moment, Dasha flinched and tore off running for the house. "Kira!" she screamed.

A beat slower than her, I finally felt the strains of Kira's aura. It surged with terror and chased fire through my veins. I bolted for the door with Dasha.

Before we made it there, the little girl darted outside. "Dasha!" Kira's eyes flared. "I knew I felt you! Help me! There's a—"

The bounty hunter emerged and caught the back of Kira's shirt. She shrieked and flailed as he raised his knife.

"Don't hurt my friend!" Dasha released a mangled cry. "Let her go!"

Like a fist to the gut, the bounty hunter's aura struck my

awareness. His trembling fury vanished, replaced by a harrowing remorse. Without a word, he dropped Kira.

"You're a bad man!" Dasha shouted. "You should hurt yourself, not her!"

In the flutter of an instant, deadly self-hatred seized him. He threw back his head, his eyes filled with anguish, and plunged his knife into his own chest.

CHAPTER THIRTY-ONE

I FELL TO MY KNEES. KIRA WRENCHED INTO A TIGHT BALL. Dasha's body jerked.

The bounty hunter's fatal pain bounced between the three of us like an echo chamber.

His face twisted in agony as he careened to the ground and landed on top of his knife. The blade drove in deeper, and we all lurched. He convulsed once, then fell still.

Aura gone. Pain gone.

Relief overwhelmed my horror—a terrible reaction to watching someone die. *Kira is safe*, was all I could think of. *The man who hunted Genevie and killed her friends is gone.* But as the bounty hunter's blood soaked the snow and Kira whimpered and Dasha clamped a hand over her mouth, both girls' shock pummeled me with dizziness and remorse.

"Dasha," Kira croaked. She pushed to her feet, though she could barely keep her balance.

Dasha burst into sobs and ran over to her. Kira took her into her arms, and Dasha wept so hard she choked for breath. "I—I'm sorry. I didn't mean to do that. But he was hurting you. I thought he would kill you." She rattled like a leaf in a windstorm. "You felt it, too, didn't you? He was bad. He was . . ." Her voice went hoarse. She looked between Kira and me and clutched her braided crown at her scalp. "What did I do?"

My heart broke for her. I knew this pain. Profoundly. I had also killed unintentionally. A convent full of Auraseers. Nadia's mother. I carried each death like stones on my back. "I understand how this feels, Dasha. I'm so, so sorry."

She looked at me—really looked at me, like she'd never truly seen me before. Her aura reverberated a deep, unsettling awe. "I'm sorry," I said again, because I wouldn't wish my suffering on anyone.

Valko stirred a few feet away from us. As he approached the dead bounty hunter, his own aura stoked with growing comprehension, bitter humor, and scathing anger. Each building sensation scorched my skin like hot ashes. "Dasha"—Valko's gaze thinned on her—"where is Anton?"

She gulped and swiped away her tears. "I—I don't feel him anymore. He must have run off."

The corners of Valko's mouth twitched as he struggled to maintain his grin. "You never tracked our brother here, did you, Princess? You only tracked your little friend."

She pressed her lips together and glanced at Kira, lowering her head.

Valko chuckled darkly and rubbed a hand over his face. "Oh, Dasha, you're full of surprises. An Ozerov to the bone."

Her aura squeezed my ribs with humiliation, but then she set her jaw and grabbed Kira's hand. "I missed her. You promised I could see her when—"

"—the war is *over*," Valko replied. "We can't take Kira to Torchev now."

Dasha's mouth fell open. "But you said we were winning."

"I said we had *almost* won. I needed to defeat Anton to do that. And since you have lied to me, you've delayed our return."

"But Kira—"

"Kira is no one!" Valko snapped. "We need Anton dead, do you understand? We need Sonya dead. You can't be with your friend again until that happens."

The wet snow seeped into my boots as I stared at Dasha. She felt so conflicted inside, so unsteady, like the earth might crack beneath her feet at any moment. I feared *she* might break, and I made ready to run, ready to cast up another block to defend myself from her. More guns blasted in the distance. The noises of battle grew louder. Dasha shivered, her nose pink, her heavy breaths fogging the air. Her hands gripped the fabric of the beautiful red cape Valko had given her.

He scoffed, his patience at its end. "If you're not going to help me, then stay out of my way."

"Wait!" she said, but her wavering energy wasn't strong enough to grasp his.

He launched for our fallen weapons, his knife and my

dagger. They were closer to him—less than eight feet away—I wouldn't make it there first.

I tensed to race away—the only option left to me—when a glint of brass caught my eye. On the dead bounty hunter. Tucked in the back waist of his trousers. A handle, mostly covered by an excess fold of his shirt. But now the cloth was saturated in his blood and clung around the defined shape of a gun beneath.

My pistol.

I bounded for it, slipping on the snow-slick earth. In a matter of seconds, it was in my grip. I didn't need to load and prime the weapon. I'd done that already, just as Anton had taught me. The bounty hunter had never fired it.

I whirled to face Valko. His back was to me as he bent to grab the two blades. I drew a quick breath. Took aim. Cocked the hammer. And pulled the trigger.

I braced myself for a loud crack of gunfire. For Valko to cry out with fatal pain.

Nothing sounded.

I frowned. Pulled the hammer and trigger again.

Silence.

I frantically opened the pistol's frizzen to check the flash pan, then gasped. The gunpowder was wet with the bounty hunter's blood. I glanced back up at Valko. He grinned from only a few feet away, my dagger and his knife in his hands.

I cursed and dropped the gun, then sprinted toward the collapsed gates and open field.

"Sonya, watch out!" Kira cried.

My stomach tightened with a sudden surge of hatred—Valko's. I dropped low as his knife slashed through the air, just missing my head. The blade clanged onto the gate bars and thunked on the ground. Adrenaline shot through my veins. I didn't think. I jumped back up and ran for the knife. Valko tore after me. He still had my dagger.

"Dasha, help!" I shouted. Valko was too close. I wouldn't be able to dodge him again.

"I can't!" she yelled. "He's too strong."

Strong? I struggled to think as I spied his half-buried knife. Could strength break past Dasha's hold, *as well* as a focused mind? Is that how Valko had overcome my power when he'd shot me at the convent? By a stronger will?

I dived for the blade. Wrapped my fingers around the hilt.

The black serpent of Valko's aura bared its full fury, sharp with fangs. All his energy channeled together, preparing once and for all to kill me.

I scrambled to my feet. Couldn't raise the knife. I was too late. Valko's dagger pointed directly over my heart.

Perspiration flushed his face, at odds with the snow collecting in his dark hair. He kept walking, forcing me backward. My heel snagged on the fallen gate rails, but I caught the brick post for support. Valko grinned, teasing me now, waiting for me to fall, drawing out the moment of my death.

Noises siphoned away. I heard only the blood crashing through my ears, the primal thumping of my own heart. My bones ached with fear, but I locked my knees in resistance. I couldn't be afraid. I labored to ground myself to the space of my body, the breadth of my aura, to every organ and pulse of energy that made me *me*. Sestra Mirna's words flooded to remembrance, her answer to the question I'd once asked her:

How will I know when I've come to my last open door?

She'd taken my face in one of her careworn hands. *You will know, Sonya. Trust me. Crossing that threshold will take every last measure of your courage and your fierce desire to fight.*

Deeply inhaling, I found the steel to support my voice. "Dasha, together we're stronger than Valko! Borrow my strength! Help me!"

I didn't have her power, but she could latch on to my aura. And so I *felt*—as mightily as possible. My bravery after losing Pia. My resilience after almost dying. My fortitude after Sestra Mirna's death. My love after remembering my mother.

Stay courageous, Sonya, Sestra Mirna urged me. *Stay strong.*

Valko seized my arm.

Tears streaked down my face—from exertion, not terror.

"Good-bye, my dear sovereign Auraseer." His unadulterated hatred peaked.

I didn't let it scathe me. "I will not die. Not here. Not today."

His brow arched in defiance.

"Now, Dasha!" I cried.

I felt her energy turn outward as Valko swung with his dagger. But his driving force weakened with uncertainty. Dasha's doing. I grabbed his arm and wrenched it to his side, then raised my own knife.

Raging energy burned through me, but behind the fury was a white blaze of something nobler, something beautiful, something stronger.

I stared at Valko in confusion. This couldn't be his aura.

Pain erupted inside me. Shock lashed like a whip. Valko jerked forward, his eyes bulging wide. His stunned gaze lowered to his stomach, where a blade pierced through him, dripping with blood.

I didn't understand. I was still holding my knife.

He reached for me, but I recoiled. Unsupported, Valko's body buckled, and he crashed to the ground.

Just behind where he'd been standing was Anton, his hair fallen across his flushed brow.

My grip went slack. My blade dropped in the snow.

"Are you all right?" Anton asked, his face pale and stricken.

"You're here," I gasped, seized by light-headedness. "How—how are you here?"

Anton wasn't in Estengarde. He stood right before me.

And he had just stabbed his only brother.

"I found Tosya." He swallowed, his chest heaving for breath. My legs went weak with his distress as he looked down at Valko. "He helped me track you—to my old home, of all places."

I scanned the field beyond and found our regiment out there fighting Valko's men and gaining the upper hand.

"Where is the bounty hunter?" Anton asked me.

"Dead."

He nodded, biting his quivering lip as he cast another glance at his brother.

I couldn't look, could barely stand, barely breathe. My chest ached, tangled between Anton's sorrow and Valko's dying energy.

"Are you hurt?" He stepped closer to me, his brows hitched.

I shook my head. The tender pulse of Anton's concern made my throat tighten with emotion.

"Sonya . . ." He cradled my face with his hand, and his aura flamed brighter. I trembled and closed my eyes. I hadn't felt his love inside me for so long. I leaned my cheek into his palm, then caught myself and pulled away.

"What is it?"

"I can't . . ." I sucked in a sharp breath. "You're married now."

Anton's mouth creased into a frown. "Who told you I was married? I refused the alliance."

I blinked, even more unsteady on my feet. "But . . . you negotiated the release of the Esten Auraseers to *bargain* for the alliance."

"I did that for you," he said gently. "King Léopold only agreed to let the Auraseers go out of desperation to make me change my mind. I refused to, even when he sequestered me in my room while you were forced to leave."

My brows lifted. "He locked you up?"

"The king was mad with panic after Floquart's death; he'd never had to threaten anyone on his own. Delphine finally persuaded him to let me go."

My brain worked sluggishly past my disbelief. "I don't understand. You truly refused the alliance?"

"We can't win a war against inequality if we align ourselves with a bigoted nation. I was blind not to see that before."

"Then"—my chest tingled with cautious hope—"you're not married?"

The cast of Anton's brown eyes grew warmer, more golden. He looked at me like we were alone together, not at the ruins of a desolate place and surrounded by death. He looked at me like I was his greatest treasure. "The only person I ever want to be married to is you, Sonya. I chose *you* . . ." He took my hands and kissed each one. "I will always choose you."

Radiant heat showered over me. Every space of my heart filled with light.

Valko coughed—a horrible, strangled noise. The sound split my focus and latched me back to his aura. All my muscles seized, tensing with him.

At once, Anton knelt at his brother's side and gripped his shoulder. Valko stared up at him with dazed, livid eyes. Deep beneath his fury, threads of his regret knotted through my belly. "Congratulations, brother." Blood gurgled from his mouth. "You . . . won."

Anton released a pained sigh. His wretchedness tore through me. "I'm sorry it had to end like this."

A spasm chased through Valko's brows. His breaths came weakly, with great effort. He had the audacity to lift his chin, clinging to his pride until the very end. "You will answer to the gods for this."

"I know." Anton bowed his head. "May they forgive us both."

Valko shuddered one last time. Then his eyes went stone still, and his head listed to the side. The candle of his aura snuffed out, forever gone.

Only when he was dead did I finally pity him. His face looked as smooth as a clean slate, free of any traces of rage, demons, and regrets . . . even the heartache I'd witnessed so fleetingly during the time I had known him.

I knelt at his other side and closed his eyes. "Be at peace," I whispered to the innocent boy he once was, a child cast off by his parents to live in secret at the farthest edge of Riaznin. I reached for Anton's hand over Valko's lifeless body. "Be at peace," I told him, too. "This had to be."

Dasha and Kira stumbled over to us, their arms wrapped around each other. Anton gave a hard swallow as he met his sister's tearstained gaze. "I'm sorry," he told her.

A halo of snowflakes fluttered over Dasha's head as she stared at Anton for a long moment, taking in the sincere and remorseful pulse of his aura, then her eyes lowered to Valko. Her voice was small when she replied, "I helped you do this."

"You did what was necessary," he said.

"You were very brave," I added.

Dasha sniffed. "Valko was bad. I knew that, but . . . I tried not to think about it." She choked on a dry sob and shrugged a shoulder. "He was my brother."

A deep ache flowered in my throat and radiated Anton's empathy. "He was my brother, too," he replied. "As I am yours."

The snow swirled, the last few pops of musket fire rang out, and Dasha's mouth trembled into the softest smile.

The sweetest promise of peace.

CHAPTER THIRTY-TWO

FOUR DAYS LATER, I GUIDED RAINA AROUND THE LAST BEND of the forest road. The convent appeared in the distance, perched on the crystalline snow. Dasha gasped in the saddle we shared. "Oh, Sonya. So many Auraseers are here!"

I grinned, anxious to meet all the Esten girls and women again. "You can sense them from this far away?" Dasha's ability never ceased to astonish me.

She nodded, her aura bursting like a butterfly from a cocoon. "The convent hasn't felt this full this since before the fire."

I kissed the top of her head. "It's as it should be."

Tosya rode up to join us. Kira sat in his lap like Dasha sat in mine. Five soldiers trailed behind on their steeds, the last few members of our regiment. The rest had gone with Anton to Torchev after defeating Valko's men at Montpanon. Before he had left, Anton sent a dispatch to the capital, announcing the former emperor was dead, then set off himself to settle matters there and confront Feliks for threatening me. Valko's death meant the end of the Imperialist-Shenglin alliance, as well as the civil war. It meant our country had a fighting chance to unify and drive out the Shenglin and reclaim the rest of our cities.

Tosya brandished a hand at the convent. "And the sovereign Auraseer and the last princess of Riaznin found peace in Feya's sanctuary," he said in a dramatic orator's tone. "How's that for a last line?"

I side-eyed him and smirked. "I think the Voice of Riaznin could do better." Tosya had recently started writing a new poem, the third he hoped would be shared throughout our nation. It was about me and Dasha, how I'd exhausted every last measure of my power in my final stand against Valko, and now my power was gone—a tall tale, but I didn't mind since it demoted me from being Riaznin's all powerful savior and excused Dasha for serving as Valko's sinister counterpart. In Tosya's poem, Dasha was an innocent child manipulated by Valko and saved by her loving brother Anton. "Those words make it sound like our lives are ending at the convent, when they're just beginning."

Tosya huffed. "If you're so particular, you should write your own verses."

His teasing undercurrent tickled the back of my neck. "I would never step on your toes like that."

"Good, I'm rather fond of my toes." He flexed his boots in his stirrups. "I can hold a quill between them, you know.

Probably write a whole sonnet that way." Kira wrinkled her nose and giggled.

We rode forward to the convent gate, and the soldiers standing guard let us in and took our horses to the stable. As soon as Dasha and Kira dismounted, they raced for the convent's front doors, snow kicking in their wake.

I linked elbows with Tosya and walked behind the girls. "When will you meet with your tribe?" I asked. Motshan's caravan should have still been near the coast of Ormina, and Tosya needed to tell them of Ula's offer to welcome them in Estengarde, though with the promise of peace in our nation, we hoped the Riaznian Romska would remain safe here.

"Sometime in the next few days." He gave a noncommittal shrug. "First I want to . . ." His voice trailed off, and a sudden shift in his aura made my stomach flip.

I followed his gaze. A few feet away, Nadia emerged onto the porch and knelt by Dasha and Kira, wrapping her arms around them. The girls stiffened and exchanged bewildered glances. Neither one had spent time with Nadia since before the convent fire, and she'd never been affectionate. As soon as she let them go, they darted inside. Her shoulders shook with a little laughter, and then her jade eyes turned to us. She nodded at me, a sort of obligatory hello, but when she looked at Tosya, she blinked softly and her cheeks, already pink from the cold, flushed to a deeper rose. She drew her shawl around her shoulders and stepped back as we joined her on the porch. It wasn't until that moment that I realized my heartbeat fluttered, reacting to the energy pulsing off of *her*.

"You're emitting aura?" I asked on an amazed breath.

"So I'm told," she replied, then cocked a brow. "Wait . . . *you're* feeling it?"

I spread out my arms. "Surprise."

"What else did you learn while you were away?"

"I can't alter anyone's emotions, if that's what you're hinting at. I'm just a regular Auraseer now."

"Regular." Nadia sighed. "Wouldn't that be nice?"

Oh. Nadia couldn't sense other people. "Well, that part came last," I said. "Valko's aura was the first I felt, actually." I shivered as the wintry air bit through my cloak. "I'm not sure why . . . maybe because his was the last one I sensed before I lost my ability." Or maybe because Valko's aura had always been a dark beacon to me, one I felt stronger than any other. "Perhaps I had to relive a spark of trauma to make my awareness wake up. So there's hope for you yet."

"Wonderful." Nadia pressed her lips in a wry line. "I'll lock myself in the east wing and you can throw burning matches at me."

Tosya snorted, and I leveled a glare on him. He sheepishly tugged on his cap.

As Nadia's gaze lingered on him, the sharpest edges of her aura sanded away. Her mouth curved slightly, and Tosya responded by going completely red in the face. "I can't believe you're alive," she said. "*Both* of you," she added, flinging a brief glance at me. "And Valko is really dead." She'd heard the news already. Anton had sent a dispatch from Montpanon to Ormina, as well. "The convent truly has a chance to become a place of refuge and learning now."

"And not a prison for the next sovereign Auraseers," I felt compelled to add. "It will be the haven Sestra Mirna desired it to be."

Nadia tilted her head in contemplation. She couldn't sense the pulse of my aura, but I hoped she could read the willingness on my face to make peace with her. "Would you like to see what *I've* been doing while you were away?" she asked.

I grinned, my heart already pounding from the many Auraseers inside the convent. "Yes, please."

Lara, Muriella, Camille, Basina, Giliana, Roselle, Éloise, Jessamyn, Aveline, Clémence, Violette, Chantal, Emelisse, Secile, and Isabeau. Within a few short minutes, I had greeted all fifteen Esten Auraseers. And there were others—six Riaznian Auraseers Nadia had found with the help of Sestra Mirna's journal: a bronze-skinned woman named Tamryn; twins a little older than me, Ilona and Irina; Neva and Anya, young cousins whose great-grandmother was an Auraseer; and Mei, who had a Riaznian father and a Shenglin mother. Twenty-five Auraseers in total, including Nadia, Dasha, Kira, and me. Heat radiated through my chest to see every wing of the convent in use. I couldn't believe this place had been almost empty a few weeks ago.

"They're helping me complete their genealogies," Nadia said, nodding at Tamryn, who sat in the library and drew out her family tree. "We hope to find many other girls and women, and I haven't even heard back from all the letters I sent out. I plan to—" She was interrupted by nine-year-old Anya tugging on her skirt.

"Sestra Nadia, Sestra Nadia," the girl said, bouncing on her toes.

My brows darted up. "*Sestra* Nadia?"

Nadia pulled in a deep breath, her energy emitting both embarrassment and pride. "Some of the Auraseers have taken to calling me that."

"It suits you," Tosya replied. When Nadia's forehead crinkled, he was quick to add, "It has an elegant ring." That made her smile, and she stood a little taller.

"When can we tell her?" Anya whispered to Nadia.

"Tell me what?" I asked, noting the girl's enthusiasm warring with her instinct to be covert. Between the two sentiments, I wanted to dance and hide at the same time.

Nadia put her hands on her hips. "Do I *feel* ready to tell her?"

Anya fidgeted with the ends of her braids. "Um . . . yes?"

Nadia gave her a pointed look.

"No?" Anya guessed again.

Nadia released an exasperated sigh. "By the end of tomorrow you're going to learn the difference between anticipation and readiness or you won't get supper."

That didn't seem to faze Anya. "So can we tell her now?"

Glancing up at the ceiling, Nadia shook her head. "I

suppose, since the surprise is now spoiled."

Anya squealed and clapped her hands. "She's in the kitchen. We told her she couldn't come out yet."

"Who is in the kitchen?" I frowned at Nadia.

Her mouth lifted in the corner. "Go and see for yourself."

Warily, I made my way there with Nadia, Anya, and a train of Auraseers following. When I came to the door, Dasha's and Kira's distinct auras emanated from within, as well as another I'd never felt before. She must be an Auraseer, though; her energy had that certain resonance that only came from those with our abilities.

I turned the latch and peered around the door at the table.

I drew in a startled breath. Palpitations skipped across my chest. I stood speechless, blinking in disbelief.

She wore a daffodil-yellow Esten dress that brought a touch of springtime to winter. Her autumn-brown shawl matched her lovely eyes. Much of the black dye had faded from her hair, and it now gleamed in mahogany waves. Her mouth dimpled at the corner when she saw me. My throat closed when I tried to say her name.

Genevie.

She set down her steaming mug and rose from where she had been sitting next to Dasha and Kira. "I feared I would never see you again," she said, her aura glowing with tender happiness.

My eyes burned as I rushed over and threw my arms around her. "You're alive!"

She squeezed me back, her joy spilling over into laughter. "Thanks to Delphine."

"Delphine?" My amazement doubled. "She convinced King Léopold to set you free?"

"He didn't set me free." Genevie pulled back and coyly tucked a lock of hair behind her ear. "Delphine helped me escape the day before my execution. She flirted with a young guard and offered him expensive jewelry until he agreed to assist her. When we staged my escape, we pretended he was smitten with me, instead of her, so it looked like the two of us had run off together."

I raised my brows, impressed. "Now all we have to do is pray the king doesn't send any bounty hunters."

"Delphine promised her uncle is done bothering with Aura-seers, which means others might have a greater chance to leave Estengarde, if they want to. Delphine said she will work with Madame Perle to help them."

I shook my head in astonishment. I never imagined I'd feel such affection for the king's niece. I wished Delphine were here so I could thank her in person. "We may need to build another wing on the convent."

"We may need more sestras," Nadia quipped from behind me.

Genevie's smile lit up her face. "I am more than willing."

Three weeks later, I walked across the convent grounds, taking a quiet moment to be alone. While I delighted in having the convent so full, I was still learning to acclimate myself to being encompassed by so many auras.

I breathed in deeply and took in the beautiful scenery around me. Snow sifted through the air and settled over the landscape like dusting sugar on gingerbread. Winter had decided it was here to stay, despite the pleadings of autumn. I didn't mind. Winter brought a hushed sense of peace that Riaznin desperately needed.

The sound of sleigh bells drew my attention to the road beyond the gate. Around the bend, gliding through the snow, came a brightly painted troika. I focused on the driver, the only person inside, and I broke into a wide smile.

Anton had returned.

He gave the horses a light whip to urge the troika along. He was clean-shaven, and his longer, windblown hair softened his appearance, a regal bearing I doubted he would ever lose.

As the guards opened the gate and Anton passed through, I stepped closer to the drive leading to the stable. His gaze shifted to where I stood in the snowy field, fifteen feet away.

Warmth trickled through my limbs, despite the cold. I had first laid eyes on Anton like this, as he'd driven a team of three horses. I'd never guessed the stoic prince who came to fetch me from the convent, bringing the emperor his next sovereign Auraseer, would capture the deepest reaches of my heart.

He pulled the horses to a halt and grinned, his eyes crinkling in the corners. "Can you sense me from here?"

I nodded, drawing my braid in front of my shoulder,

suddenly shy and unsure what to do with myself. I wondered if I looked presentable or if I resembled an icicle wearing a sarafan.

"What am I feeling, then?"

The rush of thoughts I'd just had made better sense. I'd absorbed *his* emotions. "Nervous. But why?"

He ducked his head a little. "Because now you'll be able to scrutinize every last whit of my aura. I was rather enjoying the freedom I had around you."

I bubbled with laughter. "Admit it, you missed this Sonya." I waved a hand at myself.

Anton's eyes grew soft, and I shivered under the power of his adoration. "I missed *you*, regardless of your abilities, though I'm glad they bring you happiness."

I closed the distance between myself and the troika. "Are you going to make me climb up there to say a proper hello?"

He nodded. "I was hoping you'd join me on a romantic, fifty-yard journey to the stable."

I offered my hand, and he lifted me onto the platform of the sleigh. "I should warn you," I said, joining him on the bench seat, "I'm known to behave strangely while riding in troikas. I'm liable to fall into a fit of hysteria."

His mouth quirked. "Don't worry, I've been told I have very distracting eyes, the color of butter when it simmers in a pot and smells dark and nutty."

I snorted. "Did I really say that?"

"You did." His gaze grew intimate with the memory. "I might have fallen in love with you then." He made a clicking sound with his tongue and snapped the reins. The three horses broke into a light run and pulled the troika down the drive.

A few moments later, we came to a stop inside the darkened stable. The smell of hay surrounded us, along with floating dust and the gentle auras of horses. Anton didn't unhitch his team from the troika just yet. He drifted closer to me, found the end of my braid, and untied the string holding it together. He tenderly unwove my hair and kissed the tender spot on my neck just below my jawline. Our lips met next, and our hands twined together.

Soon our noses were no longer cold and our bodies were warm. The horses nickered, and the late-afternoon sun shafting through the stable dimmed to the delicate twilight of winter. My fingers trailed across Anton's inner forearm and brushed over his lynx-shaped birthmark. "I love you," I said. "My heart is full."

Anton was needed back in Torchev soon, but he promised to stay with me for as long as possible. I walked on light feet while he was at the convent, sure I must be radiating a rosy glow for how fluttery and warm and wonderful I felt.

He spent time with Dasha, too, so she could get to know him better. Three days after his arrival, Kira and I tiptoed to the upstairs study hall, where the two of them had been spending the afternoon together. I labored to keep my breathing steady while Kira did the same, her mouth pursed in concentration. "Are you ready?" I asked her. She nodded and adjusted her grip on the tray in her hands. I knocked on the door.

"Come in," Anton called.

We stepped into the room and found Anton and Dasha seated at two desks drawn together. I exhaled, focusing on the even cadence of my heartbeat, and gave what I hoped was a natural, inconspicuous smile. "Kira and I baked something, and we want you two to be the first to taste it."

Dasha's head popped up from the drawing she'd been working on. "What is it?"

I prodded Kira forward and lifted the lid on her tray. "Cake," I replied, revealing a large slice for them to share.

"I glazed it myself," Kira added, her voice flat.

Anton grinned and set down his quill. "It looks delicious."

"Thank you," Kira replied without looking him in the eye.

I pulled two forks from my apron pocket and passed them over. "You should both taste it at the same time."

They dug in, lifting generous helpings to their mouths. I bit the inside of my cheek and tried to stay composed. My emotions must have slipped, however, because Dasha's fork paused before the cake reached her tongue. Anton, on the other hand, began chewing with gusto. One second later, he blanched and started coughing.

Kira and I snorted, erupting into giggles.

Anton's eyes watered, and he covered his mouth, gagging down a hard swallow. I cringed with his aversion, but couldn't stop laughing. "You've poisoned me," he said, chuckling with us. "What is this?"

"A cake to honor Feya," Kira said.

"Baked with salt instead of sugar," I added. Kira and I had made the cake to honor Sestra Mirna, as well.

"Then the goddess might spend her holiday with a bellyache," Anton replied, which made Kira giggle even harder. Today was Feya's Holy Day, an occasion I doubted anyone beyond the Auraseers at this convent celebrated. According to legend, on this very day, centuries ago, Feya blessed the first woman, Darya, with the gift to sense aura. "Please tell me you're not serving this at the party."

Kira set her tray on a nearby desk. "We baked a regular cake, too."

"For those with weak stomachs," I said, throwing a teasing glance at Anton. "Maybe I'll give you a slice if you dance with me tonight."

He lifted a brow. "A price I'll gladly pay."

Dasha sniffed the bite on her fork. "Can I try the good cake, too?"

"Only if you dance with someone, too," Anton replied. "I hear the blacksmith in Ormina has a boy near your age."

She pulled a face. "Boys are disgusting."

He looked affronted. "Even me?"

"You don't count." She dipped her quill in an inkwell to resume her sketching, then snuck a peek at the drawing Anton was also working on. "Though you're not a very good artist."

He tilted his head at his parchment. A lock of dark hair fanned across his eye. "I agree."

She shifted to sit taller in her chair, and the strings of her cap swung back and forth. Dasha had taken to wearing the hat Sestra Mirna had given her so she would break her habit of hair-pulling, this time of her own volition. "You're pushing too hard on the tip of your quill," she said matter-of-factly. "That's why your lynx looks like a fat blob."

A couple of days ago, Anton had told Dasha the story behind their matching birthmarks, and since then she'd become obsessed with lynxes. "A female lynx can give birth to as much as four kittens in her litter," she'd announced to anyone listening in the convent library yesterday. Glancing at the book she was reading from, she added, "Lynxes can also walk on top of snow. Do you know why?" No one did. "Their round feet act like snowshoes." A couple of Auraseers nodded appreciatively, humoring her. Dasha then turned to Nadia. "Do we have any snowshoes?"

I'm not sure if Dasha understands that the shape of our birthmarks isn't the point, Anton had confessed to me last night, feeling nervous about building a strong relationship with Dasha, especially after all the damage Valko had done to her.

I'd laughed and kissed Anton's cheek. *She just wants to bond with you over something. Let it be lynxes.* He'd taken my words to heart, for here he was the next day, drawing fat blobs with his sister.

"I'll help you with the whiskers." Dasha set her small hand over his and guided his quill. "See how much nicer that is? But next time we should use charcoal. Valko says . . ." As soon as Valko's name spilled from Dasha's lips, her hand froze over

Anton's. She pulled her lower lip between her teeth.

He glanced down at her, his eyes full of compassion. Their shared grief tightened my chest. "Did Valko draw with you, too?" Anton asked, no judgment in his tone.

"No, but one time when we had to camp with his army, I got bored, and so he found me some paper and charcoal."

Anton nodded. "I have nice memories with Valko, too," he said, and told her the one he had told me, about him fishing with Valko at the pond on the palace grounds. "I'll take you there sometime. We can *feed* the fish instead of catch them. That way you won't feel any pain."

Dasha looked up at her brother with her large gray eyes. Her aura warmed. "Tonight I can dance with you, too, if you want."

Anton wrapped his fingers over hers. "I would be honored."

When the time for the celebration drew near, the Riaznian Auraseers asked me to reign over the festivities representing Darya, the first Auraseer, but I never wore the juniper-and-cedar wreath crown. Instead, I gave it to Nadia. Maybe a gesture of kindness could help heal old wounds as well as a spark of trauma. "Thank you for all you have done for the convent," I said to her. "Because of you, Sestra Mirna's legacy lives on."

"Because of *you*, too." Nadia arched a brow. "I certainly don't intend to manage this place alone. Though I *will* wear this crown." She smirked and placed it on her head.

I laughed and helped her set it at the most flattering angle.

Her burn scars and swirling tattoos appeared different some-how, less threatening, more beautiful—marking a past she'd made peace with. "It looks lovely with your eyes," I said. "Tosya will be smitten."

And he was.

He returned that evening, after days of visiting with the Romska, and when he saw her again, supervising a group of girls as they laid evergreen boughs on the tables, warm tendrils of his aura spread toward her.

At the feast, they sat beside each other, across from where I was seated between Anton and Genevie. Candles arranged in greenery glowed from every table in the dining hall, and the falling snow outside collected in corners of the windowpanes. "Look at them, all together here," Genevie whispered to me, her eyes traveling over each girl and woman in the room. "This is what we worked for, Sonya, and it is even more wonderful than I imagined."

I took her hand and lightly squeezed it. "And all the more wonderful because *you* are here to share it with me."

As everyone ate, Nadia recited the origin story of Aura-seers, and the twins, Ilona and Irina, sang a duet to honor Feya, as well as an old Riaznian folk song. It was a haunting melody, but it also retained hope, as the notes lifted from a minor key and brightened in a resounding major chord. Anton listened intently, leaning back in his chair. When the song ended, he stood and cleared his throat, his aura simmering with anticipa-tion. I raised my brows. I didn't know he had planned to speak.

"Some of you may know that, a few days ago, the Duma agreed to admit another member onto their ruling council." He lifted his glass to his best friend, seated across from us. "Congratulations, Tosya."

I grinned, nudging Tosya's leg under the table with my foot, and he winked at me.

"While I'm grateful someone of Romska blood will be advocating for the nomadic tribes," Anton went on, "they aren't the only group of people who have been denied representation in our government until now." He looked at the twenty-six girls and women in the hall. "You have been, as well. I've pleaded to the Duma on your behalf, and they have consented not only to grant the Esten Auraseers full citizenship in Riaznin, but also to admit an Auraseer governor onto our council."

Gasps sounded throughout the room, followed by a rush of excited whispers. Everyone's buoyant energy tumbled inside me. I stared at Anton, my smile broadening. Under the empire, Auraseers had been little more than a class of slaves. Now we could take an active role in government and help shape the future of Riaznin.

"There is much yet to do in our nation," he said. "Conflicts still besiege us. The imperialists are unsatisfied with the outcome of the civil war. The Shenglin are steadily retreating, but we may have to grant them land along our eastern border to settle old quarrels. Not everyone on the Duma sees eye to eye."

Feliks immediately sprang to mind. His extreme measures would always pose a challenge. But when Anton had returned to Torchev, he'd accused Feliks of all his trespasses in front of the Duma. And although Anton couldn't prove that Feliks was guilty in every instance, Feliks had, nevertheless, become more restrained since that time. The growing peace in Riaznin and Tosya's new poem should also make him stop hounding me and threatening those I loved.

"Learning and growing from other people is the beauty of democracy, even if that growth is painful," Anton continued. "We could use your help in this work. And so, if you find the idea agreeable, I propose that you discuss the matter over the next few days and elect one of your own to represent Riaznin's Auraseers on the Duma." He smiled warmly at everyone and bowed his head to show he was done speaking.

As soon as he took his seat, Nadia said, "It should be Sonya."

My fork clattered to my plate. "What?"

"You have the most experience in government." She shrugged indifferently, but the earnest pulse of her aura reached the core of my fluttering stomach. "You served under the emperor, and you were in Torchev during the transition to the new regime. You're the most qualified."

"I agree," Genevie said from beside me. "Sonya also has made the most sacrifices to help Auraseers *and* your nation— *my* nation," she amended, her cheeks flushing.

"But . . ." Tension corded my muscles. I glanced at the hushed women and girls. "Doesn't anyone else desire to be nominated?"

Two tables away, Lara set down her glass. "We Estens still

need to learn how to be Riaznians before we consider governing them."

"And we Riaznians came here for sanctuary and learning," Tamryn added. "We aren't ready for anything more."

"Don't you *want* to be a governor?" Anton asked me.

I turned suspicious eyes on him. "Did *you* put them up to this?"

He held up his hands. "I believe in the freedom of choice . . . although, I admit, I did hope." The side of his mouth lifted. "What's holding you back?"

I looked at Dasha and Kira at the other end of my table. The girls sat so closely their shoulders touched. I had braided ribbons through their hair today. Yesterday, I'd taken them on a ride to the coast on Raina. The three of us had laughed, trying to squeeze into my saddle together. "They need me," I whispered to Anton. I twisted my fingers in my lap and added, "*I* need them."

"You could still live here." He placed his hand on my knee. "The Duma convenes for a few days every month. The rest of the time you could live at the convent."

A tingling sense of hopefulness danced across my skin. "I suppose serving on the Duma *would* put me in the best position to ensure Auraseers' equal rights and opportunities." Especially Dasha's and Kira's.

"It would." Anton's golden eyes drifted deeper into mine. My pulse slowed to match his balanced heartbeats. I didn't feel pressure from him, only calm confidence and faith. His belief in me was unshakeable. "You were born for this, Sonya."

My mind cleared like the sun on summer solstice. I was about to declare that I'd accepted—I *would* be governor, but then I realized . . . "Don't they need to vote?"

He grinned. "Yes, they do."

He took my half-curled hand, and I opened it. Our palms slid together.

"Raise your hand if you elect Sonya Petrova to represent the Auraseers on the Duma as we usher in a new and free Riaznin," Anton said, addressing all the women and girls in the dining hall.

I gazed over each of their faces, those who had lived in hiding like me, those who hadn't yet learned to train their abilities, those who had felt lost, alone, abused, disheartened, or afraid. I identified with each of them. I understood the flowing pulses of their auras, not only because they glided on the waves of my awareness, but because I also had so much in common with them. The people of Riaznin still had much to learn about unity and peace, but here in this room, harmony and respect abided. Anton was right. Auraseers could offer a great deal to our nation, if Riaznin would give us the chance. I vowed to do everything in my power to make that happen as I advocated for my sisters.

They must have felt the strength of my determination. I hoped they also felt my sincere respect.

Every Auraseer raised their hand.

Warmth pulsed over me in waves, reverberating as our shared joy coursed through the unbroken chain of sisterhood.

In that moment, I knew I loved every one of them.

And I knew, here among them, I had found my true home.

ACKNOWLEDGMENTS

I've written a trilogy! I could never have done this alone. Many hugs and endless gratitude goes to:

My editor, Maria Barbo, a brilliant lady who I've come to love so much. Thanks for understanding and championing Sonya.

Stephanie Guerdan, Maria's wonderful and timely assistant.

My publisher, Katherine Tegen, and her warm and amazing team at Katherine Tegen Books.

Josh and Tracey Adams, my agents and two of the most incredible people I know. I'm indebted to you both.

Jason, my loving husband. Anton doesn't hold a candle to you. Thanks for your pure belief in me.

My children, Isabelle, Aidan, and Ivy. You bring me joy and laughter and keep me grounded.

Sara B. Larson, my author bestie and the biggest cheerleader of this trilogy since day one.

Emily R. King, my dear friend. When I paint myself in corners, your brilliance saves me.

Erin Summerill, the queen of extroverted authors. Thanks for always keeping your writing couch welcome to me.

Ilima K. Todd, my author "sister" and a steady force in the whirlwind of publishing.

Robin Hall and Emily Prusso, my first and forevermore critique partners and friends.

Sara Keller Jensen, a longtime friend and brilliant professor of the Russian language.

Oksana Anthian, my French translator. You conjugate verbs with accuracy and class.

My mother, who makes me feel saved and loved and gives the world's best pep talks.

My angel father. I feel you helping and cheering me on every day.

My brother Gavon who spoke encouraging words when my father couldn't.

My brother Matthew. This book is dedicated to you. You know why.

My readers. You rode a roller coaster of emotions with Sonya and stayed with her. She thanks you, too.

And to God. Once I get out of my own way, you're always there and always will be. Thank you for this adventure.